Caribbean

Dreams

Reviews for Karen Klyne's Works

Come Dream with Me

This is the first book I've read by Karen Klyne and it hasn't disappointed. I do love an author that can take a difficult, emotive subject and weave it seamlessly and sensitively into their story. **Queer Literary Loft**

True Karma

Karen Klyne knows how to write an ice queen. I enjoyed this book and the intelligent and emotional storytelling. **Kitty Kat's Book Review Blog**

I adored this story from Karen. Klyne. With each new release, Karen brings fresh, realistic, but imaginative stories. **LesBi Reviewed**

Sliding Doors

Ms Klyne's skilful storytelling took me on a journey where my preconceptions were turned on their head. It was a wonderful story, full of magic and wonder and mystery. It was also, ultimately, beautifully romantic and I defy anyone not to have a wee tear in their eye. I absolutely loved it. **Kitty Kat's Book Review Blog**

Karen's stories just keep getting better and better, and each time she brings us a new one I am blown away by the amount of imagination. An excellent story from Karen, and a brilliant addition to her growing catalogue of novels. **LesBi Reviewed**

Love for Auction

I really enjoyed the story; it had the perfect amount of romance and drama to make it believable and exciting.

Phil and Kim had quite a good friendship, and a very hot attraction to one another. They weren't able to keep their hands off of each other, and it was quite apparent how well suited they were for one another, even when they were misunderstanding each other. I loved how they just got on and complimented each other, even though they were so different in personality.

A great story, that I thoroughly enjoyed! **LesBi Reviewed**

An Opening in Time trilogy
Parallel Lives: Book One

Parallel Lives is an exceptionally well written story of love, personal discovery and passion. I adored it. Karen Klyne has a very impressive turn of phrase, one that is irreverent and wicked and conjures up just the right image. Her world-building is deftly done and made me want to know more. I didn't want to put it down! It was an excellent story, very emotional at times and I literally can't wait for the next one in the series. **Kitty Kat's Book Review Blog**

Crossing Over: Book Two

I so enjoyed book one in this series, 'Parallel Lives', and have been eagerly awaiting the release of 'Crossing Over'. I was certainly not disappointed. By the end I knew that I wanted more from this series. In a good way. I will be counting the days until book three comes out. I have grown to love these characters and want to find out what happens next. **Kitty Kat's Book Review Blog**

Destiny of Hearts: Book Three

Truly a unique and fantastic example of world building, and a brilliant read. **LesBi Reviewed**

By the Author

Come Dream with Me
True Karma
Sliding Doors
Love for Auction

An Opening in Time trilogy
Parallel Lives
Crossing Over
Destiny of Hearts

Caribbean Dreams

by Karen Klyne
2021

Butterworth Books is a different breed of publishing house. It's a home for Indies, for independent authors who take great pride in their work and produce top quality books for readers who deserve the best. Professional editing, professional cover design, professional proof reading, professional book production—you get the idea. As Individual as the Indie authors we're proud to work with, we're Butterworths and we're *different*.

Authors currently publishing with us:

E.V. Bancroft
Valden Bush
Michelle Grubb
Helena Harte
Lee Haven
Karen Klyne
AJ Mason
Ally McGuire
James Merrick
Robyn Nyx
Simon Smalley

For more information visit www.butterworthbooks.co.uk

CARIBBEAN DREAMS

This trade paperback original is published by
Butterworth Books, Nottingham, England

Cataloging information
ISBN: 978-1-9150091-0-4

CREDITS
Editor: Jan Stone
Cover Design: Nicci Robinson, Global Wordsmiths
Production Design: Global Wordsmiths

Acknowledgements

I so enjoyed writing Caribbean Dreams. You see, I've always loved my cruising trips and all the wonderful places they've taken me. But one of the best parts is meeting such a variety of people from all over the world—and they've never failed to fascinate me! I just love people watching…so a big thank you to all those captivating fellow passengers…you know who you are!

Jeez, what would I do without my editor? Sometimes she's so cruel, but all the same, I love her to bits. Perhaps I'm a masochist! However, she continues to teach me all the things I've already been taught but often forget.

And wow, Nicci; the cover is terrific! It really depicts the idea of romance on the Caribbean Seas. Global Wordsmiths are amazing! They look after development, production, and all my marketing…fist pumps!!

ARC readers play a very important role, and I offer my thanks for your patience and wonderful reviews.

Thanks again to Maggie Burris for the copy editing and proofreading, and to my wonderful sensitivity reader for checking that the content in and around the Caribbean was acceptable.

To all you amazing readers, your reviews make it all worthwhile.

Dedication

*For all my readers and friends who have
supported me throughout my journey.
A big thank you.*

Chapter One

CORI LEWIS SAT ON the edge of her bed. She covered her face with her hands and felt the wetness of her tears on her palms. She sobbed. What the hell was she thinking? This was no time to go away. How callous. It had only been six months since her partner had died. What the hell would people think? Why had she listened to her friend Liz? It must have been a moment of weakness, or maybe it was the wine Liz had plied her with the other night, when she'd told her to take some time out. To stop blaming herself and go chill in the sunshine. Whatever, whenever, she should never have listened. It was all a whim, and she was far from being a whimsical person. She looked at the suitcase on the bed. Empty. No. She'd ring and cancel. She wouldn't get her money back or anything like that, but at least someone, who really deserved a holiday, would be able to get her cabin. After all, there was a long waiting list. Christmas was the time everyone wanted to get away, particularly if they didn't have anyone to spend it with. Or anyone they *wanted* to spend it with, anyway. The Caribbean. As if. But what about her trip to Jamaica? She desperately wanted to see everyone. She flopped backward onto the bed, turmoil making it impossible to move in any direction.

She jolted when the doorbell rang. Who the hell was that? No one really ever came around. They didn't know what to say to her since her partner had died, so they stayed away. She got up, ran down the stairs and opened the door.

Liz stood on the other side clutching a bottle of wine. "Surprise, surprise. Thought we might share a bottle. A sort of pre-cruise celebration."

Cori managed a smile. "Come in, you daft bugger."

"Jeez, thanks for the terms of endearment." Liz followed her into the kitchen. She got out two glasses and placed them on the counter-top and Liz unscrewed the top. She poured wine into the glasses and handed one to Cori. She lifted her glass and clinked. "Here's to a memorable vacation."

Cori raised her glass but couldn't raise a smile. She hesitated. "I don't think I can go."

Liz slammed her glass on the counter. Some of the wine swished over the top of the glass and spilled onto the surface. Liz fished out a tissue and mopped it up. "That was a waste of good red wine, and what exactly do you mean?"

Cori wiped the back of her hand across her nose and sniffed. "It's disrespectful."

"Disrespectful, my arse. I'm sorry…I have to say it. When exactly did Dusty respect you?"

Cori massaged her temples. "She did, in her own way."

Liz walked around to Cori. "Babe. It happened. It was an accident. You can't blame yourself. You have to move on."

Cori didn't reply. She couldn't. She felt guilty for a number of reasons, and she hadn't discussed it with anyone…not even her best friend, Liz. "To be honest, I think I'd prefer to spend Christmas at home, you know, with Mum and Dad, and come around to your place for the Boxing Day party."

"Bollocks to that. And what about your other family?"

Cori looked back at her wide-eyed. Liz hardly ever swore. "I know. I desperately want to see them. Maybe I'll leave it a couple of months and get a direct flight."

Liz picked up the glasses. "No way. You'll never go. C'mon, we're off upstairs to pack. You can do that other stuff any year. You need this more than you know."

"Like a hole in the head."

Liz shook her head. "I didn't hear that."

All the same, Cori followed her. The lure of seeing her grandparents and brother was way too powerful to ignore. It had been so long. When they got upstairs, she downed her wine for courage and opened her wardrobe. "If I go, what shall I take?"

"No "ifs" about it. You're going."

There was no point in arguing with Liz and deep down, Cori knew she was right. It didn't take long before Liz had laid all her outfits on the bed along with everything else she needed.

"I figure if you take a few pairs of trousers, you can mix and match with the tops. The same with shorts and tees."

"Whatever you say. Anyway, they have laundry rooms on each floor if I run out." Cori looked at the mixture of clothes on the bed; Liz seemed to have covered every occasion.

Between them, they packed most things in the case and the other bits in her carry-on. Liz lugged the large suitcase downstairs, and Cori took the small one. Liz knew her well. If she left the cases upstairs, Cori might change her mind again.

When they got down, she picked up a file from the coffee table. She took some sheets of paper out and handed them to Liz. "My flight times and a copy of my itinerary."

Liz scanned the cruise route and whistled through her teeth. "God, I've always wanted to go to St. Barts and Antigua." Her shoulders slumped. "And the rest. And bloody Jamaica. You must invite me one day."

Cori grinned. "That would be fantastic. You'd love it. You could have come with me. That would have been such fun. And I wouldn't feel like such a loser going by myself."

Liz scratched her chin. "Just a slight problem in the shape of my wife. Don't think Gem would have been too pleased me taking off with you."

"She could have come too, and anyway, she knows we don't fancy each other."

Liz wiggled her eyebrows. "Anything can happen on New Year's Eve."

Cori punched her on the arm. "It never has done before."

"Nah, and it never will but it's good to keep her on her toes."

Cori hugged Liz, unable to express how grateful she was to have her there in that moment.

"It's a great itinerary, but why didn't you go on a lesbian cruise? There are loads around."

Cori pulled away. "You're joking. I want to rest and relax. I don't want to be chased around by a herd of cattle."

"Charming. Is that how you view dating?"

"Sorry, Liz. I'm not ready to meet anyone else yet. Maybe I never will be. Oh, I don't know. I want time to think. Anyway, they all had loads of passengers on, so I opted for a smaller ship."

Liz held her palms up. "Okay, okay. Message received and understood." She looked at her watch. "Best get going. Promise you'll message me and send loads of pics?"

"Course I will."

"Are your mum and dad taking you to the airport?"

Cori shook her head. "No, I opted for a taxi. I said my goodbyes earlier. Couldn't face leaving them at the airport."

"Christ, woman. You're only going for a few weeks."

"Over three, to be precise."

"Okay, but it'll go by in a flash. You're gonna have a brilliant time. Now give us a snog, and I'll leave you in peace."

She stepped up to Liz and engulfed her in her arms. She kissed her on the cheek and pushed her away. "Go, before you have me in tears."

Liz opened the door. "It'll be fabulous. Just don't sit in your room all day."

Cori laughed. "Course I won't, I've got a balcony."

"You know exactly what I mean." She blew a kiss and left.

Cori went back upstairs, collected some toiletries and put them in her bag. She set her alarm and got ready for bed, once again thankful for Liz's help in getting ready. If she'd put it off until bedtime, she definitely wouldn't have done it at all.

She flicked through some photos on her phone and found the one of her grandparents and brother. She smiled, kissed her finger, and placed it on the screen. *See you soon.* She didn't think she'd get any sleep, so she picked up her Kindle and began to read. It wasn't long before she felt her eyelids going heavy, so she put the Kindle down and switched the bedside lamp off. Still, she woke every hour and checked the clock. She kept nodding off, but her fitful sleep was filled with guilty dreams and recriminations.

She awoke feeling like she'd done several rounds in a boxing ring and was sure it was Dusty wearing the gloves. She wiped the sleep from her eyes and remembered what was happening today. The alarm hadn't gone off yet, but she jumped out of bed and took some deep breaths. She had to snap out of this despondency. It was time to put her low spirits into a bottle and toss them out to sea. The odds of that happening were virtually zero, but she could always dream.

After a light breakfast, she packed the last of her items and waited by the door for her taxi. A car horn tooted, and Cori wheeled her suitcases to the car. Joanne was her local taxi driver, and she knew her quite well. Whilst Joanne was loading the luggage, Cori went back to lock up. She took a last look around. It felt like she was deserting her home. Abandoning the memories of Dusty. Her stomach churned, and the nausea crept up to her throat. Her head was spinning, so she held on to the door for support and waited for it to pass.

Joanne touched her arm. "Are you okay, Cori?"

She wasn't okay. She was far from it. Her heart was pounding, and she began to tremble, her legs wobbling like jelly. She took some deep breaths. "Thanks. I'll be okay in a minute. Just feel a bit queasy."

"I'll get you some water."

Cori pointed to the fridge. "There are some bottles in there."

She returned and passed Cori a bottle. "Here, drink this. Do you want to sit for a while?"

Cori shook her head. "No, I'll be fine in a minute." She drank some water, and it wasn't long before her tummy settled a little. "I'm fine now, thanks. Let's go." She knew if she didn't go now, she'd chicken out.

Joanne grabbed another bottle from the fridge. "Best take one for the car."

Cori nodded, locked the door, and followed her to the car. She didn't look back.

Joanne slowly pulled away. "Just put your head back and relax. I'll have you there in no time."

Cori wasn't sure if that's what she wanted. Right now, all she could think about was curling up in a ball on her bed and making the world go away. That wasn't going to happen, so she did as she was told and closed her eyes. When she opened them and looked out of the window, she saw the signs for the M1 south. She glanced at Joanne, who was humming to some music on the radio. Lucky, because Cori didn't feel like making conversation. She lay her head back and closed her eyes again. When she opened them, they were sitting in a queue of traffic on a major road with six lanes.

Joanne must have seen her stir from the rear-view mirror. "Bloody M25. It's always the same. Still, we're almost there now. It's the next turn-off."

"Terrific." She wasn't sure it was. She'd have liked to prolong the journey forever and disappear into oblivion, but that wasn't an option. She had to overcome this. When they arrived at the departure terminal, Joanne unloaded her cases, fetched a luggage trolley, and put the suitcases on.

"Thanks so much, Joanne." Cori handed her an envelope with cash and the details of her return flight. They said their farewells, and she fought the absurd desire to see if Joanne wanted to come with her. When had doing things on her own become so hard?

This was it then. No going back. She checked her case in and made her way through security, then got herself a coffee and a panini and took a seat at a small table. She could see the departures board and so far, her flight to Miami looked like it was on time.

The announcement for her flight was called, and the butterflies in her tummy stirred. She knew they had tiny legs, but they seemed to have clogs on and were doing a tap dance on her insides. However, she took a deep breath and made her way towards the gate to join the queue. She'd opted to pay a little more and booked in World Traveller Plus. She'd have liked to have tried business, but she really couldn't justify spending that sort of money. Dusty would have reprimanded her for even upgrading to this one. Anyway, the cabin looked nice on the pictures. There was extra leg room, and the seats seemed quite a bit wider and reclined. That sense of betrayal to Dusty's memory rose again when she considered the bit of extra luxury.

When they boarded, she found her seat on the front row by the window. She almost prayed that the person sitting next to her had cancelled. She doubted it. It was only three days before Christmas, and the plane was full to bursting. However, she was pleasantly surprised when a young man checked the seat number and smiled at her. He was well dressed, alone, and didn't look like he'd be a threat. He put his rucksack into the hold, sat beside her, and fastened his seat belt.

He looked at her. "Hi. My name's Matt. I guess we're going to be travelling together."

He didn't look like trouble but who could tell? Dusty always said you couldn't trust anyone, no matter what. "Hi, I'm Cori." She returned the smile.

"My mum lives in Miami. I'm going to spend Christmas with her." He grinned and was almost bouncing up and down in his seat with excitement.

"That's lovely. I'm sure you'll have a great time."

"What about you?"

"I'm going on a Caribbean cruise tomorrow, and then I'm meeting up with some of my family in Jamaica."

"Wow, awesome." He looked across at the other row of people. "Are you travelling with friends?"

She shook her head. "No, I'm going on my own."

His eyes widened. "Cool. That's brave."

Alone. She didn't need the reminder. "I suppose so. It's the first time

I've tried it." She and Dusty hadn't taken any exotic holidays together. Instead, they went to the same mobile home park in Eastbourne every year and met up with Dusty's friends. Dusty didn't even like tennis though that was the reason she gave for going there. She supposed it was because the event attracted a lot of lesbians. As far as a cruise was concerned, Cori had never taken one before and she'd never visited her family in Jamaica. Of course, she'd seen them when they'd come over to the UK, but it wasn't the same as seeing them in situ.

"Welcome aboard, folks." The steward shut all the overhead lockers. "We're ready for take-off. I'll be back with you shortly."

Cori looked out the window. They were on the runway, moving forward, and then they lifted off into the sky. As they got higher, the fields and buildings disappeared into the clouds, and she could feel herself leaving her old life behind. Simultaneously, she wanted to cry and laugh. When they'd levelled out into a clear blue sky, the seatbelt light went off and the steward came around to take their drink and dinner orders. Cori didn't drink during the day but made an exception on this occasion, hoping it would settle her nervous tummy.

She chatted with Matt over lunch. He told her about his plans, and she shared her cruise itinerary with him. It passed the time nicely and eventually, they both settled back with their individual TV screens. There were lots of films to choose from, so she began with one of the Star Wars movies, something she'd always wanted to watch but Dusty had said they were a waste of time and had ridiculed her desire for such base escapism. A few hours later, Cori had loved it so much, she'd decided to buy the whole set when she got back home. As the credits rolled, she yawned and blinked. She guessed the tiredness must be down to the drinks. She reclined her seat and closed her eyes.

When she opened them, she looked at her watch which she'd already adjusted. She was surprised to see there were only a couple of hours to go. After a light snack, they began their descent into Miami airport. She couldn't help but smile. She'd made it, and all by herself. Dusty would never believe it. Cori wished she could get her out of her mind, but there was no chance of that. She waved Matt off and thought briefly of the way people connected during travel, never to see each other again. It pinned that sense of loneliness to her chest like a note anyone really looking could read.

The queuing at immigration and customs took forever, no doubt because it was Christmas. The officer wasn't very friendly either, not like the ones in England. Even when she wished him a merry Christmas, all she got was a grunt. Next stop: luggage. She held her breath and became more and more nervous until her case finally appeared.

She was shattered now. Her body told her it was the small hours of the morning, but her watch said it was ten p.m. In the meantime, she had to locate her hotel. She'd opted for the one in the airport. It wasn't exactly the most welcoming, but all she really wanted was a bed for the night. And that's all she got. But the depth of the exhaustion meant no more lying awake, thinking about all she'd lost in the last year. In the morning, after some breakfast and a self pep-talk about the fact that she'd come all this way and she could definitely keep going, she studied her itinerary and took a walk around the airport to kill some time before she ordered a taxi. Embarkation was at midday, and it only took half an hour to get to the cruise terminal. When the taxi drove along the waterfront, she gasped. There were six massive cruise liners sitting there and thousands of people milling around. She mentally cursed Liz for getting her to think this was a good idea. She was a pea in a sea of marbles.

The taxi driver half turned to her. "Which ship did you say?"

"*Caribbean Dreams.*"

He pulled up outside the passenger terminal, a long, squat building that didn't speak of dreams worth having. And there it was, just on the other side of the building. The ship looked small in comparison to the others, but she'd heard that some of them carried anything between three to five thousand people. She shuddered at the thought. Even seven hundred seemed too many for her. The driver unloaded her cases and placed them on the quayside. She paid him and waited. What was she supposed to do now? She gripped her manilla file folder until it began to fold in her hand.

A man with a clipboard strode towards her and smiled. "Good afternoon, ma'am."

Ma'am? Surely, she didn't look that old. Still, this *was* America. Cori smiled back. "I'm not sure what the procedure is?"

"Well, if I can take your name, we can get things moving."

"Cori Lewis."

The man checked his list and ticked her off. He waved a guy over who took her suitcase and loaded it onto a conveyor belt. "Right, Ms Lewis, if you go through that door to the left, you'll see the registration desks."

Cori smiled and thanked him. She looked back at her luggage, wondering if she'd ever see it again. She entered the large hall and joined the queue to register. There were plenty of people ahead, mostly in couples or groups, but it wasn't long before she reached one of the desks. They took her photograph, kept her passport, and handed her a key card.

"You'll get your passport back on board." The young man pointed to the card. "You'll need this every time you get on and off the ship, and it's also your room key." He smiled. "Take good care of it, Ms Lewis."

She held it like a lifeline. "I will."

"Okay. So, you can board the ship now. Up the stairs and across the bridge. The rooms won't be ready for a while, so if you want to go have some lunch in one of the restaurants first, they'll announce when your room is ready. Have a great time."

"Thanks." Cori followed the route. This was it. Her luggage was gone, and her passport had been taken. There was no turning back.

She stepped on board *Caribbean Dreams* and couldn't believe her eyes. She'd heard it was one of the most luxurious ships ever built but she wasn't prepared for this. A young lady offered her a glass of champagne and welcomed her on board. Cori murmured a response, mesmerised by her surroundings. She took a sip from her drink and twirled around in a circle. The soaring atrium made a powerful first impression and she looked up to see a vast crystal chandelier hung over a dramatic curving double staircase. She wondered how anyone could possibly clean all that glass. The floor was inlaid marble and looked like something you'd see in an Italian palazzo. There was way too much to take in at first glance.

She put her drink down on a tray. She wanted to savour every moment with a clear head. She rummaged in her rucksack for her plan of the ship's layout. She'd made extra notes because she was sure it would take her a while before she became acquainted with everything. She scanned her map, slung her rucksack over her shoulder, and made her way to the elevators. They were those sort that were all glass, and she could see all the floors and the opulence as she travelled up to the eleventh floor. When she got out, she headed for the deck. The swimming pool looked inviting with plenty of sunbeds. At the far end were a couple of hot tubs. She couldn't imagine she'd ever be using them, but they did look inviting.

There weren't too many people around yet, and it looked like she was one of the earlier arrivals unless, of course, the ship was just so big that it would always feel like she had plenty of space to herself. It was a deflating thought. The last thing she wanted was to feel alone in the middle of seven hundred people. She inhaled deeply and the smell of the barbeque filled her nostrils. She'd save that experience for another day. Right now, she fancied sitting inside and having a light snack. A quiet table on the perimeter would suit her nicely. She didn't feel like mingling just yet. She wanted to sit, observe, and orient herself. The reality was that she'd forgotten how to mix with groups, apart from Dusty's friends, and she usually made a hash of that.

A waiter held the door open, and she spotted a table for two by the window. She left her bag underneath it and headed towards the buffet. When she got around the corner, her jaw dropped. There were counters covered with food of every description that stretched right across the ship. She walked one way first and at the end she saw that it was an identical set-up the other side. She picked up a plate and loaded it with a variety of salad stuff. She added king prawns, smoked salmon, and crab onto her plate and took some bread. She hardly ever ate fish because Dusty had hated it, and now she couldn't wait to savour every bite. She stopped and stared at one of the counters.

"Would you like to try the roast of the day, or perhaps you'd like to choose some fresh fish and we'll bring it to you?" a young man asked.

"Thank you. Another time maybe." *Oh. My. God.* The choice of food was simply amazing. Now she was thinking about her waistline and how much weight she'd be putting on over this vacation. She didn't care; it was Christmas. When she sat down, she was offered wine but stuck with water. Wine would only make her sleepy, and she'd paid way too much to sleep through the whole experience.

The lunch was as good as it looked, and she rounded it off with some cheese and biscuits. The restaurant had begun to fill up. The laughter and jovial voices spread throughout the room, and everyone who passed by smiled and greeted her. She could have struck up conversation with any of them, but figured she had plenty of time over the coming days and didn't want to rush it. She couldn't help but notice that she seemed to be the only one sitting at a table alone. So be it.

She was delighted when an announcement was made over the tannoy. Their rooms were now ready, and their luggage would be delivered in due course. She grabbed her bag, made her way to the elevator, and pressed for floor seven. When she got out, she stared both ways. Odds left, evens right. She was in room seven-four-nine, halfway down the softly lit corridor. She tapped her key card on the metal strip and the light turned green. She tentatively walked in, once again feeling like she was doing something she shouldn't be.

The paperwork had told her she had to place the card in the holder inside the room to get power and light, so she popped it in. Luxury beyond her imagination made her knees weak, and she leaned against the wall as she took it all in. She peeked in the bathroom. Two sinks, a bathtub, a toilet, and a massive shower. It was nearly bigger than hers at home. Another door was a huge walk-in wardrobe. Around the corner was a king size bed set into an alcove and beyond that was a big vanity unit with a built-in fridge and another vanity on the other side. It was all elegantly decorated in a cream and coffee palette with deep blue accents. In the middle of the room was a table with a bucket with ice and a bottle of champagne. She shook her head. That would last her the whole trip.

And then there was the balcony. It wasn't enormous, but there were two wicker sunbeds and a small table. She looked around the room again, ignoring the fact that everything was meant for two and she was just one. This ship was definitely a floating luxury hotel.

She bounced on the bed. So comfortable, and big enough for three, let alone two. Maybe you'll get lucky, Liz would say. She tutted. So far, she'd not seen anyone of interest and that suited her just fine.

She unpacked her rucksack and put all her valuables in the safe in the wardrobe. She had a good hour to relax before the muster drill. Apparently, everyone had to attend prior to embarking on a voyage. The lifeboat drill supposedly prepared passengers for safe evacuation in the event of an emergency and it familiarised crew and passengers with escape routes. Thoughts of the *Pirates of the Caribbean* drifted through her mind. Yes, she certainly needed to know where the lifeboats were.

She saw a white invitation card on the table addressed to her.

I'd be delighted if you would join me and fellow single guests in the Spiral Galaxy lounge at seven p.m. for cocktails and dinner later in the Magnetic Arc Restaurant. Looking forward to meeting you.

Your hostess, Rafaela Rojas.

She tilted her head. Maybe that was a good idea for the first night. She didn't know anyone, and if she didn't click with them, she didn't have to do it again. After all, she could always eat in her room or on the deck. And the ship was certainly big enough to find spaces to be on her own. But she was so very tired of being on her own.

The doorbell rang, indicating someone had delivered her suitcases. She wheeled them in, lifted the large one onto her bed and quickly unpacked, placing her clothes in colour-coordinated stacks. She stowed her suitcases beneath the bed. Organization and tidiness were important to keep an uncluttered mind. Then she sat on the bed, unsure what to do next and trying hard to push aside all the thoughts telling her this had been a silly idea. She brushed away the few tears that rose and went onto her balcony, where she tilted her face to the sun and concentrated on the lapping water below.

When the alarm sounded through her room intercom, she grabbed her lifejacket, removed her key card, and left the room. Members of staff were there to direct everyone to their designated station, and she followed everyone down the stairs to deck five and into the coffee shop. She took a seat with a couple who introduced themselves as Ron and June from Alabama. They made polite conversation, and she was glad they didn't ask her if she was travelling with anyone. It took about half an hour to get through all the instructions and then they had a quick recce onto the deck, where they were told which tender to head for in the event of an emergency. And that was it. She made her way back to her room, took a shower, and put her bathrobe and slippers on. The freedom to do what she wanted left her feeling a little dizzy and out of sorts.

What should she wear tonight? Liz had packed a couple of short dresses but mostly light slacks and tops. There seemed to be quite a strict dress code unless you were eating on deck. The restaurants stated either dresses or smart casual wear for ladies. She preferred the latter but thought she'd wear a dress on Christmas Day and New Year's Eve. She stared at the bottle of champagne. Why not? She popped the cork and poured herself a glass then stuck the stopper on and put the bottle in the fridge. She took a sip. Not bad. She raised her glass and looked in the mirror. *Happy holiday, Cori.* Emotions were messy little gremlins. How could it be that she felt both free and guilty at the same time? How could it feel so exciting to be doing something so decadent while also feeling like she was doing something so selfish? She drank the glass of champagne and turned on some music to drown out the beastly little emotion gremlins. She was here and that needed to be her focus.

She finished her hair, applied some make-up, and placed her outfit on the bed. She'd opted for a cream tunic with colourful swirly designs and a pair of cream slacks and sandals. She checked herself over in the mirror and was happy with the result. Dusty always told her she was way too vain. Maybe she shouldn't look in the mirror as much as she did. She shrugged. For once, nobody else could see her.

She made her way through the corridor to the elevators and up to deck eleven. Nerves made her neck tight as she thought of joining a group of people she didn't know. She took several deep breaths and entered the lounge. She had no idea who she was meeting and where they'd be sitting but as soon as she'd taken a couple of steps forward, a woman sprang from her seat and came towards her.

She smiled. "Are you looking for the singles' group, by any chance?"

Cori nodded.

The woman stuck her hand out. "I'm Rafaela Rojas. Call me Raf."

She wiggled her eyebrows in a suggestive way, and her large, dark brown eyes seemed to become even larger. Cori felt her cheeks burning. Raf flicked a strand of hair from her face. It seemed to obey her wishes and joined the rest of her carefully coiffed style which draped its way just below her shoulders.

"I'll be looking after you during your trip." She lightly touched Cori's arm. "Come on, hun, come and meet the rest of the gang."

Cori followed her to a large table and tried to breathe normally.

"Okay, everyone. Listen up. This is Cori, and if I'm right, she's from across the pond." She pointed from left to right. "This is Lena and Dorothy, they're sisters from Canada." She laughed. "They can't help that though. This here is Patti, and she's from Texas, and Mike here is from California."

Mike stood up and stuck his hand out. "Hi, Cori. Good to meet you. Come and sit by me."

He patted the seat next to him. Patti, who was sitting on the other side, looked a bit miffed. Cori wanted to say, *he's all yours.* Wrong gender, wrong age, wrong everything. She didn't want to sit next to Mike. She wasn't sure how old he was, but his skin was stretched like rawhide by one too many facelifts. He also looked kind of slimy. However, she didn't want to be rude. Not just yet. She sat down beside him, near enough to smell his overpowering cologne but far enough that she wasn't touching any part of his anatomy.

Raf touched Cori's hand. "What can I get you to drink, hun?"

"I'm not sure." She stared at Raf's glass. "What are you drinking?"

"Cosmo. I'll order you one. They make the best here."

Raf called a waiter over, and it was only minutes before he returned with her drink.

Raf raised her glass. "Here's to a memorable vacation."

They all clinked glasses, and Raf winked at Cori. It was one of those flirty winks that communicated some sort of innuendo. Maybe she was reading too much into it but one thing was for sure, Raf certainly thought she was the *hostess with the mostess*. Still, she seemed like fun, and that was exactly what Cori needed from this trip.

Chapter Two

Steph Graves couldn't believe her luck. She'd put her name down on several wait lists for a Christmas Caribbean cruise. She was certain nothing would come of it, but then two days before one of them was due to set sail, she got an email. Someone had cancelled and was she interested? It was short notice, but hey, she only had to throw some clothes into a suitcase, so it was no big deal.

She contacted them immediately and said she'd take it. It was vastly reduced and although there seemed to be a long wait list, she supposed a lot of people had made other arrangements by now. Unlike her, they couldn't up and leave at the drop of a hat. The daytime flights were all full, but they managed to get her a late flight with one stop off the night before the cruise started. They assured her she'd get there in plenty of time before setting sail. The overnight flight didn't bother her, she'd be able to sleep on the plane. Maybe. Depended on whether she started her celebrations early.

She ran full speed down the stairs and into the living room. Her mother and father were sitting either side of the table. They didn't look up and seemed engrossed in their daily ritual of entering "events" into their massive diaries. She waited by the side of the table, gave a small cough and they both looked up simultaneously.

Her father put his pen down. "Yes."

Steph grinned. "There was a cancellation. I'm off on a cruise for a couple of weeks."

Her father looked skyward and held his hands together. "Thank you, Lord. Our prayers have been answered."

No, he wasn't saying it in jest, his expression was humourless, per usual. "Yes, I thought you'd be pleased. The ship's called *Caribbean Dreams*."

His eyes narrowed. "Dream? You're more of a nightmare."

"Jeez, thanks, Dad."

"Our once-proud name has fallen into disrepute. A reputation your mother and I have worked years to build up. You ruined us."

Steph's shoulders slumped. "I don't know how many times I can say sorry, but I'll say it again, I'm sorry." Shit, she hadn't murdered anyone. It was hardly the end of the world.

Her mother shook her head. "If any of this gets out, we'll—"

Steph rested her hand on her mother's shoulder. "Mum, it's not going to get out."

Her mother sighed. "In the chapel of rest, of all places."

"Christ, Mum, it was only a kiss." That wasn't exactly true, but you couldn't see what had gone on behind the plinth once they'd hit the floor.

She raised her voice. "Is that what you call it? Well, it was caught on CCTV."

"I hardly think the police are going to request it. It wasn't that good a kiss."

Her father banged his hand on the table. "Don't be facetious. Say she goes to the papers?"

Steph couldn't help the small laugh that escaped. "I don't think that's likely. What's she going to say? I kissed her in a funeral home? Hardly headline news."

Her father still looked solemn. "Anyway, when are you going?"

"I have a flight tomorrow night."

"Well, I can't take you to the airport. We have way too much on."

"I didn't ask you to. I'll leave my car there."

Her mother cleared her throat. "Hopefully, all this will have blown over by the time you get back. Being out of the public eye will help us make things right."

Jeez, she felt like a little kid. Hell, she was thirty-one and she'd done with being chastised. If she stayed in this room any longer, she'd say something she'd later regret. "Right. I'll go and make some arrangements."

Her mother and father nodded and returned to their work. She was effectively dismissed, just as she'd always been.

She ran up the stairs taking two at a time and whistled a happy tune. She reserved her car parking and then pulled her suitcase out from under her bed and dusted it. She still had her old room in their house for early morning funerals and she stayed over there on the odd occasion if it was really necessary. It was a big old Victorian house, which hadn't changed much inside or out since the nineteenth century. Even her parents seemed like relics who had come with the house when it was built. They ran their business from it and lived there too. Steph always thought of it as the city of the dead.

She checked in her wardrobe but most of her clothes were in her apartment, so she grabbed the case then poked her head around the door before she left. "I'll drop in tomorrow morning before I leave." It seemed like the right thing to say.

Her dad didn't look up from his paperwork. "Unnecessary. We'll see you when you get back."

She felt the words like the punishment they were meant to be. "Yup, okay. See ya." Then she dashed out of the door before they could add anything more.

She chose outfits from her wardrobe and folded them as neatly as she could, though she wasn't a great packer. She thought about her parents' reaction to the drama she'd created. Yes, she was fully aware that she was in the wrong, but their response was a bit over the top. She'd made a fundamental business error. Having an affair with a client had been a bad mistake. Well, she wasn't exactly a client, since those were usually in coffins, but whatever, it was a total no-no, and it certainly wasn't something she'd done before, or ever again. Lust had got the better of her. It had all gone tits up and she'd realized she'd made a big mistake after discovering the woman was bat-shit crazy. She could laugh about the bondage part now, but at the time, it was fricking scary. However, said woman hadn't taken kindly to being binned off and had reported her to the firm for gross misconduct. Luckily, it was her family. Well, not that lucky. God, she needed this time out and getting away might save her skin, and the embarrassment to her parents and sister.

Good news obviously travelled fast because her sister, Hill, paid her a visit the following morning.

"Have a good holiday, Stephanie…and perhaps this will be a good opportunity to reflect on your life and where it's taking you."

Holy moly, she wished she knew where life was taking her. Still, she smiled. "Thanks, Hill. I'll try. And I hope you all have a jolly Christmas and New Year without my joyful presence."

Hill shook her head. "Life is just one big blast to you, isn't it? And will you stop calling me Hill? My name is Hillary."

Steph saluted. She'd often wondered if she belonged to this family. Maybe they'd taken the wrong baby in the hospital? She'd heard that could happen. "Sorry, *Hillary*. You of all people should know, life's a one-way street, and we have no clue what's at the end of it. All I do is try to make it an awesome adventure."

Hillary folded her arms across her cassock. "It's not all about adventure. It's time you considered other people's feelings. You're not a teenager anymore."

Steph didn't want to get involved in yet another argument with her sister, so she bit her lip and held back. "Point taken." She looked at her watch. "Must dash. Got to get petrol."

Her sister tutted, exactly the way her mother did, and it made Steph wince. Such a small sound to create so much judgement.

"At least think about it," she said as she got into her sensible family car. "You have to grow up sometime."

Steph waved her off. "At least I'm not just living like I'm waiting to crawl into a coffin," she said softly.

As soon as she began her journey, she played her Christmas music collection and sang at the top of her voice until she reached the airport. The car park was easy to find, the transfer was good, and the check-in was quick. Very soon she was through security and into the departure lounge. Now she could relax. She'd still got a few hours to kill so she got an energy drink and a box of cookies, and then went online and booked all her free excursions for each island. There wasn't a great choice. She guessed most people would have booked theirs months ago.

Every so often, she glanced at the departure board, but no information was up. She felt sure there should be by now. Then it appeared. A delay of two hours. Typical. Still, she'd be okay timewise. She chewed her nail. What about her connection? Whatever, she couldn't do a thing about it. She knew loads of other people were flying to Miami, so she'd have company. Maybe she'd even find an attractive woman to spend some time with.

Eventually they boarded and she settled into her window seat next to a man who was busy working on his laptop. They served a meal of sorts, and she ordered a brandy in hopes that it would help her sleep. She reclined her seat as far as it would go, but it wasn't long before she felt someone kicking the back which jolted her back and forth. She looked around. Children. Little darlings were obviously just as excited as she was. She couldn't help but notice how their parents smiled and looked after them, keeping them entertained and even reading books to them. What a strange childhood that must be.

After a few hours, she wasn't so enamoured, especially when they started screaming. Nothing quite like grouchy kids. Bawl, bawl, bawl. That's all they did all the way to Orlando. If she had behaved that way, her parents would have thrown her from the plane. But just a stern, cold look from her father had always kept them from stepping a toe out of line.

Finally, they arrived, and she did manage to get a connection, but it was cutting it a bit fine, and the time issue was worrying her all the way to Miami, which kept her from flirting properly with the quite pretty woman sitting beside her. She kept looking at her watch. Would she make it? She had to be on board by four p.m. Granted, it was a domestic flight, so all she had to do was collect her case and meet someone in the terminal. Luckily, it went smoothly, and, in the terminal, there was a representative waiting for her, along with another couple. He ushered them out quickly and into a luxury SUV. God, it was plush. It was a Lincoln Navigator and if she'd had more time and felt less shitty from the long flight and lack of water, she'd be asking loads of questions.

They made it on board by the skin of their teeth. It was all too hectic to take in the surroundings, but from what she could see it was pure luxury. It took her ages to find her cabin. It wasn't on the main corridor but miles down an offshoot that resembled crew quarters. Her suite was right next to the laundry room. Still, that'd be handy. *Let's hope it's soundproofed.* Once inside, her cabin looked okay, but nothing like the photos in the brochure. And what the fuck was that on her balcony? She stepped outside. If there was sunshine on this side, she'd certainly never see it. Still at least if there were problems, she'd have instant access into the lifeboat, because one of them was virtually on her veranda. Too late to complain now. Maybe when she was more compos mentis, she'd see if she could swap rooms. She grabbed a quick shower and put her bathrobe on. She had nothing fresh to change into as her luggage hadn't been delivered to her room yet. With her luck, she doubted she'd see it again. She looked at the invitation card on her table. Singles get-together with dinner after. Why not, she didn't have anything better to do, and maybe there'd be someone interesting to take her mind off the fuck-twaddle her life at home had become. Then there was this fire-drill thing shortly. Hell's teeth. She was glad she was in good physical condition, because she'd hardly slept for what seemed like two days and it looked like it was going to be a marathon of a night.

She changed back into her dirty clothes in preparation for the fire drill, and when the emergency alarm sounded, she made her way to her station.

A woman smiled. "Room number and name, please."

"Steph Graves, room 620."

"I'd better get you a life jacket." She gave a half-smile. "You were supposed to bring it with you."

Great. Disappointing someone on her first day. Perfect. "Oh, sorry. It was all a bit rushed. Haven't long been on board."

The woman nodded and handed her a jacket.

She stood at the back hoping that she'd be able to make a quick getaway. She also had a good view of some of her fellow passengers. They looked okay. Some looked like they might not make it through the trip, but then…what a way to go. There were a few youngish couples in her group and four women together who looked to be in their forties. They seemed fun, and she liked older women. Alarm bells rang in her head, as she cast her mind back to her last affair with an older woman and where that had got her. Best stay away from them. In fact, best stay away from all women. For a while. A few days, at least.

When it was over, she made a quick exit back to her room, but her luggage still hadn't arrived. She lay on her bed and closed her eyes. When she opened them, she had no clue where she was. Then it hit her, and she glanced at her watch. Six thirty. She jumped off the bed and ran to her door. Thank God her suitcase was there. She slung it on the bed and rummaged around for something to wear. She went for a black pair of trousers and a loose cream top. She stared in the mirror. Her coffee-coloured hair was supposed to be a choppy pixie style, but parts were flattened or floppy where they shouldn't be, and she just didn't have time to find her styling clay which was no doubt lurking somewhere at the bottom of her luggage. Sod it. Who was she trying to impress anyway?

She left her suite and made her way up to the Spiral Galaxy Lounge. She drank it in, loving all the architecture and lighting and not in the least bit daunted by the kind of luxury she wasn't at all used to. It was another adventure, after all.

She hurried into the lounge and glanced around. There were quite a few people there, so she hadn't got a clue who was who. Then she saw a woman wave from a table not far away. The woman got up and beckoned her across. She stuck her hand out. She was smiling but the smile didn't reach her eyes. "Hi, you must be Steph?"

Steph shook her hand. "Yup…that's me." She ran a hand through her hair and looked at the group. "'Scuse the hair. No time to find my repair kit. And sorry I'm late, guys, both of my planes were delayed. Nearly missed the boat, then there was that bloody fire-drill. Then my suitcase didn't arrive." She waited, hoping someone might offer sympathy. "Anyone else have that problem?" They all shook their heads. "So, had to do a quick change, and here I am. By the way, my name's Steph Graves."

The woman who'd greeted her rubbed the back of her neck. Possibly wishing she'd missed the boat.

"Well, you're here now. I'm Raf Rojas, your hostess. Take a seat and I'll introduce you to the gang." Raf pulled out a chair for her. "What can I get you to drink, Steph?"

She shrugged. "Dry white wine would be great."

Raf almost sneered. "White wine? Champagne, Prosecco, or any particular grape variety?"

Steph shook her head. "Nah. As long as it's wet and dry."

Raf raised her eyebrows, called a waiter over and ordered her a dry white wine. The waiter asked about her preference, but Raf told him any would do.

She did that false smile again. "Introductions." She pointed to the far end of the table. "Lena, Dorothy, Patti, Mike, and Cori." They all said hi.

Steph liked the look of Cori. Raf had certainly saved the best for last. She looked about the same age as her, possibly a bit younger. Those sapphire blue eyes were mesmerizing and complimented her wavy blond hair. There was only one guy there, Mike, the facelift man. She found it hard not to stare because his face looked like it had been through a press one too many times, although they'd forgotten to put his neck through as well, leaving it looking like a worn-out accordion. Maybe he'd run out of money or something.

The waiter brought her wine, and she raised her glass. "Cheers, everybody. Here's to a great trip."

They all raised their glasses. Then the ship's horn sounded several times. Steph jumped up. "Are we leaving?"

Raf nodded. "It appears so."

Steph ran to the windows that stretched the entire circle of the lounge. She waved her hands in the air and sang that good old favourite from

Rod Stewart. The one about sailing, and she didn't care that some people were watching her, clearly bemused. Strangely enough, it wasn't long before she was joined by Cori. She plucked up the courage and put her hand on her shoulder and they swayed in time to the music. Cori laughed shyly and sang quietly, but she seemed up for the fun. Unfortunately, all the others joined them a moment later. Then Raf barged in on the other side of Cori and put her hand on her other shoulder. Steph couldn't help noticing that it was more like a caress than a touch. It was a bit like saying, "She's my property—keep off." For all she knew, she could be Raf's girlfriend. Gawd help her. Steph had known plenty of women like Raf. Women who thought they were the hottest thing on the menu and better than anyone else around them. A grown-up mean girl. They were sometimes good for a night, but never good for more than that.

When they'd finished their song, Steph watched Cori walk back to the table. She sure as heck had a curvy figure on her, and she knew how to dress too. *Enough!* She wasn't here to ogle women. Not yet, anyway. She should relax without any complications for a while. And women were always a complication.

They all sat down again and Raf looked at her watch. "I've reserved a table for seven forty-five in The Magnetic Arc restaurant." She looked at everyone and her eyes rested on Steph. "Of course, if you've made alternative arrangements, there's no problem."

Steph jumped in. "I'm game." She looked across at Cori.

Cori nodded. "No, nothing arranged. Love to."

All the others said they'd like to eat there too. So off they went. The restaurant was really something. It was elegant, spacious, and featured a massive sparkling-blue Murano glass ceiling. The brightly coloured glass balls hung down looking slightly precarious, and Steph decided she wouldn't want to be sitting here in a bad storm.

Raf steered them over to a large table in the centre of the room and before Steph could take a seat, Raf suggested the seating arrangements. Of course, she was put next to one of the sisters, Dorothy, and on the other side was Mike, the facelift man. She made a mental note not to keep calling him that just in case it slipped out one day. Dorothy, Steph, Mike, Patti, Cori, Raf, Lena. Nice one. Still, at least she was opposite Cori.

She glanced at Cori and wondered. Her gaydar was never great, since women of all sorts seemed to like her attention and she never had to figure out whether they were gay or not, but looking at Raf, and watching her ogling Cori, she was convinced where her preferences lay. Still, a bit of healthy competition never hurt anyone. As long as she won. She tried to quieten the mischievous voice in her head. Anyway, she wasn't up to much now. If it hadn't been for her interest in Cori, she'd have possibly declined the dinner invite and had a quick meal at the deck bar, then taken an early night.

She thought she'd better be polite and chat with Dorothy, though it was hard going because Dorothy seemed to be captivated by the glass ceiling and couldn't take her eyes off it. She asked her a question, but Dorothy just glanced to her right at her sister as if she needed help in translation, then her gaze returned to the ceiling.

Dorothy nudged Steph and said in a loud voice. "Are those dangly bits supposed to be testicles?"

Steph nearly knocked her glass of water over. She couldn't help but laugh. "Yeah, they do bear a remarkable resemblance, I agree." Dorothy either had a wicked sense of humour or an unusual way of thinking. She suspected the latter.

Lena tried to distract her sister, but Dorothy's eyes remained glued on the dangly bits.

She glanced over at Cori who was being monopolised by Raf. So far, Raf had the upper hand, but she was sure by tomorrow she'd be back on form. Anyway, she and Cori were both guests, so Raf would be otherwise engaged with work at some point. She gave herself a mental shake. She wasn't here for more drama. But something about Cori seemed…nice. And Steph hadn't been around a lot of simply nice people lately. Maybe she'd try something new and get to know a woman as a friend.

The sommelier took orders for wine and returned with a variety of red and white. Steph picked up one of the decorative plates on the table and turned it over. "Wow, are these really Versace?"

Raf half smiled. "Of course. They're custom-made for the *Caribbean Dreams*. Incidentally, they're for decoration only. You don't eat off them."

Patronising woman! Although it was good she'd said so or Steph might have used it as a bread plate. Still, she didn't like the presumption that she didn't know better.

They were presented with menus, ordered their meals, and Raf launched into conversation.

"So, what does everyone do for a living?" She looked across at Lena and Dorothy.

Lena answered. "We used to own a dog grooming salon."

Steph stifled a chuckle. They both had hairstyles a little like poodles. She saw Cori purse her lips and look down into her lap and wondered if they shared a similar humour. She really hoped so. A sense of humour was essential to Steph. Almost as much as fancying someone. She loved laughter and the two together were a must.

Mike leaned forward. "I'm a retired financial adviser. But should any of you wish to seek advice, I'll be more than happy to assist."

Steph sat upright. "Hey, do you deal in Bitcoin?"

Mike sneered. "No, I do not."

Whatever he dealt in, Steph suspected he'd spent a lot of his commission on stretching his face.

Patti flashed her hand around which was covered in diamond rings. "I was in real estate."

That figured. And judging by all the gold dripping from her body, she must have been successful.

Steph rubbed her hands together on her lap. Now for Cori. She tried, but she couldn't guess what she did for a living.

Raf turned to Cori. "And you, Cori?"

It was strange. Cori really blushed. Maybe she had an embarrassing profession, like a chicken sexer, or a deodorant odour tester, or worse still, a bull semen collector. Laugh one may…but one of her buddies had that occupation. Apparently, the cattle industry was extremely profitable, and the seed of bulls was like gold. He'd told her that five litres of bull semen could fetch tens of thousands of pounds. She always thought five litres was an awful lot, but then bulls were large creatures. The thought made her squirm. No, she couldn't really see Cori in that job, so why was she blushing profusely?

Cori cleared her throat. "I'm a li— well, I was a librarian, but I now write children's books."

There were murmurs of appreciation at Cori's revelation, but she just blushed some more and put her head down.

Why had she started by saying she was a librarian? And why had she blushed so? *A writer, eh?* She'd have been dead proud to announce that. She'd never met a writer before. It always sounded like a glamourous career. She wondered if Cori was in the same boat as the other guests seemed to be…or maybe she'd done the same as her and got a vast price reduction? Whatever, why had she looked so awkward?

Cori still looked uncomfortable and didn't seem to like the attention she was being given, so when it came to Steph's turn, she thought she'd take the heat off Cori. "I'm a sex-toy tester." It seemed to work because Cori laughed. "Great, innit? I get to pleasure myself and make damned good money too."

Raf smiled and stared at her with a hint of challenge in her gaze. "Do you have to evaluate your orgasms?"

Steph grinned. "Yeah, it gets a bit tiring, but I'm usually in the mood. Anyway, a job is a job."

Mike turned his chair towards her and leaned an elbow on the table. "How fascinating. Is that really your profession?"

"Actually, no, I'm a florist but the colours are much the same." Everyone seemed to find it amusing, apart from Raf.

Mike grinned. "I suppose the other one's your dream job?"

Steph shrugged. She nearly said no, she did that for pleasure, but thought better of it. "Strangely enough, Mike, I enjoy being a florist. I love flowers and the joy they bring to people." She omitted telling them that the florist shop was part of the family business and she only helped out there, along with the main business at the funeral home. Most of the flower arrangements were for people who'd passed away. She was sure Raf would have taken the piss, especially as her surname was Graves. She'd never have let that one go by. She could take a joke; all her friends took the piss, but she didn't want to take it from *her*. However, it was a damned good business, and paid her a good salary, but sadly, she didn't get much fulfilment from either of her jobs. She just rolled along with it because she had no idea what she really wanted to do in life.

Patti leaned back in her chair. "I love flowers. When I show my clients around a property, I always place a great big vase of flowers in an appropriate place, it always pleases people."

Very quickly, Patti turned her attention to Raf, obviously bored with flowers.

"How long have you worked on cruise ships, Raf?"

Raf raised her arms in the air. "Since…whenever. As long as I can remember. I began in entertainment and now I cover many areas. I love it. It's my whole core."

Now it was Mike's turn to fawn over Raf. "You have an American accent, but am I correct in saying you're Latina?"

"Very observant, Mike. My mother is American, and my father is Venezuelan. They live in America now, but of course, travelling around the Caribbean as I do, I get to see a lot of my family. Some live on the islands and some in Caracas."

Very observant, Mike. Fricking hell, it wasn't rocket science. Her features were dark, her eyes were big and brown, her hair was dark with a touch of red, and unfortunately Steph had to agree, she had a natural beauty. But what did they say? Beauty came from within, and so far, she hadn't seen much of that. Well, it certainly hadn't been aimed at her. She seemed to be storing it all up for Cori. She only hoped Cori could see through it. And this was only the first night.

Mike fawned over her. "How fascinating, Raf. You must tell us more on another occasion."

Yes, but not now. Steph put a hand to her mouth to smother a yawn.

Raf must have seen. "You look tired, Steph. Don't let us keep you up. It's a sea-day tomorrow. Plenty to do, and as I always say, Sea days are Raf days."

Steph suspected every day was a "Raf day." However, she had to admit, she was shattered. This was a holiday she'd looked forward to and she didn't want to ruin it by staying up just to flirt with someone. She stood. "You're right. If you'll excuse me, I'll take an early night. Catch you all tomorrow." Her gaze rested on Cori, and at least she gave her a little wave.

When she got back to her room, she put the Do Not Disturb sign on her door. She moved her suitcase off the bed and threw all her clothes onto a chair. She briefly thought about Cori, but it wasn't long before she drifted off into a deep sleep.

Chapter Three

CORI WATCHED STEPH LEAVE the restaurant. She seemed nice and was incredibly attractive. Not as though Cori was looking for anyone, just merely observing, that's all. She didn't look like a florist, but then she hadn't got a clue what a florist should look like. What she had appreciated was Steph coming to her rescue. It hadn't gone unnoticed. Her face had burned like a furnace when Raf had asked her what she did for a living. Why the heck had she said librarian, and then added writer? It must have sounded ridiculous. Perhaps they'd think she was lying or something. Of course, she knew why. Dusty's words echoed in her mind. *Don't mention what you do, either on holiday or to our friends. You know how people are, they'll make a fuss because they'll think you're a celebrity of sorts. You're only a little fish in a little pond.*

That's why she'd said she was a librarian, which was true, but that had been many years ago. Well, she didn't have to worry about that anymore. There was nobody there to chastise her. Apart from in her head. It seemed sneaky though, like she was going against Dusty's wishes, and that had made her self-conscious. What a joke. She'd lived with Dusty for eight years. Her family and friends told her it was water under the bridge now, but she couldn't let it go and as the water flowed it turned into rapids. Nothing was going to be easy. She couldn't wipe all that control away with a spray of Flash. And part of her wondered if some of what Dusty had said was true…

"Are you going to the show?"

Cori was immersed in thought. She turned to Raf. "Sorry, I was miles away. I'm a bit jet-lagged so I think I'll take an early night."

"Yeah. I don't blame you. It's Christmas Eve tomorrow. You don't want to miss out on all the fun, do you?"

"Why, what's happening?"

"There will be a daily events paper on your bed when you get back. Nothing too exciting, just games and things. There's carol singing by the tree. Don't miss that. I've organised it."

Cori shook her head. "I certainly won't. I love singing carols."

"Good, you can come join me in the Atrium. I'll need all the help I can get."

Cori held up her hands. "No. I don't mean I can sing. I mean I love joining in. It reminds me of when I was a child."

Raf touched her hand. "Then we shall all be children together and enjoy."

Mike pushed his chair back. "Will you excuse us, folks? We're off to the show."

Raf hung back. "Enjoy. See you all tomorrow. Remember, there's always a table set up here for us, breakfast, lunch, and dinner. I'm afraid I won't be able to join you until the evening. I have loads of other activities to organise, with it being Christmas. But we can meet in the Spiral Galaxy in the evening, same time."

They acknowledged and waved their goodbyes.

Cori stretched and got up. "Right. See you tomorrow, Raf. Thanks for the entertaining evening."

Raf got up too. "I'll walk with you."

When they left the dining area, Cori hesitated. "Is the Connoisseurs lounge near the Galaxy?"

"Yes. The smoker's lounge. Do you smoke?"

Cori grimaced and felt ashamed. "Only a few a day, four max. You know, one after coffee and lunch and dinner." Dusty hadn't had complaints about that habit, since she was a smoker too.

Raf winked. "And the other after sex?"

Cori's face burned again, and she looked away. Raf was rather forward, for someone she'd only just met.

Raf touched her arm. "Sorry, only pulling your leg. Anyway, that's great, I'll join you. I always have one after dinner."

Cori smiled. "Great. Nice to have company." She wasn't sure if that was true. Raf seemed to be paying her way too much attention. She wasn't used to it. Dusty would have said she was encouraging her, and she certainly didn't want to do that.

They took the elevator up, went into the lounge and took a table by the window.

Cori looked around. "Hey, it's really nice in here. You can hardly smell any smoke at all."

"They keep it well ventilated. Have to. There's a lot who'd like the ship to be non-smoking but there are also a few important guests who like the odd cigarette or cigar. And why not. I hate being told what I can or can't do. I'm an adult and I can make my own decisions."

Cori nodded. "I agree. We're not really hurting anyone. I wouldn't dream of having one in front of other people." She opened her handbag, took out her case and removed a cigarette. Raf leaned over and flicked her lighter. Then she opened her bag, took out a box and removed a small cigar. She lit it and inhaled deeply. "My family still make these in Venezuela. It used to be a big industry years ago. No more. They still produce a few for the affluent Venezuelans though."

Cori breathed in. "It smells lovely."

A waiter walked in carrying a tray. "Can I get you ladies anything to drink?"

"Cori, a nightcap perhaps?"

"No, thanks. I wouldn't mind a Diet Coke with ice and lemon though."

"Make that two," Raf said. "So, have you got all your excursions booked?"

Cori shrugged. "To be honest, no. I booked this cruise, then I had second thoughts, so I didn't bother. My mind just wasn't on it."

Raf smiled. "No worries. Do you want to go on the excursions? They're excellent on this trip."

"I'd have liked to, but it's too late. I thought I'd go down to the destinations desk tomorrow and see what they've got left."

Raf held her hand up. "Leave it with me. I'll make sure you get some good ones."

Cori sat up straight. "Really? That would be terrific. Thanks, Raf."

Raf grinned, and it wasn't hard to see the flirtation in her eyes. "My pleasure."

They finished their drinks and headed to their cabins, and Cori managed to keep enough physical distance that Raf couldn't touch her again, which she seemed prone to do. Cori wasn't the touchy-feely type in general, but even less so with strangers.

She lay in bed thinking about the events of the day. All in all, she'd had a great one and the evening had worked out so well. She'd met some nice people already and all her fears of being alone had diminished. She picked up her phone and texted Liz to tell her all about it. She didn't expect a reply because it was the wee hours of the morning in England, but at least she could let her know she was safe and sound and mixing with people. She was sure that would please her. She mentioned neither

Raf nor Steph personally. Liz didn't need that kind of encouragement. She smiled, curled up on her king size bed and closed her eyes. When she awoke, she checked the clock. Seven a.m. It was possibly the best sleep she'd had for months. She phoned the galley and ordered herself a pot of tea then crawled back into bed after opening the balcony doors to the ocean breeze. Waking up in a place without any bad memories was a luxury she hadn't had in far too long. She closed her eyes and felt the gentle sway of the ship and listened to the sound of the water beyond her balcony.

God, it was Christmas Eve. It hit her, and melancholy covered her like fallen stars. What would she normally be doing? Mostly, she'd be dashing out and getting last minute gifts. Perhaps queueing at the supermarket for food she'd forgotten, or something that Dusty specifically wanted at the last possible moment. Then later she'd be wrapping presents, and then in the evening they'd go out to the pub and meet up with a few of Dusty's friends. Never her friends. Most of them she'd dropped because Dusty didn't like them. Either that or Dusty had caused friction between them all, making things uncomfortable and awkward.

Still, she'd managed to hold on to Liz. It had been hard work, but despite Dusty's protestations, she'd managed to keep that friendship going. No, she didn't see her as much as she'd wanted to, but at least they did manage some clandestine meetings at lunch time. The idea that she no longer had to keep anything a secret was both elating and uncomfortable.

When the doorbell rang, she slipped her dressing gown on, and the waiter set her tray down on the table. She poured herself a cup and heard her phone ping. She opened it up and laughed. As predicted, there was a text from Liz.

So, have you met anyone?

She texted back. *Being well looked after by the hostess. There's also another youngish single woman in the group.*

The response was immediate. *Tell me more?*

She visualised Liz rubbing her hands together. She'd let her stew and talk to her again later.

She put some light jeans and a T-shirt on and made her way to the restaurant she'd had lunch in. In the daytime it was called The Balcony, and in the evening, it changed its name to The Brindisi. There were also three other speciality restaurants. Le Petit Chateau, Island Prime, and

Pacific Coast. The latter three had to be booked, but she dared say she wouldn't bother. She didn't want to eat alone, and apparently most of the food there could be ordered in the main restaurant anyway.

She opened the door to the outside deck and the warmth hit her. It was so deceiving because the air conditioning in her room and all around the ship didn't prepare her for the real conditions, even though she'd opened her balcony doors. Maybe she'd change into shorts after breakfast.

She found a table outside, left her bag on the seat, and made her way to the buffet. She always took a bag with her. Key card, phone, tissues, cigarettes and lighter. She'd feel bereft without her bag. It gave her a sort of security. She could always rummage in her bag if she felt lonely, or if she thought someone was staring at her, possibly thinking she was a sad sight sitting there all alone.

When she turned the corner, the aromas were tantalising. There was everything one could imagine, and you could also order anything your heart desired. It seemed decadent, and it was a little overwhelming.

She loaded fresh fruit into a bowl for starters, and when she'd finished, she returned to the buffet and tried to decide what to choose. She heard laughter and looked around to see Raf and a few other official-looking crew members chatting together. Raf spotted her and came striding over. She put her arm gently around Cori's shoulder. "Good morning, sweetheart. Did you sleep well?"

Cori nodded, wishing there was a polite way to shrug off the arm that draped over her shoulders like a weight. "Terrific, thanks."

Raf pointed to another area. "Are you going to try the eggs Benedict? It's absolutely wonderful."

Cori rubbed her tummy and tried to shift away from the contact by pretending to look at the buffet. "I couldn't manage that right now. Maybe I'll try it later in the week. Thought I'd plump for some scrambled egg and ham. Have you eaten?"

"Yes, I ate with the guys. Usually take my meals with them apart from in the evenings."

"Sounds good to me." Cori concentrated on the array of food before her. She filled her plate and added a bagel, hoping she'd take the hint.

Raf took her plate from her. "Here, let me, ship's a bit rocky this morning. Where are you sitting?"

"Outside." She sighed internally. So much for a quiet moment to herself.

Raf followed her and set her plate down.

"Thanks, Raf."

Raf hovered. "Did you get the itinerary for today?"

"Yes. There's loads to do, isn't there?"

"Absolutely. It's fun-packed. Which reminds me, I've put you down in my team for the putting competition at eleven thirty." Raf waved to one of the crew and finally made to leave. "Enjoy your breakfast, and don't be late."

Cori waved back. She had the impression this cruise was going to turn out to be a lot of fun, if she let it. But she didn't like people encroaching on her time or space, and she hoped that Raf would be busy later.

After breakfast, she went back to her suite, changed into her shorts, and opened the door to the balcony again. She leaned on the wooden rail and looked out to sea. She pinched herself. Was she really here, or was this an illusion? No, she was here all right. She breathed deeply and sighed as the breeze stroked her face. She could smell and taste the salt water. She stared at the myriad of shining blue and green gems touched by the sun. It was so quiet apart from the swishing of the waves and the sound of the birds. She closed her eyes and felt the peace. She fell in love with the sea from that very moment.

She jolted and glanced at her watch. Enough of this dreaming, she had things to do. She headed for the sports deck which was on the top floor and stopped to look at all the options. There was a golf net, which she wouldn't be using, shuffleboard, a bocce court, whatever that was, paddle tennis, and a putting green. Raf saw her and beckoned her over to the back of the ship. There were quite a few people around and she began to get nervous. She hated crowds, but luckily, she spotted Mike and Patti and went to join them.

Mike handed her a putter. "We're in teams of four. We're with you and Raf."

Cori took the putter. "Great."

Just then, Steph came running down the deck towards them. It sounded like a stampede. She huffed and puffed. "Am I too late? Had a terrible night. Had some breakfast in my room then must have fallen back to sleep."

Cori and the others laughed. So far, Steph seemed to be late for everything. She wondered if she was that kind of person, a bad planner. Then she remembered the ordeal she said she'd been through. As far as she recalled, she'd had a night and day of travelling and nothing had gone smoothly. And anyway, running a floristry was a responsible job. She'd have to be up early and highly organised, so this was likely out of character. Still, she looked good now. What made her think that? Well, she couldn't help but notice how her body was well toned. *For God's sake, Cori...stop staring.* Steph must have noticed because she gave her a broad grin. And then she felt the heat rising on her neck. Shit, she wished she didn't blush so much. Dusty said it signified guilt. *Stop thinking about Dusty.* She was possibly right, though.

Raf joined them. "Morning, Steph. I'm afraid we're only in fours. Do you want to join the guys at the back?"

Steph shrugged. "Sure."

Cori swung her putter back and forth. "I've no idea how to putt. Apart from crazy golf when I was a kid."

Raf took Cori's hand. "Aww, sweetheart. Don't worry. I'll give you a quick lesson." She put a ball down on the green and stood behind Cori. She wrapped her arms around her and put her hands on top of Cori's. She moved the putter back and swept through pushing the ball towards the hole. Cori could feel her breath on the back of her neck and her mouth was awfully close to her ear. It sent a tingling sensation throughout her body, though it was more from discomfort than pleasure.

She whispered, "There, just like that."

When she looked up, Steph was watching. Her lips were pursed, and she had her hands stuffed in her pockets.

Steph coughed. "So, you play golf, do you, Raf?"

"No. But I know putting is all about rhythm...and the way you stroke it. I'm an expert. I always find the hole." Raf laughed. It was one of those dirty laughs full of innuendo. Eventually, she let go of Cori. She turned her attention to Mike. "You look like a golfer, Mike. Do you play?"

Mike puffed out his chest. "Yes, and if I say so myself, I'm pretty handy with the driver."

Raf grinned. "So, you'll know the answer to this. What's the difference between a G-spot and a golf ball?"

Mike chuckled. "No idea."

"A guy will actually search for a golf ball." Raf punched Mike on the arm and snorted.

Everyone laughed at Raf's joke, apart from Steph. Somehow, Cori didn't think that Raf and Steph were going to become the best of friends.

And in truth, Cori felt that Raf was a little over the top when it came to her attentions.

They finished their putting competition, and much to Raf's annoyance Steph and the three guys won. She reluctantly handed them their prizes, and smiled whilst doing so, but it looked incredibly false.

Patti rubbed her hands together. "Hey, you guys. I'm starving, shall we all have lunch together?"

Raf tilted her head and gave a little smirk, as though she assumed a response to what she was going to say. "As I mentioned yesterday, I'm pretty busy so I won't be joining you for meals." She paused, as though waiting for some disappointed reaction, and when she didn't get one, she frowned slightly. "But we'll meet up tonight, yes?"

Steph glanced at Cori, perhaps to see her reaction. Cori nodded along with the others, and Steph followed suit.

"See y'all in the Galaxy lounge then. And don't forget the carol singing by the tree at five. It's only for about half an hour." Raf blew a kiss as she strode off.

As soon as Raf disappeared, Steph smiled. It was the first time Cori had seen her smile today and it lit up her face like the sun breaking through the clouds.

Patti motioned upward. "Right, gang, shall we eat in the Balcony restaurant?"

Steph nodded. "I'm game."

Cori and Mike nodded approval and they made their way down to the buffet. They chit-chatted over lunch, mainly about the food and the splendour of the ship. When they'd finished, they went their separate ways apart from Steph, who hung back to walk with Cori.

"So, what are you doing now?"

"I thought I'd go lounge on my balcony for a couple of hours and catch up on some texts back home. This is great, but there are people I'm going to miss over Christmas."

"Yeah…I might do the same. Anyone special you're missing?"

"Yes. My mum and dad."

Steph nodded but didn't say anything else.

Cori thought it was a bit odd that Steph hadn't mentioned anyone she was missing. But for all she knew, Steph may not even have a family, or perhaps she would have spent Christmas on her own anyway. They got in the elevator together and Cori pressed the seventh floor and Steph the sixth. When it pinged, the door opened, and Steph held it open momentarily. "Are you going to the carol service?"

Cori smiled. "Yes. I want to feel Christmassy. What about you?"

Steph nodded again, though she looked distracted. "Me too. See you down there."

Cori wandered back to her suite. When she got inside, she took her iPad and went to sit on the balcony. She replayed the conversation about missing anyone and wondered if Steph was doing a bit of fishing. Maybe. Not that it really mattered, but she did like Steph and thought maybe they could do some things together as friends. There could be nothing more. Her head wasn't in the right place, and after all, it had only been six months since Dusty had died. Anyway, for all she knew, Steph wasn't gay. So why did she seem to get annoyed when Raf gave Cori attention? Oh, God, she wished Liz was here. She'd be able to decipher all these mixed messages. She was rubbish at all this stuff. After all, she'd only had one partner.

She'd met Dusty when she was twenty-one, at the library where she'd worked. Dusty had flirted with her. Of course, she'd always thought that her preference was women, but she'd led a sheltered life in her early days. She wasn't a party animal and although Liz had taken her to one of the gay clubs, she didn't feel comfortable in that atmosphere. Her other few friends were straight, and there weren't any women in the library she'd been attracted to. Dusty had chatted her up and asked her to dinner, and she'd wooed her and wowed her and eventually seduced her. The following year, she'd moved in with Dusty. It was amazing. Dusty had treated her like a queen. She seemed to worship her. Everything seemed to be perfection. *Until.* First it was her friends. She'd disliked them, particularly Liz. Then she'd discouraged her from seeing too much of her mum and dad. She'd said that Cori preferred her parents' company to hers. Of course, she didn't, but she loved her mum and dad, and they'd always been so close. It was like asking her to choose. She loved Dusty, so she visited her parents on her own mostly. Just as she did with Liz. She let the iPad rest on her lap as she remembered that conversation. Her mum and dad had quizzed her about her solo visits. They'd been having coffee and it all came out of the blue.

Her mum grimaced. "Why doesn't your girlfriend ever come with you?"

Cori crossed her arms. "She's my partner, Mum, not my girlfriend, and her name is Dusty."

Her mum shrugged. "Whatever. It's the same difference."

Cori shook her head. "It's not, actually. When I met Dusty, I introduced her as my girlfriend. It was the beginning of our relationship, and I wasn't sure if there was anything long term. We live together now, and we've planned our life together. That makes her my partner."

Her dad cleared his throat. "Does that mean you'll be getting married one day?"

"Blimey, Dad. I don't know. We haven't thought that far ahead. Don't you like her?" Cori looked from her mum to her dad.

Her dad clenched his fists. "If anything, we think it's she who doesn't like us."

"Dad, that's unfair. She does like you…it's just that she doesn't really know how to act around you. You know she spent most of her life in care. She was farmed out to foster parents and had a terrible childhood."

Her dad nodded. "Yes, I know that, and she obviously had an awful time. Listen, Cori, all your mum and I want is for you to be happy, but she seems to have driven a wedge between us, and we don't want to lose you. She seems to have so much influence over you."

Cori got up and hugged them both. "You're wrong about her influence. And as for the wedge, that's not going to happen. I promise you. She'll come around gradually, you'll see. She just has to learn to trust." Cori knew that wasn't true. Dusty had no intention of doing so, and that's why she was a bag of nerves, always clock-watching and dashing off before Dusty got home from work.

As for being in care…that had all been a pack of lies. Everything about Dusty was lies and deceit. But she'd found out too late. She didn't think she'd ever be able to trust anyone again. Ever.

She covered her face with her hands. Her happy mood had now turned to melancholy.

Suddenly there was a commotion. Shouting came from the balconies on either side of her. She jumped up and leaned on the handrail.

The people next door pointed out to sea. "Dolphins," they shouted.

Oh my God, there they were. A pod of about eight of them. They were amazing. It was like they were putting on a synchronized dance display for them, and they were so close to the ship. She reached for her iPad and took a video. They turned and went out to sea and Cori thought that was it, then they glided around and returned even closer, jumping now. Their tails moved rhythmically, and the faster they got, the quicker they propelled themselves through the water. They were flipping and jumping and as they moved closer to the surface, they gave powerful flicks of the tail and leapt into the air. She'd never seen anything like it in her life. She laughed freely, openly, for the first time in ages. She'd send that to her parents and Liz. She was sure they'd be as impressed as she was. Imagine, Christmas Eve and seeing that magnificent spectacle. It was as if someone had organised it especially for her. Whatever, or whoever, her mood had changed from melancholic to joyful within minutes. "Thank you," she whispered.

Later, she showered, and laid some clothes out on the bed, ready for later. There was a slight wrinkle in the shirt, though, so she put it aside to iron later, and chose something else. She put on casual slacks and a simple shirt and walked down to the fifth floor. From the balcony she had a terrific view of the Christmas tree. She could see Raf and about ten other members of staff gathered around the tree on the floor below. In the centre of the atrium, there was a table which stretched about six metres long. She couldn't believe her eyes; it was a replica of a village made from gingerbread, and a little train ran all the way around the houses. Once again, she took her iPad out and videoed the scene. Someone had gone to a lot of trouble, and it wasn't wasted. She spotted Raf waving to her and beckoning her down.

She shouted up. "Come on, Cori. We need some help here with the carols."

Cori grabbed hold of the stair rail and made her way down. Granted, Raf might be a little overzealous, but at least she never left Cori to stand around on her own. "I love singing carols, but I'll get nervous in front of all these people."

Raf put her arm around her shoulder. "Don't be crazy, honey. Just join in. Everyone else will." She handed her a sheet with all the words of the carols they'd be singing. She looked around feeling self-conscious and glanced upstairs and saw Steph leaning on the balcony above her. Cori waved and Steph came running down. She had a pair of mint green jeans on and a tank top that matched. She looked fixedly at her and couldn't help but notice her well-developed muscles. She must be in the gym every day to get a well-toned body like that. She quickly averted her eyes, realising that she was gawping at her.

Cori cleared her throat. "You can share my carol sheet if you like."

By that time, Raf was organising everyone. She moved closer to Cori, and they began to sing. First up was "O Come All Ye Faithful." It was a happy song, and everyone sang at the top of their voices. Steph didn't need the words and seemed to know them all off by heart, which surprised Cori, though she didn't know why. They went through their repertoire and ended. It was all so uplifting, and everyone seemed to be sad when it came to an end. They all congregated for a while. Nobody wanted to leave.

Raf held her hands high. "Okay, one more then. Do you know the words to 'Joy to the World'? Don't know about you, but it seems like an appropriate song to finish with. I wish you all joy." Raf began and everyone followed. Steph and Cori sang at the top of their voices. Unfortunately, she only knew the first verse, but she hummed the rest. Once again, Steph knew all the verses.

Raf came over to them. "See you girls later. Duty calls." She pecked Cori on the cheek. But not Steph.

Steph grimaced. "She's a bit overfamiliar, isn't she?"

Cori laughed, although she agreed entirely. "I think she's trying to wind you up."

Steph crossed her arms. "Why, though?"

Cori shrugged, embarrassed by the assumption she'd made that Steph might be interested in her. "No idea." She looked at her watch. "God, look at the time. I should go. Got to get ready."

Steph nodded. "See you up in the Galaxy."

Cori waved. "See you there."

She wasn't sure why she'd told Steph that Raf was winding her up. She guessed it was true, but all the same, why had she bothered? Possibly because she liked Steph. She ran up the stairs with a spring in her step and a smile on her face. It felt good to be alive and it was a long time since she'd had that feeling.

Chapter Four

STEPH LOOKED BACK ON the day so far. It seemed like she'd only had a couple of hours' sleep when she'd heard buzzing in her ear. Breakfast. She grabbed her robe, slipped it on and ran towards the door, stubbing her toe on the vanity unit. Good start. She opened the door and managed a smile at the young waiter.

"Good morning, ma'am. Shall I set your breakfast up on the veranda?"

Steph remembered her poxy veranda. It was more like a sardine can. "No, thanks. The table will be fine."

He left and she poured herself coffee. She lifted the lid off one of the two plates, remembering she'd ordered an assortment of pastries. She wasn't that hungry, but thought she'd find room for her favourite breakfast. She bit into the salted egg croissant. It was so buttery, and the gooey egg filling ran down the side of her mouth. She caught it with her finger and licked it. She managed the chocolate one too which was equally as yummy but couldn't manage the Danish. After a quick shower, she set off on her mission. The door was open to the suite on the other side of hers and the cabin stewardess stepped out.

"Morning, Ms Steph. You good this morning?"

Steph looked at her name tag. "Yes, I'm good, thanks, Vaz." The room looked empty. "Hey, Vaz, is that room occupied?"

"No. Not taken, Ms."

This could be her lucky day. She scooted along the corridors and walked a couple of flights down to Reception. She smiled broadly at the receptionist. "Hi, Josy, my name is Steph Graves and I'm in room six-twenty. I've got a balcony, but the view is obscured," she laughed, "there's one of those big tender things hanging in front." Josy didn't laugh. "I was wondering if there are any other rooms available? I saw that next door wasn't occupied."

Josy tapped away on her PC. "I'm afraid there's only that one free."

Steph's eyes sparkled. "Can I swap rooms then, please?"

"Yes. No problem." She smiled. "I can arrange an upgrade for you."

Steph tilted her head. "An upgrade?"

"Yes. It's the Master Suite."

Josy mentioned a figure to upgrade, which ran into thousands of dollars, so after she'd picked herself up off the floor, she declined the offer. Her shoulders slumped. "But it's really depressing looking at that thing. I didn't see any of that in the brochure."

"I'm afraid that's the room you paid for, Ma'am."

The way she said it made Steph feel like a second-class citizen. "No worries, I'll make sure I check it out next time." She turned and walked away. "Snotty cow." She hoped Josy could hear her. She took the elevator to the upper decks and stared through the glass as she ascended. She felt like one of life's losers.

Things improved, though. Golf and lunch went well. She considered going to the gym but instead, she'd stripped off and changed into her bikini. She lay on the sunbed, minus the sun, clutching her iPhone, and jotted a few texts to her friends.

She turned her head from side to side to alleviate the tension creeping up her shoulders. Aargh. Just thinking about Raf's arms around Cori while they were golfing made her jaw clench. Teach her to putt? Huh, she knew exactly what Raf wanted to teach her. She'd made that obvious. Or maybe that's how she always was. A flirt. Putting things into perspective, she'd only just met Cori, but she liked her, and she thought during the trip they may become friends and have some fun together. That was all. Yes, she was attractive, but it was early days, and anyway, she shouldn't be thinking about anything more. She'd made a big mess of things at home, and this was supposed to be a vacation to reflect on her life. She laughed. Some chance.

Cori was right though, Raf was winding her up, but why was she letting it get to her? Because she didn't like Raf, she didn't trust her, and she was definitely interested in Cori. *Fuck it. Don't let her bug you.* Time to chillax, or at least pretend it didn't bother her.

She was bored then so she got up and leaned on the balcony rail. She stretched forward and looked at the balcony next to hers, the one that was vacant. It looked so inviting. There was a divider between the balconies and that's all that separated them. She looked it over. One bolt at the top and one at the bottom. No harm investigating. She slipped the bolts and quietly folded the door back and latched it. She checked around. Nobody there and the curtains from the sliding door were closed. Bloody hell, the balcony alone was huge. It was one of those wraparound balconies that extended around the corner. And there was the sun! Not much, but enough for her. There was no furniture, but who cared. She went back, fetched her towel and sun cream and spread the towel on the deck. She lay down and began to giggle. Why shouldn't she? Problem solved. *Let's hope I don't get caught.*

Later, the carol singing had gone well and at least Raf hadn't been able to monopolise Cori all the time. It was much more fun than singing in a church, and at least there were no sermons. She flipped through her pics and videos of the singing and gingerbread village. Now that was cool. She posted them in emails to her mother and father, along with her sister and uncle, even though she wasn't sure they'd bother to watch them. She wished them a Merry Christmas. Somehow, she thought she might be having a better one than them. Frivolity was frowned upon in their households.

She wondered if they'd forgiven her yet. She doubted it, but at least she was out of their way and wouldn't be a cause for embarrassment. She was certain her absence wouldn't be noticed. The blunder with the woman was just a one-off and strictly speaking, she wasn't the client, so nothing was untoward, not *really*. They were making a mountain out of a molehill. The woman, Jocelyn, had come into the office with her friend, who was arranging her father's burial. She'd caught her unawares, and maybe she'd been a bit flattered that the woman had paid her so much attention. She was gorgeous and incredibly sexy. Jocelyn had caught her eye…and those eyes, they were so wild and beguiling. Then she came into the florist to order flowers. She was her kind of woman, and what was the harm in getting to know her a bit better? On reflection, she should never have succumbed, and certainly not in the Chapel of Rest. Funerals were serious occasions, so yeah, maybe sex in that haven of meditation hadn't been the best move.

They'd dined out, laughed a lot, and seemed to get along fine. Jocelyn invited her around for dinner, one thing led to another, and they ended up in another room. And that's where it all went tits up. It wasn't that Steph was prissy, far from it. She liked to experiment and spice up her sex life, in fact there was nothing better. But with a new woman, she preferred to get to know them a little before adding kink. At least until the second date. However, Jocelyn had different ideas. Bizarre things happened. Luckily, she'd escaped.

Unfortunately, Jocelyn was pissed with her attitude. She kept leaving messages and naked pictures of herself on Steph's phone. Eventually she blocked her. Then a few days later, Jocelyn made the complaint. Still, that was history now. New beginnings, she hoped.

She showered, washed her hair, and applied the styling clay. She picked out some clothes to wear and opted for tight black trousers, a white blouse, and her black and white striped waistcoat, which was her favourite. She was happy with the reflection in the mirror and left before she changed her mind.

She got up to the lounge early tonight and there was only Dorothy and Lena there so far. "So, ladies, how was your day?"

Lena clasped her hands together. "Oh, it was wonderful. We both love playing cards and we found this lovely little group, didn't we, Dorothy?"

Dorothy nodded chirpily. "And we went to the carol singing."

"Yeah, that was terrific. Got me all in the Christmas mood." Steph glanced around. "Talking of Christmas, I'd love a drink."

Lena stood and waved to a waiter. "They're ever so good. So easy to catch their eye. You'll get used to it. We've been on every ship now and they're all the same. So kind and attentive."

Steph imagined they had to be. This was no cheap cruise, but luckily, she'd got it at a fraction of the price. How did the sisters manage to go on cruises like this all the time? Grooming pooches was obviously lucrative.

The waiter greeted her. "What can I get you tonight? A white wine perhaps?"

Steph shook her head. "I fancy something a little more exciting tonight." After all, she'd be having wine later with her meal.

"The Black Russian is excellent."

"Really. What's in it?"

"Vodka, coffee liqueur, ice and a maraschino cherry."

Steph grimaced. "Sounds potent."

"What about making it a long drink and topping it up with coke? Makes it into a Dirty Black Russian."

"Sounds perfect." Otherwise, she'd end up having two and be shit-faced before dinner. She spotted Cori from the corner of her eye. "My friend has just arrived. Would you mind waiting so she can order?"

"Of course not, ma'am."

Steph stood. "I've just ordered. What would you like, Cori?"

Cori smiled. "Thanks. Can I have a cosmopolitan, please?"

"Of course. Be right back, ladies."

Cori sat down next to Lena, and Steph sat the other side of her. Her plan had worked. This arrangement meant Raf wouldn't be able to have those exclusive chats with Cori and leave everyone else out. As she sat down, by accident her hand briefly touched Cori's. Bats began to flap in her stomach. Oh, God, that was a sure sign that she was crushing. Still, why not, it was Christmas. Everyone should have a crush at this time of the year. It wasn't like she had to do anything about it.

Patti, Mike, and Raf walked in together. Raf looked a bit miffed at the seating arrangement, but still plastered that fake smile on her face. Their drinks arrived and the others ordered theirs. The chat was animated as everyone reported on their day's events.

Raf took a sip of her drink. "So, did everyone see the school of dolphins?"

"Pod," Steph corrected. She wished she hadn't when Raf gave her a look reminiscent of the one her mother often gave her.

Raf shrugged. "Pod, school, who cares. Did you see them, though?"

Steph shook her head. "No."

Raf leaned back in her chair with a look of satisfaction. "Ah, no, of course you wouldn't. You're on the wrong side of the ship." She laughed. "And there's not much of a view or any sun."

Ha ha! Not true anymore. And how did she know where she was?

Cori sighed and tilted her head. "They were wonderful. They danced like ballerinas." She took her phone out of her bag. "Here. I should be able to get them up in my album." She eventually leaned in towards Steph. "There they are. I've got several videos."

Steph tilted her head in to look and moved the phone closer. She touched Cori's hand again. A tingling sensation shot up her arm like she'd been prodded with little needles. "Wow, that's awesome. Don't suppose you could send them to my phone?"

Cori nodded. "I'd be happy to, but I don't know how to do that. I'm not really into that techy stuff. Someone always looked after that side of things for me." She handed Steph her phone. "Will you do it?"

So, who was this someone? She hoped she'd find out, but in the meantime, Steph shared the photos and videos to her phone. At least that way Cori would have her email.

Dorothy sat forward and so did her sister. "Can we see too?"

"Sure." Cori passed them her phone.

Lena pouted. "Ah. We missed them. We were playing cards."

"So, you found the bridge club?" Raf asked.

"Yes, thank you, Raf. A lovely bunch of people." Lena turned her head and whispered, not too subtly, "Dorothy has a bit of a memory problem, but it's amazing how well she does in bridge."

Raf grinned. "How is sex like a game of bridge?"

Lena gave a little chuckle but looked uncomfortable. "Oh, I wouldn't know."

"If you have a good hand, you don't need a partner."

Raf laughed at her own joke and Mike did too and punched her arm playfully. "You are a one, Raf."

Steph wasn't sure what "a one" was but wished "one" would put a muzzle on her.

Raf looked at her watch. "Okay, folks, time to eat. I've booked us in at The Brindisi tonight. Promises to be a good evening."

Everyone seemed to be happy with the arrangements and they made their way to the next floor.

The head waiter greeted them. "I have the best table reserved for you beautiful ladies." He showed them to a table outside on the balcony. He spotted Mike. "You are one lucky man. Is this your harem?"

Mike puffed his chest out and did a little shuffle. "Yes, it's my Christmas present to myself." He laughed and looked triumphantly happy.

Steph fought the urge to roll her eyes and say she wasn't harem material but chose not to make a big deal of it. Instead, she focused on the restaurant. "Wow, this is awesome. Christmas Eve and dining al fresco." What could be more romantic? Well, take away the sisters, Patti, and Mike and of course Raf, now that would be romantic. Not that romance was part of this trip, but still. She'd try and capture the memory in a photo. Maybe she could ask Raf to take the shot? Though she was sure Raf would muscle in on every photograph.

"Raf!" Someone called out to her from another table. She turned around, sighed heavily, and walked over to speak to them.

With Raf out of the way, Steph thought she may be able to organise the seating again. Their table was oval and one of those where you had to slide into the upholstered leather seating.

Dorothy and Lena hung back. "Do you mind if we take the chairs? Much easier for us oldies," Lena said.

"Not at all." Cori slid in and Steph followed. Perfect. It sat four so Mike and Patti joined them. There was plenty of room, but Steph sat as close to Cori as she could. The cocktail she'd had was strong and had made her lightheaded and brave.

It wasn't long before Raf returned. She looked across at Steph and gave her one of those feigned smiles, then sat on the other chair. She picked the wine list up and handed it to Steph. "What shall we order tonight? Do you have a preference?"

Steph felt the beads of sweat forming on her brow, but she tried to remain composed. "I think we should stick with the sommeliers' recommendation, they're far more knowledgeable than me." Fuck. Until this cruise, she'd never come across a sommelier. She'd had to google it. Pretentious pricks. Why couldn't they just call them wine waiters? She'd got through that one, but Raf seemed to be going out of her way to show everyone that she was a pleb. She was proud of who she was, but it still made her feel inferior.

They all nodded, and when the waiter came along, they ordered their appetisers.

All the food was amazing and after two other courses, their entrée was served. Cori deliberated and eventually chose the chicken. Steph rarely had duck, so she plumped for that with an assortment of vegetables and dauphinoise potatoes. Steph tucked in. So far, she couldn't find any fault with any of the food she'd had. It was like eating in a Michelin star restaurant three times a day. She usually settled for a ready meal and a glass of plonk at home in the evening.

The waiter topped everyone's glass up and the conversation around the table became more animated with each glass. At some point, they all raised their glasses. "Merry Christmas, everyone." Yes, so far, it was proving to be an incredibly happy occasion.

Cori rested her knife and fork on the side of the plate. "Hey, Raf. Thanks so much for all the trips you booked. They all look spectacular. I can't believe it." She wiped her forehead with the back of her hand. "Do you know, I've never done ziplining before. It looks scary."

Steph sat up straight. "Ziplining? They didn't offer me that one. Said it was full."

Raf dabbed the corner of her mouth with her napkin. "Yes, it was the most popular. Why, did you want to do it?"

Steph leaned forward. "You bet."

Raf smiled. "I'll see what I can do. I can't verify it until later tomorrow, but if it's on, I'll get someone to slip the confirmation under your door. Keep your fingers crossed."

"Wow, that would be fantastic. Thanks, Raf."

"Don't mention it. Don't anyone forget, you must check in for all the excursions at the Solar Theatre. You exchange your ticket, and they'll give you a coach number. Make sure you're on time though, and if you want to take the trip with friends, one person should take all the tickets to check in."

Steph perked up. Maybe Raf was having her on, but she seemed confident about the ziplining. Perhaps she wasn't so bad after all? Maybe she'd allowed her penchant for drama to paint Raf in a bad light. She reached into her bag and got her phone out. "Would someone take some pics for me? It's Christmas Eve, we're in the Caribbean. I mean, what could be more exotic?"

Mike took her phone. "I'll take lots, then you can forward them to all of us."

Raf held her hand out. "No, you get in the photos too, Mike. I'll take them." She danced around taking shots of them from all different directions. "Smile. Move in closer, everyone. Lean in, Dorothy, otherwise I'll cut your head off."

Dorothy covered her mouth with her hand. "Oh no! Not like Anne Boleyn. I've never been adulterous, incestuous, or conspired against the monarchy."

Lena patted Dorothy's arm. "It's all right, darling. It's only a figure of speech. Raf only means she doesn't want to miss your beautiful face in the photograph." She pulled Dorothy close to her and put her arm around her shoulder. Dorothy relaxed and smiled.

Raf took photos from every angle, one after the other, and then handed the phone back to Steph.

Cori nudged her. "I'd love some of those to send to my mum and dad."

Steph smiled. "Sure, I'll send them to your email. I've got your details from when you sent the pics of the dolphins."

"Brilliant."

Steph had almost forgotten that detail. Maybe some time she could message her and suggest meeting up for breakfast, or lunch, or coffee or anything. Things were looking up.

When it came around to dessert, the sisters, plus Mike and Patti, said they were skipping them, as they wanted to catch the show in the theatre. Tonight, it was some magic show and a stage hypnotist.

Mike looked from Steph to Cori. "You two coming along?"

Steph covered her face. "No way. I'm still trying to put that crazy stuff behind me."

"Why, what happened?" Mike asked.

"A hypnotist once put me under, woke me up, and sent me back to my seat. Said I wasn't a good subject. I didn't think I would be because I don't believe in all that rubbish. Next thing I know is the hypnotist calling out number three and I got up and did the chicken dance."

Everyone laughed loudly.

"Not funny. It happened loads of times, and just like you, everyone was in fits of laughter. I wasn't even aware, but I'll never live it down because one of my friends videoed it and put it on Facebook. So, no... never again." Anyway, she'd much prefer to sit there with Cori, and Raf was less of a threat than a hypnotist.

Raf snorted. She seemed to find her disaster somewhat amusing. Luckily someone tapped her on the shoulder, and she excused herself.

This was a perfect time for Steph to broach the subject of having dinner together. She might not get another opportunity, so she took a deep breath. "I wondered if you'd like to join me for dinner on Boxing Day. I managed to get a booking in Island Prime. Unfortunately, it's an early one at six forty-five. That's all I could get, but I wanted to try it out, and it would be really great to eat with someone instead of on my own."

Cori smiled. "I'd love to. I didn't book any myself. Hopefully I'll see you on the ziplining trip, but otherwise we can meet there."

Steph grinned. "Great. That's fantastic." Maybe she shouldn't have gone overboard but she couldn't pretend that she wasn't ecstatic. She'd have liked to have got up and done the chicken dance, but that would have been overkill. So, that was that. A Boxing Day date. Could this Christmas get any better? She couldn't wait to tell her friends and of course, she'd be sending them some photos too. She didn't have a bestie, but a group of them always hung out and went to pubs and clubs together. Granted, she wouldn't call any of them if she was in a bind, but not everyone was so lucky.

Raf returned and they ordered desserts. After, they had coffee together, then Raf became a little fidgety. She made some head signal to Cori, as though she had a tick or something. Or was it a "shall we go" sign. Oh my God. Was there already something between them? Shite. She'd left it too late. In that case, why would Cori have accepted her invitation? She hoped she was imagining things, even though it was illogical to feel that way and she had no claim on Cori's time.

Raf looked at her watch. "I have to do some paperwork when I get back, so I only have about ten minutes or so."

Ten minutes or so for what? She looked from one to the other, waiting for another code, but none came.

"Or would you like more coffee?"

Steph shook her head and turned to Cori. *What's going on here?*

Cori stretched, her breasts pushing against her blouse perfectly. "No, thanks. Shall we go?"

Go where?

Raf got up and they slid out from their seats and followed. When they left the restaurant, they didn't go towards the elevator, they walked straight ahead and onto the pool deck. Steph followed, unsure what else to do and hating the feeling of having been dismissed without a word.

Raf turned to her. "We're just nipping to the Connoisseurs lounge."

Steph shrugged. "What the heck's that?"

"The smoking room." Raf looked smug.

Steph looked at Cori. "Oh. I didn't know you smoked."

Cori blushed and her body seemed to tense. "I'm sorry. I only smoke a few a day, but I enjoy one after dinner."

Steph smiled. "You don't need to apologise. It's still a free country. I'm not an anti-smoker. I think everyone is entitled to make their own choices."

Cori's shoulders relaxed. "Yes, me too. But not everyone is so unbiased."

Raf grimaced. "Tough shit. They can take a hike."

Steph shrugged. She meant what she'd said before. Everyone to their own. "What's this place like? Sounds posh."

Cori reached out almost like she was going to touch her, and then dropped her hand. "Come and have a look. It's very civilised."

Steph followed. Cori was right. It was a bit like one of those gentlemen's clubs you saw in the movies. On the floor was a luxurious carpet in swirly red patterns and there were beautiful leather armchairs and sofas. There were several people there and a lot of laughter. She guessed they all had something in common and they'd get to know each other much quicker from seeing the same people. A waiter passed by with a tray full of drinks, pushed the door open and it quickly closed behind him. Yes, it was posh all right. She didn't smoke and didn't want to smell like she did, so it was a no-go area for her. She resented Raf having a shared interest, but she couldn't do anything about it. She said her farewells and went back to her room. She sat on the bed and went through the photos on her phone. They were good, and there were plenty of them. She was relieved to see that Raf hadn't chopped her head off either. She picked an assortment out and sent them to Cori and her friends. They were terrific reminders of her Christmas, so far.

***

Christmas Day. That was the first thing Steph thought when she opened her eyes. This was the first year she'd ever spent Christmas away from her family and friends. There wasn't even a hint of nostalgia. What would her family be doing? Their traditions were the same every year. Her mum made a turkey that was always too dry, her dad commented on how dry it was, and her sister would try to smooth things over by talking about work. Because nothing said Christmas like talking about funerals. When that didn't work, they'd start talking about all the ways Steph needed to change her life, and how disappointing it was that she wasn't *someone* yet.

For once in her life, she'd broken away from the soul-crushing holiday. She ordered coffee and took it onto her adopted veranda. They were cruising the Caribbean Sea, just imagine. How blessed she was. She looked up at the sky. It was like a canvas covered in a mass of blue with an array of golden sunshine. The sea was calm, and the waves glistened silver and gold as they rippled against the side of the ship. She sighed. She wished she could paint because this was a seascape made in heaven.

She checked her phone. A nice email from her uncle, a couple from friends, and two curt ones from her parents and sister that just said Merry Christmas. Still at least she knew she'd be having one, and the turkey was bound to be better than her mother's. Her stomach rumbled and grumbled so she went back to her suite, quickly dressed, and made her way to the restaurant. There weren't many people around and she guessed a lot of them were having their breakfast in bed. Perhaps she should have opted for that, but it would be no fun on her own. She could hardly ask them to set it up on her new balcony and eating on her own deck next to the lifeboat wasn't exactly thrilling, but then, being in here on her own wasn't exactly awesome, either.

She passed the central table where one of the waitresses was serving champagne and caviar. She politely refused. That wasn't her go-to this early in the day, or any part of the day really. She filled her glass with freshly squeezed orange juice and loaded her plate with scrambled eggs, sausages, bacon, and toast. It was too nice to eat inside, so she took it to a table on the veranda. She'd just begun to tuck in when she saw Cori hovering near the door. She shot up and waved to attract her attention. "Cori. Over here."

Cori spotted her, waved back, and smiled. "Can I join you?"

Steph stood and pulled out a chair. "Sure thing." She looked behind Cori and one of the waiters was carrying Cori's plate and orange juice. He placed it on the table and said he'd be back with coffee. Cori leaned in and kissed Steph on the cheek.

"Merry Christmas, Steph." It was a lovely surprise, and she took the opportunity to put her arms gently around Cori's shoulder. "Merry Christmas, Cori." It was only brief, but during those seconds, she inhaled the beautiful fragrance on Cori's neck. She'd have liked to have kissed it…possibly followed by a kiss on the lips. She took a deep breath. She must stop thinking like this. She'd already told herself that they were only going to be friends. Still, there was no harm in a little fantasy.

By the time she'd stopped daydreaming, her food had gone tepid, but she couldn't give a damn. She'd eat it frozen if it meant sitting opposite this gorgeous woman. It was the first time she'd been able to ogle her legitimately. She wanted to make a long-lasting impression on Cori and tried to hold her gaze to make that deep connection. Her sapphire blue eyes seemed to have a tint of green today. Or was that the sunlight casting a different colour? As for Cori's hair, she seemed to spend a lot of time getting it just so…almost manicured, like her hands which looked so soft and smooth. Cori said something, but she was miles away thinking about Cori's hands touching her body. Unfortunately, Steph couldn't change the habit of a lifetime, even though she knew she shouldn't even be contemplating that thought.

"Steph?"

"Sorry. Pardon?"

Cori laughed. "I asked you what you'd be doing on Christmas Day back home."

Steph looked at her watch. "Right now, I'd be trying to figure out how to get out of going to church."

"Really?"

Steph laughed. "My sister is a minister in the Anglican church, so, my family and I always go to the Christmas morning service."

"Hey, that's wonderful. You and who?"

Ah. So, she was showing some interest. She wasn't used to that. "I always pick my mother and father up and we go together. We meet up with my uncle and his family, and after the service, we all go back to my parents' house for a Christmas meal together." She omitted how grim the whole affair really was. If it wasn't for her uncle's family, she didn't think she'd be there. "What about you?"

Cori put her head down, and her arms and hands fell limply into her lap. "Not all happy memories."

Steph reached across and stroked Cori's arm. "I'm sorry."

"Maybe I'll tell you about it sometime. This year, I just want to enjoy Christmas."

"Absolutely. Just to let you know, I'm a good listener. I don't judge and I never divulge anything anyone tells me."

Cori nodded. "I believe you. I don't know you, but you seem like a genuine person."

Steph gave a small nod. "Thank you. I like to think I am. I hope I can prove that too. I'd like us to be friends." In truth, Cori was way out of her league, even as a friend.

Cori nodded. "Me too."

They were getting on fine and then Patti and Mike rolled up. She wished she could magic them away because she wanted Cori all to herself.

"Merry Christmas, girls." They gave them customary cheek kisses and hugs like they were old friends. They pulled up two chairs. "Can we join you?"

She and Cori both spoke at the same time. "Of course." It wasn't really a question because they'd already sat down.

Patti rubbed her hands together. "Did you have the champagne and caviar? It was amazing."

Cori shook her head. "Not really a caviar and champagne person."
"Me neither," Steph added.

Patti pulled a face. "What a waste. Still, everyone to their own."
Mike crossed his arms. "So, what's everyone doing today?"

Cori frowned. "Not sure. I haven't read the events sheet yet."

Mike looked at Patti. "We're going to play in the bocce ball tournament."

Cori sighed. "Don't know what that is."

Mike laughed. "I'm sure Raf will teach you."

Cori gave a half smile. "I think I'll give that a miss today."

Mike shook his finger at Cori. "Remember what sea days are?"

"Sea days are Raf days." Steph and Cori said it at the same time. They both covered their mouths with their hands and giggled. Somehow, she thought this would become an in-joke between them.

Steph caught Cori's eye. "Shall we do the Christmas treasure hunt instead? Sounds like fun." This was a small cruise ship and there wasn't that much going on. She wouldn't have minded all-day entertainment like they had on one of the bigger ships, like the wave surfing machines or the ropes course, but this was the only thing on offer at the moment. Anyway, she'd come for a break in the sun and to see some islands she'd always dreamed about. She could do that other stuff somewhere else, some other time.

"Yes, why not. I'll just go and change into my shorts. Where does it start from?"

"By the pool. See you there in about an hour."

They left the table and went their separate ways, and Steph knew it was already a better Christmas than any she'd had before.

Dead on the dot of eleven Steph waited by the pool and Cori arrived, looking beautiful in a simple shorts outfit that showed off her legs. Ben, one of the entertainment staff, handed them their Treasure Hunt instructions. Steph glanced at the list. "Shit, where the hell do we start?"

Cori leaned over. "Wow, this so reminds me of when I was a kid. My mum used to organise these for my brother and me. Bet you did this, too?"

No. Her mother had never done this. She hadn't got the imagination or the inclination. She wasn't about to admit to it. "Maybe. But it was a long time ago." She rubbed the back of her neck. "So, what do we do?"

Cori took the instructions from her. "You see, it's all blank clues, rhyming ones, mirror clues, pictures, codes, and mazes. So, all we have to do is follow the treasure map clues…and we're there."

"Right. Lead the way, Captain."

Cori threw all sorts of questions at her. They seemed to cover the whole ship. Down one corridor, up another and eventually they filled in the answers to the riddles. Steph answered a few, but mostly it was down to Cori. It seemed to take hours but eventually they arrived back at the pool deck. For Steph, it ended too soon. They laughed, joked, and found more than one little nook to take in the view of the ocean together. For the first time in forever, Steph didn't feel the need to be anyone other than who she was. When Cori laughed, it made Steph feel all warm and squishy inside. She liked it. A lot.

Ben took the sheet. "Might have guessed you two would be here first." He winked. "Of course, it doesn't mean you've won, it just means you're faster than the rest."

In fact, they didn't win, but they did come second and got a gift certificate each to use anywhere on the ship.

Steph grinned. "That was such fun." She punched Cori on her arm, then immediately felt a little silly for the juvenile gesture. "We came second. C'mon, let's go celebrate with some lunch."

Cori seemed equally elated. "That's the best Christmas morning I've spent since my childhood."

"Something to add to our new memory list, eh?" Steph wasn't sure why but the thought of creating memories with Cori filled her with a warm glow.

"You bet!"

Steph was delighted that Cori had chosen to spend time with her and not join in with the arranged events and having lunch together on Christmas Day was a real bonus. It made her feel special.

"Thanks so much for the photos. I sent them to my mum and dad, and to my brother and grandparents."

Steph was chuffed to bits. She'd been included in someone's important pictures.

Cori laughed. "My best friend, Liz, keeps messaging me and asking for some. Those should shut her up for a while."

Liz. Who was Liz? She didn't say girlfriend, she said best friend. *Stop reading into things.* Steph brushed some crumbs off the tablecloth. "So, what are you doing this afternoon?"

"Sunbathing on my balcony. Might catch up on some reading too. What about you?"

Steph pulled a face. "I'm on the other side. I don't get the sun in the afternoon." She didn't tell Cori that she'd sneaked onto another balcony. Maybe Cori would think that she was some sort of cheapskate.

"You can always sunbathe on the pool deck."

Steph nodded. "I might do that later. Thought I'd go check the gym out first."

Cori fanned herself with her hand. "Much too hot and energetic for me. Are you going to the Christmas show? It sounds like it could be fun, it's all the crew that take part. I suppose Raf will be in it." Cori smiled.

Steph grinned back. "In that case, it'll be a one-woman band."

Cori played with her napkin and glanced up shyly. "We could go together, if you want?"

Steph jolted upright. "That would be great. We can have a giggle together then. What time?"

She looked relieved. "About six outside the theatre. Then we can get out first."

"Brilliant."

Cori stood. "Right. Off now, see you later. Have a great day."

Steph waved her off. She tilted her head as she watched her leave. There was something special about this woman. There was something sad, though, too. It made her feel like she wanted to get to know her better, to talk to her, to help her deal with whatever she was going through. Now she was turning into a big softie, which was quite a novelty as she didn't usually encounter these feelings. Emotional stuff was complicated, and she didn't have time for that.

But for some reason, she wanted to earn Cori's trust and had this deep urge to defend her against the world. It felt natural, not possessive, more that she wanted to protect her. She mentally snorted at herself. Next thing she knew, she'd be throwing her coat down over a puddle so Cori wouldn't get her feet wet or standing in the middle of the road and slowing down traffic for her to cross. It would be laughable if it wasn't so true. What was it about Cori? She huffed and sighed. Like she hadn't already screwed up enough things in her life. She needed to get her shit together, and a holiday romance wasn't going to help her do that.

Chapter Five

CORI HAD A LOVELY afternoon lazing on her lounger and sending all the photos to her family and Liz. The five hours' difference in time meant they could share their Christmas wishes, and somehow, it didn't seem so far away. She'd have loved to have FaceTimed, but the Wi-Fi onboard wasn't that strong and the rules were that nobody could video chat. Cori always obeyed the rules. Of course, Jamaica was only an hour behind. She posted her photos to her grandparents and brother and immediately they replied.

Merry Christmas, Cori. Looks like you're having a wonderful time. Good to see you've met up with a nice bunch of people. You deserve it, sweet pea. Won't be long now and we can't wait! All our love, Grandma, Grandpa and Josh. xxxxx

She smiled. Sweet pea was the special term of endearment her grandparents used. It was lovely seeing those words and a surge of excitement flowed through her. It wouldn't be long, but she didn't want to rush it, she still had lots of fun to come. Although she'd hardly been away long, she felt her old life sliding from her like an old skin. Thoughts of Dusty still intruded, but the distractions available soon shut them down. The tension in her neck and shoulders had begun to ease, and she couldn't remember the last time she'd felt like she could breathe this easily.

She moved her lounger back and forth from sun to shade and when she'd had enough, she took a long luxurious soak in the tub, and she refused to stress about anything at all. After, she got ready and put some clothes on. She was going to wear her dress for Christmas Day but decided to save it for tomorrow in the speciality restaurant. She grabbed her handbag and hot-footed it down to meet Steph.

Steph was leaning up against a pillar. As soon as she saw Cori, a beautiful smile covered her face. "It's just about to start. Shall we sit on the barstools at the back?"

"Good idea."

On came Raf. She was compering the show, of course, and told her usual jokes but tempered somewhat to suit the audience.

As the show progressed, Steph covered her mouth with her hand and whispered to Cori. "Oh look, she's dancing too."

Cori giggled. "And singing."

"Is there no end to this woman's talents?" Steph chuckled and nudged Cori. "Guess what sea days are?"

Cori replied. "Raf, Raf, Raf days."

Steph let out a snort and the people in front looked around and grimaced.

Cori smacked Steph on the arm. "Shush." But it only seemed to make her laugh more.

Steph winked. "Looks like it's coming to an end. Shall we do a runner?"

Cori nodded and they crept out the back of the theatre. "We should make it to the lounge before the masses arrive."

There was hardly anyone there, so they ordered their drinks at the bar and found themselves a nice table by the picture window. There was a small stage in the centre of the room and a quartet were playing quietly.

Steph rubbed the back of her neck. "I can't remember. Are we meeting the gang here tonight?"

"No, they're all going straight to the dining room."

"Good. I don't think I could deal with the adulation from Raf's fans."

Cori smiled. "Hopefully, that will be over with by the time we meet." She shook her head. "Does it feel like Christmas to you?"

"Nah, I suppose it's the climate and lack of family drama." She grinned. "But I'm still having a great time."

"Me too. Thanks for hanging out with me."

"Hey, I should be thanking you. I must have come over as a right jerk on the first night."

Cori laughed. "Well, I did wonder."

"Oi. You weren't supposed to agree with me."

"Only joking." They sipped their drinks in companionable silence for a while, and while Cori couldn't think of any non-intrusive questions to ask about what Steph would normally have been doing today, it wasn't uncomfortable to simply be with her. What a lovely change. Eventually, she glanced at her watch. "Whoops, we're late. Best go join the gang."

They arrived at their table and luckily there were two chairs left, side by side. Everyone was there, including Raf.

Cori tried to appear serious. "The show was terrific, Raf. You're so multi-talented." Steph kicked her on the ankle, but she managed to keep a straight face.

"Well, thank you sweetheart. I'm glad you enjoyed it." Raf grabbed the menu. "I don't know about anyone else, but all that singing and dancing has made me famished."

Without exception, they all ordered the turkey and ham. It was washed down with copious amounts of good wine, and over dinner they made light-hearted chatter.

Lena placed her knife and fork down on her plate. "So, what would everyone be doing today if they weren't on board ship?"

That was what Cori hadn't been able to bring herself to ask Steph outright, and she was glad someone else had brought it up. It wasn't in her nature to pry, but she was undoubtedly interested in knowing more about Steph.

Raf flicked her hair from her face theatrically. "Can't remember not spending Christmas on a ship. But of course, the company is far better this year."

I bet she says that every year. Yes, they were a great bunch of people and she felt comfortable with them, but Cori wasn't sure if Raf was sincere. Perhaps she never got to spend time with her family…and really this ship and all the crew were her family. That was quite a sad thought.

Lena smiled. "Of course, we feel the same. I can't recall the last time we spent Christmas at home—" She turned to Dorothy and touched her hand. "We can't remember either, can we, Dorothy?"

Dorothy smiled. "I love Christmas."

Mike looked at Patti. "What about you?"

Patti shrugged. "I'm divorced, but I have two children. I think I'm a burden to them. 'Who's going to have Mum this Christmas? You have her Christmas, and we'll have her New Year.' I can always read between the lines. So, this year I thought, sod them! I'm going to do something for me." She smiled. "And here I am."

Mike stroked Patti's hand. He didn't seem to be a bad guy after all. In fact, all of them seemed quite caring people. She wasn't sure about Raf, but her life was so different to theirs, and she had a totally different perspective.

Mike slumped in his chair. "I lost my wife a few years ago. I tried Christmas at home last year—" He looked and smiled. "Of course, I have lots of friends and they were so kind, but I had a miserable time, so this year, I thought I'd try a cruise. I have to say, I feel much better."

Patti stroked his arm. "I'm so sorry. Difficult times with so many memories. What about you, Cori?"

There was no way she was going to tell them the truth. Some things were far too personal to share with strangers. "I've always spent it with my mum and dad, but this year, I really felt I needed some sunshine, so I'm killing two birds with one stone."

"How's that?" Steph asked.

"I'm going to see my grandparents and brother in Jamaica."

Steph elbowed her. "Hey, that's brilliant."

Cori smiled. "Yes, it'll be lovely to see them again. What about you, Steph?"

"Family on Christmas Day, and then the usual parties with friends. Nothing special. Wanted a change this year, though."

Steph gave her a quick smile before she concentrated on her drink, and it was clear there was more to her story that she, too, didn't want to share. After hearing their reasons for being here, Cori didn't feel quite so bad. Of course, her story was far more tragic, and she was sure they'd be empathetic if she shared it with them, but she didn't want anyone's sympathy, particularly as she'd only be telling half-truths about Dusty. She could never bring herself to admit how selfish she'd been, too. However, they all had one thing in common. They were lonely.

It was a strange evening and there was a bit of an anticlimax at dinner even though they all wore their silly Christmas hats, pulled crackers, and put on their happy faces. Eating roast turkey and all the trimmings, followed by Christmas pudding just didn't hit the spot. Steph was right, it was possibly down to the warmth of sailing through the Caribbean Sea. But what the heck, did it really matter? This was all about the vacation and the islands they were going to visit, and tomorrow it would all begin.

Despite the underlying feeling of nostalgia and loneliness, the meal lasted hours. Eventually, they said their farewells to the others and Cori and Raf said they were going up for their final smoke of the day.

Steph looked how Cori felt…gloomy. Perhaps she'd have liked to go to one of the lounges for another drink, but Cori wanted to get a good night's sleep in preparation for her first trip tomorrow.

When they got to the atrium, Steph seemed to perk up. "Hope to see you guys tomorrow on the trip." She winked at Cori. "Otherwise, see you later."

Cori winked back and both she and Raf gave Steph a wave and made their way up to their lounge.

Raf puffed on her cigar then squashed it out in the ashtray. "Sorry I can't stay longer, sweetheart. Have to be up at the crack of a sparrow's fart."

"No worries. I'm off in a minute. See you tomorrow, Raf."

She blew a kiss. "You certainly will, hun."

Cori went back to her room. She sat at her table and filled in the breakfast menu, then hung it outside her door. Once undressed, she slid under her duvet into her comfortable bed.

All in all, her day had been a good one, and she certainly hadn't missed the usual arguments. To be honest, her Christmases were terrible. Dusty had made one small concession, and that was to go for lunch with her mum and dad. She recalled their last Christmas together, unable to keep the memory from intruding.

She'd really tried hard that year to buy the right gifts for Dusty. When Dusty started unwrapping the first present, Cori felt the beads of sweat forming on her forehead. She jammed her hands under her armpits and waited.

Dusty pulled out the sweatshirt. "Ah, you remembered." She held it up in front of her and frowned. "Looks a little small to me."

"It's the size you always have."

"Depends on the shop. I'll try it later." She unwrapped the next one which was the main present.

Cori didn't think she could fail with this one. But Dusty's eyes blazed with anger. "Bloody hell, it's the latest iPhone."

So why wasn't she smiling and jumping up and down? Cori knew she'd been hankering over it for months.

Dusty shook her head and clenched her jaw. "I can't believe this. Spending all this money on me and making me look stupid. You know I can't afford to buy gifts like this!"

Cori was aware of that. She wasn't bothered how much Dusty spent on her, though she would have liked something she'd given thought to, rather than the usual Amazon voucher. "I—I thought you'd really—"

"I was saving for one myself. Now it's left a bitter taste in my mouth."

Cori slumped. "I'll get a refund."

"It's done now. Too late." She sneered. "Great start to the holidays." She looked at her watch. "We'd better get going soon. Get it over with." She sighed heavily. "God, I could really do with a drink."

"Have one. We'll take a taxi."

Dusty cackled. "That's right. Throw your money around again. Come on, let's get going. And remember, don't hang about too long. We'll leave about six so I can get back for the film and a drink."

Cori gathered the gifts for her mum and dad together quickly. Leaving at six would give them four hours together. Oh well, she could have said no altogether, and it wouldn't have been the first time.

As per usual, there were hardly any words spoken on the journey over. It was the same every year. Cori vowed she'd not rise to the bait, but each time, Dusty caught her out. God, she wished she hadn't bought her the phone. She thought she was doing something nice but looking back it was thoughtless and had made Dusty feel small. She'd been inconsiderate and it was all her fault. Mostly, she felt sorry for her poor mum and dad. Seeing Cori and Dusty at odds made them so unhappy.

Then there was Boxing Day. Her friend Liz's family always had a party. Had done since they were kids together. But today was Dusty's day. They did at least pop in for a quick drink, and then went on to her friends. Cori had to drive. It was bad enough not being able to have a drink, but she had absolutely nothing in common with them, and of course, she wasn't allowed to talk about her writing as that was a forbidden subject. Dusty said it made her sound pretentious and bored people.

Today had been such a contrast. She did miss her mum and dad, and she'd have loved to share it with them, but they wanted her to do something for herself and stand on her own two feet. Well, she'd done it. Would Dusty have liked this? Definitely not. There was no way they'd take a vacation like this. She'd say it was too extravagant and living beyond their means. And showing off. Cori could afford it, but Dusty wouldn't have allowed it. She controlled her finances and her life. Looking back, it was such a shame because they could have had a lovely life together—if only Dusty had been different. But really, that was her fault. She'd made her that way because she just wasn't good enough or right enough for Dusty.

Her phone pinged and she reached out and flipped it open, thinking it would probably be a message from her family. She was surprised to see it was from Steph.

Hey, I'm punching the air. I got the ticket for the ziplining tomorrow. Meet you in the theatre, then we can travel together on the coach?

Cori replied. *Terrific, see you there.* She was thrilled. Not only would she have some company, but she was a little apprehensive about the ziplining and was sure she could rely on Steph for moral support. Well, good old Raf. She felt guilty now. Maybe they'd misjudged her.

Images of Steph flashed through her mind. They'd spent a lot of time together today. Breakfast, the treasure hunt, lunch, the show, and then drinks and dinner. Hour by hour, she was getting to know Steph, and so far, she'd found her so supportive and caring. Was it just the company as a friend? No. There was something else. Her eyes glowed whenever she smiled. And she laughed and smiled a lot. It made such a change to share a joke and laugh with someone. Dusty had never been one of those people. She was serious. She always acted and spoke earnestly, rather than in a joking or half-hearted manner. Cori guessed she'd made her that way. Of course, she was so different with her friends. With them she was the life and soul of the party. At first, she hadn't noticed. She supposed love was blind. And then love turned to fear. It wasn't that she was a timid person, it was just that Dusty always made her feel like she was in the wrong. Possibly she was. She hated upsetting her because then she'd go into those rages and storm out of the house. She'd be gone for hours. Then there'd be the silent treatment. In the end, she didn't know why but she always ended up apologising, even though she didn't think it was her fault.

Liz said she revisited the bad memories too often, and the more she dwelled on them, the stronger they'd become. Maybe she was right. Oh, how she wished she could stop looking back. Something always triggered it and then she felt riddled with guilt. If it hadn't been for her, Dusty might still be alive today. She hugged herself and tried to rid her mind of the thoughts. Would there ever be a time when the bad memories would cease to plague her? If there was, she imagined it was an awful long way off.

She plumped her pillows up and took a deep breath. *For God's sake, stop feeling sorry for yourself. Look around, and look at your environment.* Why couldn't she rejoice in all the positives of her life? In the future, she should surround herself with confident and happy people. People like Steph, who were always cheerful and looked on the bright side of life. She imagined Steph's glass would always be half-full. Yes. She'd try to do that. Tomorrow was a new day and at least they'd be on the same excursion. They'd spend all day together and then have dinner in the evening. She put her hands behind her head and leaned back onto her pillow. If that wasn't upbeat, then she didn't know what was.

The next thing she knew was the alarm clock ringing in her ear. She blinked and looked around. Her sleep had been sound. It must be the sea air or something. She took a deep breath and smiled at the lack of tension in her shoulders and the knowledge that there was a wonderful day ahead. She leapt out of bed and pulled the curtains back. Her mouth gaped and she slid the balcony door open. They were due to dock in San Juan, Puerto Rico, and as they approached, the views were stunning. Multi-hued houses covered the hillside like something from a children's painting, vibrant and bold. Blue, red, green, purple...the blocks of Crayola colours made her heart sing. The turquoise water and strand of white sand was something out of a travel brochure. She took her phone out and quickly captured the photos that didn't really do it justice. She couldn't believe that the fortress could look so captivating. It must be El Morro, though she never expected to be passing by at such a close range. She could carry on taking pictures, but she had to get a move on. This was a big day, and it had all the makings of an awesome one.

She skipped to the bathroom, took a shower, and put her bathrobe on. The door buzzer rang, and she let the waitress in. She set up her table and wished her bon appétit. Breakfast in her room seemed extravagant but it was a good choice today. Then she could dress and go straight down to the theatre. She lifted the lid off her plate. "Yummy." Poached eggs and a couple of sausages. She wished it was bacon, but there were mainly Americans on board, and they seemed to cater for their tastes, providing mostly streaky bacon or cooked ham. She'd kill for some lean back bacon, but that wasn't going to happen. She shouldn't complain because the choice of food was phenomenal. She tucked in and washed it down with a few cups of tea.

When she arrived at the theatre, it was filling up. There were loads of tours going out and she hadn't realised just how many people there'd be. There was only one entrance, so she found a seat at the rear. That way she'd see Steph when she entered. A young couple sat next to her and started to chat. It turned out they were also on the ziplining trip. They seemed nice and full of life.

The guy stuck his hand out. "I'm Nyall, and this is my partner, Jess."

She shook hands. "Hi, I'm Cori."

Nyall jumped up. "They've just called out our trip number. Shall I take your ticket and we can travel together?"

"I'm supposed to be meeting my friend. She's on the same trip." Cori scanned the theatre in case she'd missed her. There was no sign. Her shoulders slumped. Either Steph was late, and she'd dash in at the last moment, or she'd overslept.

Nyall slapped his thigh. "Listen, you stay here in case your friend shows and I'll take the tickets down. There's quite a line-up, so it could be ages yet."

That sounded like a perfect idea. "Thanks, Nyall." He took it and joined the queue.

Jess smiled. "You from across the pond?"

"Yes. I guess I am. I know you're American, but which state?"

"Illinois. I'm from Chicago. And you?"

"Leicestershire."

"Hey, we've been there. Went to King Richard's visitor centre. It was awesome. And we went to The National Space Centre."

"No kidding. I live there and yet I've never been to the space centre."

"Well, honey, you should give it a go."

"I'll do that."

It wasn't long before Nyall returned, and he handed her the coach ticket. "We're on number three and it's due to depart at ten thirty."

Cori nodded, but at the same time she looked back hoping to see Steph running through the entrance.

She didn't appear, and it wasn't long before the destinations team shouted that coach one was ready to leave. The instructions were to form an orderly line-up and make their way off the ship. There were a lot of older people around, but boy, could they run.

Nyall covered his mouth with his hand, but Cori could see he was laughing. "Did you see that? There was about a dozen of them with walking sticks, but they lifted them and ran like the wind to get to the front. There's a few miracles today." The three of them laughed out loud. "Hopefully, there won't be too many of those on our trip."

Cori suppressed another laugh. "God help us if there are."

Nyall nudged her. "Well, we know who'll be in the lifeboats first."

He seemed to be on her wavelength, at least. His partner was quiet, for the most part, but seemed nice enough. However, as the minutes ticked by, she became more anxious. The second coach was called and then it was their turn. They walked towards the exit and Cori took a quick glance over her shoulder. She knew if Steph was there, she'd have seen her.

They walked along the dock and into the terminal where they queued to show their passports. Once through, they headed across the tarmac towards their coach. When they boarded, Raf greeted her. Cori was surprised to see her, but then again maybe not.

Raf removed her bag off the front seat. "I've saved you a seat."

"Hey, thanks so much." Cori pointed to her newfound friends. "This is Nyall and Jess from Chicago. Can we sit together?"

"Sure, they can sit opposite." Raf checked her list and ticked them off. "I'm taking the tour today. Unfortunately, with it being Boxing Day, there's a shortage of regular guides."

Cori shook her head. "You're quite amazing. Is there anything you can't do?"

Raf grinned. It was one of those suggestive grins. "Very little, actually."

Cori shook her head and settled in her seat. "Steph said she'd got a ticket for the ziplining, but I haven't seen her, have you?"

Raf held her palms up. "You wouldn't. They put an extra one on due to high demand. Couldn't get her on this one. It was booked to the hilt. It leaves an hour later than us, but I know she really wanted to do this."

Cori lowered her head. She'd thought it was too good to be true. Anyway, that explained it. She couldn't blame Raf because the trip was, and always had been, full. She'd been so looking forward to having Steph beside her for this. And that was silly, really. They'd only just met. Glomming onto someone new when she was in such a vulnerable state was a bad idea. Maybe this wasn't such a bad thing after all.

It wasn't long before the bus filled, and the doors closed.

Raf grabbed the microphone. "If there's anyone here who hasn't had the pleasure of my company before, my name's Raf. Being Boxing Day, there's a shortage of staff in Puerto Rico, but don't worry, I've done this trip many times."

She broke off and chatted to the driver in Spanish. Then she turned around and winked at Cori. "You okay, hun?"

Cori smiled. "Very impressive. Any other languages?"

"My dad insisted I learn Spanish, with it being his language, and I speak Italian, Portuguese, and French. It certainly stands me in good stead on the cruises."

"Wow. I'm envious. I've got a bit of schoolgirl French, but that's it."
"Well, that'll certainly help in St. Barts. They tend to insist on using French." She winked again. "Mind you, you can always stick with me. I'll take care of you."

Cori sensed the colour rising in her cheeks. God. She wished she didn't blush so much. Unfortunately, it was something she'd suffered from since she was a kid. She imagined she'd have got over it by now, but no, it wasn't to be and was a source of continual embarrassment.

Raf picked the mic up again. "Right. A little about the trip. It takes between an hour and an hour and a half to drive from San Juan to Toro Verde in Orocovis. All depending on the traffic and of course as you can imagine it's mostly winding mountain roads. The mountainous municipality, known as the heart of Puerto Rico, is the geographic centre of the island and located amidst the Sierra de Cayey. Toro Verde is the largest adventure park in the Caribbean and Americas, and boy, are you going to see some spectacular views. I can tell you this trip is going to leave you breathless. However, if you do decide to visit again, I can recommend the sport fishing and kayaking, but today, we're ziplining."

Everyone on the coach cheered.

"Ha! You may not be doing that later. You could be cursing me."

There were rumbles of nervous laughter.

"Now I hope everyone's read the notes. Only closed-toed shoes are allowed." She looked down at Jess's sandals and raised her eyebrows.

Jess pointed to her rucksack. "Don't worry, I have them."

"Good. So, today we're riding The Monster which is the longest zipline at the park. It's more than a mile and a half long and you're going to reach speeds of more than ninety miles per hour."

Now there were cries of horror.

Cori covered her mouth with her hand and could feel her eyes bulging.

Raf reached over and stroked Cori's arm. "Don't worry, hun. I'll look after you." She cleared her throat. "You can only ride the Monster Supergirl style." She laughed. "Oh, sorry, guys. Guess you'll want to be Superman. Whichever you choose, you'll travel in a horizontal flight position. You'll wear helmets and goggles in addition to your harness, and gloves are also provided. Just fly and feel the adrenaline pumping through your body. You don't have to be brave…just live it." She paused and smiled. "So, any questions?"

Cori raised a hand. "Can I back out now?"

Raf shook her head. "No way."

A man at the back shouted. "Can we leave stuff on the coach?"

"Best if you do. There will be bottled water in the shuttle bus that takes you to and from the platforms. And when we've all finished, there will be a snack in the café. There are public restrooms there too…which you'll possibly need." She snorted.

The more Cori heard, the more scared she became. She so wished Steph was here as she was sure she'd give her words of encouragement and strength. However, time passed quickly and the nearer they got to their destination, the more anxious she became. Particularly when she looked out the window. Granted, the scenery was amazing, but they were climbing, and she'd always had a bit of a thing about heights. What had she been thinking? The thought of the ride made her tremble. Still, Raf said she'd look after her, and she certainly needed some moral support.

Very shortly, they pulled into the park and then everyone got off, transferred buses and off they went. When they reached the platform, they were given a briefing and were kitted up with all the equipment. Cori watched as the first of their group left the platform. She had to do this. It promised to be an experience of a lifetime and certainly one she could share with her family. *They'll never believe me.* She didn't want to be afraid anymore. Not of anything, or anyone.

Raf pushed forward. "Okay, hun. I'll go first and meet you at the bottom. You'll be fine." She laughed and wiggled her eyebrows. "Spread out and fly."

Raf took off and yelped at the top of her voice. Then it was her turn. She did as she was told, almost feeling outside herself as they got her rigged up, and the next thing, she was soaring like a bird through the sky. Her stomach lurched when she looked down at the land far below and she quickly squeezed her eyes shut to concentrate on the other senses. It was nerve-racking, but hell, was it exhilarating. She was flying at heart-pounding speeds with the warm tropical air against her face as she zipped down. If it could be summed up in one word, it would be "freedom."

She dared to open her eyes and stared down as the mountains, forests, and rivers sped past her. It seemed like hours, but then she suddenly reached the summit. A guy grabbed her, steadied her, and helped her out of her harness.

Raf jumped forward with her phone. "Got it all on camera, hun. You're gonna love these videos."

Cori was a bit disoriented, but the experience had been amazing. Now she was back down to earth and safe. Raf steadied her and put her arm around her waist. "So how was it?"

Cori shook her head. "Awesome. Definitely checking this off my bucket list."

"Told you, didn't I?"

"Wow. I'm lost for words. Did you really take photos?"

"Of course. I videoed you all the way down. You'll have to give me your email and I'll send them to you."

"That would be fantastic. My family will not believe this. I usually err on the side of caution." That was putting it mildly. She hated taking risks. Elation spread through her as she thought of what she'd done.

"Well, you did it, hun. Give me your email and I'll send them."

Cori gave her address and Raf guided her from the platform. "Told you. A once-in-a-lifetime experience." She hooted with laughter. "A bit like me."

Cori laughed. "Yeah. I'll second that."

"Go take a seat. Just got to wait for the others, then we'll go get a bite to eat."

Cori wasn't sure if food was on her to-do list right now, given the excitement still trying to burst from her skin, but she didn't feel queasy, so that was a plus. She sat on the bench and waited. She shook her head. This was only their third day. Could it get any better? Yes, it could have been if Steph was there. Still, no matter, she'd see her tonight and they'd have the entire evening together. They could share their experiences. She wasn't sure why it mattered. But it did.

Eventually, everyone arrived at the lower platform. They had a light lunch and then boarded the coach back to San Juan. All the way back, there was animated chatter. Along with all the others, she was on a high too.

When they arrived back at the ship, Raf tapped her on the shoulder. "Just gotta check this lot in. See you at dinner, hun."

Cori felt her cheeks colour. "Sorry. Can't tonight. Steph has a booking in Island Prime, so I said I'd join her. Might see you in the Connoisseurs club later, though."

Raf's eyes narrowed ever so slightly, but she gave a false smile and jerked her head in the direction of some passengers. "Sure. Have a great time."

She sighed internally as she made her way back to her room, slightly deflated. She seemed bound to disappoint. But why should she be worried about disappointing the cruise guide? Anger made her clench her fists. She didn't want to be worried about things like that anymore. Slowly, she took deep breaths and unclenched her fists. She was overreacting. The day had been fun, and she didn't want to lose that.

And she was looking forward to having a long soak in her bathtub now. Maybe she'd order some tea after and sit on her veranda. Yes, she'd do that, then she could look at the video and send it to everyone. After that, she had the Island Prime to look forward to. What a day this had turned out to be.

After writing her emails, she debated whether to wear a dress tonight. She'd fully intended to but now she was getting cold feet. What if it sent the wrong message? She got it out of the closet and hung it up on a rail. It was a little black number. The other was a sequin one and she wanted to save that for New Year's Eve. She held her palms up. Why not? After all, it was a special occasion. It slid on like silk, making her shiver. She looked in the mirror. It seemed shorter than when she'd bought it and she tugged it down a bit. Dusty would never have allowed her to wear it. She'd call her a tease. To hell with it, Dusty wasn't here, and after all, she was on vacation.

She left her suite and made her way up to deck ten, trying to still the unexpected butterflies in her tummy. She was a little early, so she sat on the sofa outside the restaurant. She waited a while, then looked at her watch. Six fifty-five. She was sure Steph had said six forty-five. She decided to go in and check with the maître d'. He confirmed the booking and said that unfortunately he could only hold the table for another five minutes. Now she was worried. Steph certainly wouldn't have forgotten, but maybe she'd fallen to sleep or something. She paced a little then sat back down on the sofa.

Raf passed her, did a double take, and walked backwards. "You okay, hun?"

Cori grimaced. "I was supposed to meet Steph here, but she hasn't turned up."

"Jeez. I heard something earlier." She rubbed her neck. "Give me a minute. I'll just check." She turned her back on Cori and made a call. Raf shook her head. "Sorry, hun. Seems like their zip trip was delayed. Think their coach broke down or something. Should be here in about fifteen minutes. The ship's had to delay departure."

"God. Poor Steph. She'll be beside herself."

"She'll be fine." Raf looked her up and down. "Wow, you look good enough to eat."

Cori looked down and shuffled her feet. "Thank you."

Raf patted her arm. "You might as well come and join us then."

Cori looked up. "Is that okay?"

"Sure it is, honey. Not gonna have you eating alone when you look so gorgeous."

Cori felt her ears burning. No, she didn't want to eat alone, and she didn't want to go back to her room either. But she couldn't quite let go of the idea she'd be letting Steph down, even if she wasn't around.

When she got up, Raf linked arms with her, and they walked one flight up to the lounge.

Cori pulled her shoulders back. She'd had such a wonderful day and didn't want to ruin her elation. She'd had enough of that. Perhaps meeting up with Steph alone just wasn't meant to be.

Chapter Six

WHAT A CATASTROPHIC DAY. Steph rubbed at her sore head and wondered how it had gone so wrong.

When she'd received the ticket for the ziplining she was on cloud nine, but when she'd arrived down at the theatre, it was a different matter. Apart from the hordes of people sitting waiting for their tours, no matter how much she looked, she couldn't spot Cori. She walked down to the front and scoured the room. If Cori was there, she'd see her. But nothing.

One of the destinations staff must have seen her anxious look. "You okay, ma'am?"

He must have been referring to her, but ma'am made her feel so old. "I have a tour at eleven thirty. It's the ziplining one."

"Yes, we're just organising that one. If you give me your ticket, I'll swap it for coach one."

Steph frowned. "I was meeting my friend, but I can't see her anywhere. She was on the same trip."

"Don't think so. Everyone's checked in. She wasn't on the earlier one, was she?"

"Earlier one?"

"Yes, it went an hour ago. We put this one on as an extra because it was so popular. Here on the *Caribbean Dreams*, we try to fulfil everyone's dreams."

Steph tried to muster a smile at the cheesy line. It wasn't their fault and they had tried to please everyone. Shit. No wonder Raf had been able to get her on it. She took all the good thoughts about Raf back.

Despite there being no Cori, she'd had a fantastic day. The ziplining was mind-blowing and she'd met a great group of people, too.

That is until the poxy bus broke down. That in itself was bloody frustrating, but it was right on a hairpin bend. They were ushered off and had to wait on the roadside in the heat of the sun, and there was hardly any bottled water left. The driver assured them that another bus would be sent. It was, but it took ages and then they got caught in the Boxing Day traffic. She panicked like crazy and kept looking at the time, but it didn't help matters. There was no question she was going to miss her dinner with Cori, not to mention she was starving. Eventually, they arrived back at nearly seven thirty. She went straight to the restaurant, despite her sweaty hair and rumpled clothing, and the head waiter told her about Cori having stopped by. She explained the circumstances and luckily, he squeezed her in the following night a bit later. She hoped Cori would understand.

It was too late to go up to the lounge, so she went up to her room, had a quick shower and threw some clothes on. She'd go straight to the dining room. It seemed like she was making a habit of turning up looking like she'd been dragged through a hedge backwards, but she didn't have any options.

When she got to the Magnetic Arc they were already seated. Mike stood and offered his chair and Raf organised another setting. The little fucktard looked so smug. Still, she guessed it wasn't really Raf's fault. She briefly related her story, but it seemed like everyone already knew.

Cori looked really concerned. "Fancy having to go through all of that."

Raf cocked her head. "Anyway, at least you've caught the sun." She gave a small, irritating laugh.

She returned a lacklustre smile. *Why doesn't she go bond with a piranha?* Although she suspected Raf would bite the piranha first. She could easily give a suitable retort, but why sink to her level? There were other ways of winding her up.

She punched the air with her fist. "That trip was unbelievable. Thanks for getting me the ticket, Raf."

"My pleasure."

"Sorry about letting you down, Cori, but I have to say, The Island Prime were brilliant and managed to find a table for tomorrow at seven fifteen. How are you fixed?"

Cori smiled. "Wonderful."

"Great. Shall we meet at six forty-five for cocktails in the Caribbean Dream Lounge for a change?"

Cori bit her nail. "Where's that?"

"Deck four."

"Sounds great. I'll see you there."

Yes, it was childish, but she could see by the expression on Raf's face that she'd managed to rattle her.

Cori looked a bit fidgety and kept glancing at both Raf and her. Then she fiddled with an earring. "So, what's everyone doing tomorrow?"

Dorothy looked at Lena. "Where are we tomorrow? Is it Puerto Rico?"

Lena patted her arm. "No, darling. That was today. We did the city tour. Tomorrow we're in Basseterre, St. Kitts, and Nevis. We're doing the St. Kitts scenic railway."

Dorothy's eyes lit up. "Oh. That sounds exciting. Is it on a train?"

"Yes, that's right, love."

Cori sat forward. "I'm doing that one too. We can go together, if you like."

"That would be wonderful, Cori. Give me someone to talk to." She winced slightly. "Of course, I have Dorothy, but we see each other every day."

"Great. We'll meet in the theatre, and I'll take your tickets so we can sit together." She looked across at Steph. "Are you on that one, too?"

Steph raised her eyebrows. "Nah. I'm doing the Romney Manor and Brimstone Fortress. It's the only one they had left."

"Hey. We're doing that. You can join us, can't she, Mike?" Patti said.

Mike gave a wink. "Sure can. Two ladies are better than one, I say."

Raf smirked. "You bet. Always prefer two ladies." She nudged Mike. "Hey, what kind of bees make milk?"

Mike shook his head.

She batted his arm. "Boo-bees."

Mike and Raf laughed. Nobody else laughed. One of her worst ones yet. Still the two of them seemed to think it was giggle-worthy. Or maybe Mike was just being polite.

They had another wonderful meal and after they were finished, the sisters, plus Mike and Patti, headed off to the theatre. Tonight, it was the turn of the trapeze artists and acrobats. Again, not really Steph's kind of thing, but she'd heard that tomorrow night there was a tribute act to Whitney Houston. She wondered whether Cori would go with her. Tonight however, she decided to go and look at the casino. Maybe she'd play a bit of roulette or go on the machines.

Raf turned to Cori. "Ciggie, hun?"

Cori nodded and got up. "Good idea."

Steph forgot to breathe. Cori looked gorgeous. She had a little black dress on…and it was quite little because it seemed to have rucked up and stuck to her bum. Luckily Cori must have sensed it and blushed some as she adjusted the dress. Not before Raf had taken a good gawp as well.

Get your eyes off my woman. It was wishful thinking but a nice thought anyway. It suddenly hit her that Cori had worn the dress for her. Well, not specifically, but she had worn it for the occasion of going out to dine with her. It made her feel special.

She watched as the two of them disappeared into the elevator. Steph crossed the hallway and went into the casino. It was relatively lively and a good place to spend an hour or so. Mostly the tables were for blackjack and roulette, and the back was filled with loads of slot machines. She opted for roulette. It wasn't just because the croupier was female and rather attractive, but it did help with her decision. She changed some money and took a seat. The young lady's badge said her name was Annette, who smiled at her. It was one of those beautiful smiles, the ones that light up the eyes as well. Steph spread her chips around and won on one of her numbers. Good start.

Steph looked at Annette. "When's your birthday?"

Annette laughed. "Eighth of June."

Steph put a couple of chips on number eight. It didn't come up, but she repeated the process each time. Eventually the ball landed on the number. Now she had stacks of chips lined up in front of her. She decided to call it a night and cashed most of them in. She placed a few by the side of Annette, who gave a slight smile with direct eye contact and tilted her head downward. "Thank you. That's very kind of you."

"You're welcome."

"Hope to see you again."

Steph smiled. "I'm sure you will." She gave a tiny wave and left the room. She hadn't really meant to flirt, but she couldn't change the habit of a lifetime. Attractive women just had that effect on her. Of course, she'd never have done that if Cori was with her. But she wasn't.

Back in her room, she opened the patio door and stared out at the water. It wasn't long before melancholy began to make her soul itch, and she sighed as she flopped onto the bed. This escape was what she'd needed. Away from the family expectations, from the job that was nothing more than a paycheck. This cruise would end, though, and she'd have to go back to all that. Even the thought made her stomach turn. But damn it, she still didn't know what she wanted to be when she grew up, if that day ever came. And the family business was…well, family. All of them.

She flipped onto her stomach and hugged the pillow. Being a disappointment sucked. Deciding not to consider the future while she wasn't anywhere near it, she pressed the TV on and soon fell asleep.

The following morning, she was up bright and early. Her tour wasn't until eleven, but she wanted to sit on her balcony and watch the ship dock. As it did so, she took loads of photos, even though she didn't really have anyone to share them with, and then went for breakfast. A little later she joined Patti and Mike in the theatre, and they exchanged their tickets. She couldn't help but look around to see if Cori was visible, even though she knew she was on a different tour altogether.

The drive to Romney Manor was, to say the least, panoramic. She'd imagined that most of the Caribbean Islands were similar as far as scenery went. But St. Kitts was slightly different. For miles all she could see were dark jade volcanic peaks which led down to lush emerald-green valleys. Suddenly someone shouted, "Monkeys!" The bus pulled up and they all piled out. Steph liked monkeys, but there was no way she wanted her photo taken with one, unlike the others. They were cute but they carried diseases and she had enough problems without catching anything.

They continued to their destination. Apparently, the estate was a former sugar plantation. Steph appreciated flowers. Working in the florist industry, she came across many of the tropical flowers that were growing in the garden. Hibiscus in pinks, reds, yellows and white, bougainvillea and tamarind. She closed her eyes and breathed in the scents. Sweet and exotic.

They meandered around the gardens which were beautifully set out and she took a few photos of the three of them for her album. After, they browsed around the Caribelle Batik. It was fascinating watching the local artists produce the batik fashions and she couldn't resist buying her mum and sister a couple of T-shirts. It was a joke, and probably a waste of money, because neither would ever wear them.

The next stop was Brimstone Fortress, which frankly wasn't her thing. She wasn't really into fortresses, but the views of the neighbouring islands were spectacular. After, they rested out of the heat and had a snacky lunch. Then they went onto their final destination. It was well worth the drive up to the Timothy Hill Overlook. It was a bit of a hike up there and she was surprised how some of the older people managed it.

She guessed they were fitter than they looked. Once there, it was by far the most memorable view of the day with the Atlantic Ocean on one side and the Caribbean Sea on the other. All in all, it would have been a good tour but a bit long, and she wished she'd been on the one with Cori. Still, this is what she'd come for…to see the Caribbean Islands. She hadn't taken the cruise to find herself a woman, otherwise she'd have gone on one of the gay cruises, and there were plenty of those around. However, the highlight of the day was going to be her dinner date. She could hardly wait for it. They were on their way down the hill when the catastrophe struck. She'd hung back taking thousands of photos and when she'd got half down, everyone had come to a standstill and were gathered in a group. She tapped Mike on the shoulder. "What the hell's happened?"

He stepped back and whispered, "Code Blue."

"Jeez, what's that?"

"Medical emergency. Coach driver collapsed. Just like that, in front of my eyes."

"Is he okay?"

Mike shook his head. "Not looking good. They've called for an ambulance, but right now, the guide from the ship is doing chest compressions."

Steph grimaced.

Patti joined them. "Nothing we can do. We've been told to go sit in the shade. Gonna be a long wait, I reckon. I suppose eventually they'll get us back to the ship." Patti stroked her face. "Hey, didn't something go wrong on your last excursion?"

Steph nodded. She wished Patti hadn't remembered.

Patti raised her eyebrows. "Hah! You must be jinxed. We'll make sure we avoid you in future."

Steph was beginning to wonder if that was true. Three incidents so far was more than bad luck.

The ambulance arrived and took the driver away, but there was no sign of his replacement. Shit. She'd planned to go to the lecture on The Pirates of the Caribbean later, but there was no way she'd make it back. She made a silent prayer. *Please get me back for dinner.*

Finally, a new driver arrived. It was a slow drive back, because again they caught all the traffic. She had plenty of time to think and wondered if there could ever be something more with Cori, or was that just the effects of the bond that tended to be created on a ship and everyone became your new family? It was odd how quickly you formed an attachment with virtual strangers. This was only a short cruise—what would it be like if the trip was a month long? She was beginning to understand why so many people treated the crew like they were their best buddies…because they were the equivalent to family, particularly at times like Christmas and New Year.

They made it back, though there was plenty of grumbling from most of the passengers. As though the poor bus driver had planned on collapsing and inconveniencing them. Fortunately for Steph, the dinner reservation was later tonight. Cori would never have believed her if she'd stood her up again. All the same, she didn't have much time to spare. She'd have liked to have given her outfit a little more thought but settled for a pair of tight white casual trousers and a black blouse and headed to the cocktail bar. She managed to get a nice sofa for two opposite the door so she could see Cori come in.

Cori stood in the doorway glancing this way and that. It was quite dimly lit, so Steph stood and waved, and she came to join her. Cori looked gorgeous. No, she didn't have the dress on that she wore last night, but she looked equally as attractive in a pair of cream slacks and a red sparkly blouse that showed some cleavage. Not too much, just the right amount. Saying that, Steph found herself staring.

She shook her head, trying to bring herself into the moment. "Hey. You look lovely." She wished she hadn't said it because Cori blushed. She hated embarrassing her but at the same time, she kinda liked her blushes.

Cori twisted the ring on her finger. At least it wasn't on her wedding ring finger, but the next one along. "Thank you. You look good too."

"Thanks. Just something I threw together for the occasion." Steph bounced on her toes. It had been a long time since a woman had given her those sorts of feelings. The ones that set off the hornet's nest in her stomach. Thinking about it, *no* woman had given her those feelings. They were unique. Usually, it was pure desire and lust. "What would you like to drink?"

"I've got into Cosmos now. Guess I'll stick with them."

Steph waved to the waiter and ordered two of the same. Over drinks, it was difficult to talk, let alone see. No wonder that sofa had been free; the music had become deafening. On top of that, there was a large group on the next table who were definitely worse for wear. Even though she leaned in closer to Cori when she spoke, it was impossible to hold a conversation. In the end, they finished their drinks and made their way to the restaurant.

The maître d' greeted them. "I have a lovely table reserved for you two ladies. I saved the best as you missed your dinner date last night."

Steph beamed. "Hey, that's really kind of you."

He pulled their chairs out for them and spread a napkin on each of their laps. "The waiter will be with you shortly. If you're having the steak, I highly recommend the Châteauneuf-du-Pape. It's a perfect accompaniment."

Steph nodded and smiled. "Thanks, we'll do that." She handed a menu to Cori and took one for herself.

Cori looked around. "It's really nice in here and they're so friendly."

"They all seem to be on this ship. They make us all feel so special."

Cori tilted her head. "I love it. I wasn't sure if I would, but so far everything has been terrific. The excursions have been great." Cori covered her mouth with her hand. "Sorry, that was thoughtless of me. Yours didn't go so well."

"Technically, the coach breaking down wasn't their fault, and I have to say the ziplining was awesome."

"It was. Something I thought I'd never do, but it was tremendous."

"Wait until I tell you about today."

Cori's eyes widened. "Tell me?"

Steph saw the waiter hovering. "Best concentrate on our menus first." Her eyes sparkled. "Yummy, there's steaks of every description."

The waiter held up his tablet. "Okay, ladies, fire away."

Cori didn't look like she'd decided yet, so Steph took the initiative. "I'm going for the large fillet steak with sweet potato fries and a salad." She looked across at Cori. "Are you happy with the suggested wine?"

"Yes, it sounds perfect."

Cori looked up from her menu. "I'm going for the surf and turf please." She handed her menu back to the waiter and he left.

"So, tell me about today's trip?"

Steph fell about laughing. "Well, the coach didn't break down."

"That's something."

"However—"

Cori leaned her elbows on the table. "Go on?"

"We had a Code Blue, that's a medical emergency." Steph related the rest of the story then pressed her hand on her forehead. "Things seem to go wrong on all my trips. Patti said I must be jinxed. Do you think so?"

"Rubbish. It could happen to anyone."

"Yeah, but so far every trip since I left the UK has gone wrong."

Cori reached over and touched her hand. "Well, as far as I'm concerned, you've brought only good luck to me."

Steph perked up. "Aww…thank you. I hope to continue doing so." She smiled. "There were some highlights before that, and all in all, it gave me a real flavour of the Caribbean islands. What was yours like?"

"Really good. Mind you, it was a bit hairy when we went over the rainforests and through the canyons. It was quite high up and I didn't realize it was only a narrow-gauge railroad. When I did open my eyes, the views were magnificent. I didn't join Lena and Dorothy on the open-air observation deck. They're much braver than I am. Then it took us around some of the coastline and the scenery was breath-taking. When we switched to the coach, we had drinks and snacks, and they even had a group of musicians playing island music. St. Kitts' southern coast was so picturesque." Cori chuckled. "To be honest, it was a bit long. I could have done without a few of the visitors centres."

The waiter came along with their wine, uncorked it, and poured a little in Steph's glass.

Steph offered it to Cori. "Would you like to try it?"

Cori shook her head. "No, I'm sure your palate is much better than mine."

It wasn't. Steph couldn't tell the difference between quality or junk, but no way would she let on. Cori would think she was a philistine. So, she sipped it as though she knew what she was doing. She nodded and smiled. "Excellent."

The waiter topped up both glasses, and then their meals arrived.

Steph picked her glass up. "Bon appétit, and thanks for joining me tonight."

Cori touched Steph's glass with hers. "Cheers, Steph. And thank you for asking me. So far, it's a lovely evening."

Steph smiled and they tucked into their dinner. "This steak is to die for."

"Mine is wonderful too and the lobster is perfectly cooked. The wine goes so well."

Steph grinned. She felt a million dollars sitting here with one of the loveliest women she'd ever met. There was nothing false about Cori. She seemed like a genuine person, although there was a sadness to her, especially when she was away from the others, that was clear. She wondered why, when, and how she'd lost her confidence. Perhaps it wasn't evident to the others. Maybe they just saw her as a shy person, but to Steph, there was something she was hiding. She hoped she'd get to the bottom of it, and perhaps she could even help her. Steph rubbed her forehead. "Can you remind me; I've already lost track. Where are we tomorrow?"

"I know, I've lost track of days too. Anyway, it's St. Johns in Antigua. I've watched so many travel programs and thought how magical it looked, and tomorrow we'll be there. I'll have to pinch myself."

Steph looked heavenward and tilted her head. "I know, it's unbelievable. I never thought I'd be doing this. I bet you're on some exotic trip tomorrow?"

"Antigua highlights." Cori hunched her shoulders. "I felt awful because Raf managed to get me on what she thought was the best tour, the Island Safari and Stingray fantasy. I honestly didn't fancy the long day. Anyway, I swapped it."

Steph had a hard time stopping herself bouncing in her chair. "Glad you did. I'm on that too."

"Which one? There's a morning and an afternoon."

She could take bets that Cori would be on the second one. "Morning." Cori smiled. "Me too."

Steph didn't jump up and celebrate. She quietly took it in and tried to remain calm, although inside, she was dancing. "Great. We'll be able to see the sights together. With a bit of luck, Raf will be on the trip she booked you on. I'm sure she'll have the stingray for lunch."

Cori laughed. "Yes, I think I'd put my money on Raf if there was a fight."

"For sure."

The waiter came around and topped up their glasses and they finished their main course. "Phew, I don't know about you, but I need a few minutes to recover before dessert."

Cori smiled. "I hoped you'd say that."

Steph rested her elbows on the table. "So, what made you come on this cruise?"

Cori fidgeted and cleared her throat. "A number of things, really."

Steph didn't press her. If she wanted to, she'd tell her in her own time.

"There were some negatives, but the positives were that the cruise stopped off in Jamaica."

Steph beamed. "Yeah, I've always wanted to visit Jamaica. Wouldn't mind a holiday there one day."

"This will be my first visit."

"Boy, you must be excited. Shame it's only a few hours."

Cori grinned. "Not for me. I'm jumping ship in Port Antonio and having a holiday with them."

Steph pressed her lips together, then forced a big smile. She hoped Cori hadn't noticed her disappointment. Once again, she reminded herself that's not what this trip was about. "That's fantastic." Steph did a quick calculation and realised Jamaica was the last stop before they disembarked in Miami the following morning, so she'd only miss out on one night with Cori.

"I can't wait. My grandparents came for a visit to the UK a few years ago, but I haven't seen my brother, Josh, for nearly four years, apart from FaceTime, which we do every week."

"Is he older than you?"

"No, he's eighteen months younger." Cori gave a small laugh. "He's lovely, and he looks after my grandma and grandpa. All my family are wonderful. I couldn't ask for better."

Steph rubbed her hands together. "Have you got any piccies?"

Cori leaned back in her chair. "You sure? I don't want to bore you."

"No, I want to see them."

Cori seemed really pleased with her response. She fished around in her bag and came out with her phone. She flicked through some photos, then reached over. "It's an old one, but that's my mum and dad, and Josh and me."

Cori seemed to be watching for Steph's response. The four people in the photograph sat on a sofa with their arms around each other's shoulders. Cori was the image of her mother, blond and white, and her father and brother were Black. They all looked so happy. She wished she could produce a photo like that to show to Cori. But there was no chance. "Wow, that's beautiful. You all look so blissed out. I'm envious."

"Yes, we always are. Wish we could have had a total family reunion, but my mum and dad were tied up." Cori smiled, and her eyes lit up.

"But I think we're going to do it next year."

"Awesome." Steph had the feeling if she didn't ask the inevitable questions, Cori would just slip the phone back and nothing more would be said. Of course, Cori may be her mum's daughter and her mum had remarried. "So how did that all pan out with you being white and your brother Black? If you don't mind me asking."

Cori tilted her head. "I'm pleased you asked that. Most people either avoid the subject or ask me if my mum married again. Truth is, Josh and I have the same parents, we just look totally different. It happens. My grandma is mixed race and Grandpa is Black." Cori whizzed through some photos. "Here's one of the three of them." She passed the phone to Steph.

"They look lovely. Wow, Josh is a good-looking guy."

Cori chuckled. "Yes, and doesn't he know it. Has all the girls after him, but so far, he hasn't settled with anyone. I guess he feels he has to look after my grandparents."

"Is it a full-time job then?"

"No, not yet. My grandpa's a bit frail. He had a fall a few years back, but Josh always fusses over them both. He took over my grandparents' business in Port Antonio. Car hire, motorbikes, scooters, and bicycles. He's doing really well, and he's just opened another in Ocho Rios."

"That's brilliant. I used to have a scooter in my younger days, before I could afford a car. Loved it." It felt like a somewhat inane response to Cori's brother's success, but it was about the only way she could relate.

A waiter stood by their table. "Excuse me. Can I interest you two ladies in one of our speciality desserts?"

Steph rubbed her hands together. "What do you recommend?"

He looked from one to the other. "Do you like toffee popcorn?"

They nodded. "Then I'll bring you our popcorn surprise."

When it arrived, Cori held her stomach. "I can't eat all that." The toffee popcorn was layered with salted caramel ice cream, fudge, and toffee sauce.

The waiter smiled. "Wait until you try it. Enjoy!"

Cori and Steph picked up their long spoons and dug in.

"Wowzah." Steph said. "This is to die for."

"All those calories." Cori laughed. "But who cares?"

They scraped around their glass dishes until there was nothing left. Steph stopped the waiter as he was going by. "Can we order this in any restaurant?"

"Sorry, ladies. Only here in Island Prime. You'll just have to book again. I'm sure we can fit you in before the end of the trip."

Steph didn't want to think about the end of the trip. "Yes, we'll do that." She licked her finger and pressed it onto a piece of popcorn on the tablecloth. She noticed Cori was laughing. "Sorry about that." She looked at her watch. The show would be halfway through, so she decided against that. "Do you fancy having a drink up in the Galaxy? Then you can pop in and have a ciggie before."

"Sounds great. You don't mind?"

"Of course not." *If Raf isn't there.*

They left and made their way up the stairs. Steph peeked in the smoker's lounge. She'd like to go in, but she hated the smell of smoke on her clothes. However, one day she might, if only to keep spending time with Cori. That would piss Raf off. "What shall I get you?"

"I'd love a coffee. Maybe one with Tia Maria in it."

"See you soon. Don't rush."

It was busy in the lounge, but most people were crowded around the dance floor. Steph gave her order and chose Grand Marnier with her coffee. She picked a table at the back away from the crowds so they could talk and actually hear each other's response. She wanted to know as much as she could about Cori. So far, she found her unlike anybody she'd ever met before. However, she couldn't help but wonder if she'd measure up to Cori's expectations? Her family sucked, she had no career prospects, and she just didn't feel worthy. Once outside this bubble, surely Cori would see she wasn't up to her calibre. The thought sent her into a melancholic mood, but as soon as she saw Cori walk through the door, her spirits lifted. For now, she didn't need to think about what would happen when the bubble burst.

Chapter Seven

So far, the evening with Steph had been wonderful. They got on so well and Steph seemed to be genuinely interested in her life. Doubt crept in. Dusty had been like that when they'd met. She couldn't get enough of her. And then—

But why was she comparing Steph with Dusty? The problem was that she'd had very little experience with women…with relationships, and she only knew the one she'd had with her late partner. God. What if Steph asked about her old life? Would she be able to tell the truth, or would Steph run in the opposite direction? Oh, how she wished she could get rid of these negative thoughts. She so wanted to believe that Steph, and people in general, were better than Dusty, and yet fear was getting the better of her. She stubbed her cigarette out and went into the lounge.

It was so crowded. She'd never been up here at this time before and was surprised how popular it was. The band were just coming back on stage, and everybody began to applaud. She wished they'd chosen a quieter place to sit. She'd dearly love to have a conversation with Steph. She glanced around and Steph was waving. Luckily, she'd picked a table miles away from the stage. Just as she arrived, the waitress brought their drinks.

Cori took a seat opposite Steph. She was nervous and picked up her glass of coffee. Steph picked hers up too and they both took a sip.

"Ooh, this is lovely." Cori wiped some cream off her lip with her fingertip. "I've really enjoyed this evening, thanks so much for inviting me."

"Me too. It's been terrific. Can we do it again? Maybe we could try a different restaurant."

"I'd love to…really." She meant it.

"So, tell me more about what you were like as a kid." She paused. "I hope you don't think I'm prying. I'm really interested…that is, if you're happy to talk about it."

"Absolutely. I've never been ashamed of my parentage and the fact that we're mixed race. I know that Josh and I were treated differently, and it was hard for him. Luckily, I was the elder, so when we went to school, I was able to look out for him. It wasn't so bad in primary school but when we went on to secondary school the problems increased. And then whenever my mum picked us up or dropped us off and they saw she was white, everybody assumed that Josh was either adopted, fostered, or our mum was on her second marriage."

"Poor guy. Was he bullied?"

"Yes, terribly. There weren't a lot of Black kids in our school, so he stuck out like a sore thumb. I got a lot of stick too because nobody believed he was my birth brother. They used to taunt me, saying he was adopted. I took photos of our family to school, I didn't want to hide them away, but they still didn't believe me. I have to say there was a lot of prejudice and I never had that many friends. To be honest, I didn't want to become part of the clique if they couldn't accept me for what I was, and when they treated my brother the way they did."

Steph shook her head. "Kids can be so cruel. Saying that, sometimes they don't improve when they grow up, they just become bigger bigots. How did your mum and dad cope?"

"They were great with us kids and we had a lot of family discussions and always addressed our problems together. Mind you, they had their own issues from the Black community too. When my dad took us out together, they used to stare at me a lot. They didn't believe I was my dad's real daughter. I suppose in a way it was good, because at least I could understand how Josh felt."

"I'm surprised you ended up so well adjusted."

Cori shrugged. She'd had no real hang-ups about her upbringing. It was later that she'd developed her dilemma, but she wasn't going to go down that road with Steph. Not yet, anyway. In fact, she doubted if she ever would.

"So how do you describe yourself, if you have to?"

"I'm very proud of my heritage. Everybody assumes I'm white, but really, I'm mixed race."

Steph nodded. "Did Josh go to live with your grandparents because of the bullying?"

"Partly, yes. He went out for vacations and fell in love with Jamaica. He adores my grandparents, practically worships them."

"You have such a lovely story to tell."

"Thank you. I like talking about my family if someone's willing to listen." Cori loved showing her family off, and it made her warm inside to see Steph's respect of the situation. Generally, people paid lip service. She'd like to say other people's opinions didn't matter, but they did. But in this instance, Steph seemed genuinely interested, and that was important to Cori. "Anyway, enough of me. Tell me about your life."

Steph held her head in her hands and laughed, but there was real pain in her eyes. "Where do I begin?"

"Wherever you like."

"I'm afraid I told a bit of a fib when we introduced ourselves. I said I was a florist, which is true to some extent, but it's only a part of the family business."

Cori's eyes narrowed. "Really, and what's that?"

Steph glanced around. "Just checking Raf isn't here 'cos she wouldn't half take the piss. My family are funeral directors."

Cori chuckled. "No kidding. So, what's your job in the business?" Cori silently prayed Steph wouldn't say she was an embalmer. There was something a little creepy about that position, even if it was a necessary part of the process.

Steph laughed. "Generally, they shove me in the flower shop out of the way. I'm a pretty good florist. At the funerals, I walk in front of the cars and lead them to the church or the crematorium."

Cori smiled. "I can see you doing that, top hat, stick, and all."

Steph chuckled. "Yeah, that's the bit I like. We keep everything in the family. I think I told you, my sister is a minister, and my uncle does the catering."

Cori laughed. "Sounds like you've got the market cornered. Are you happy in your work?"

Steph's shoulders dropped and she rested her head against the booth. "No, is the short answer. Things have happened recently, and it's made me question where I'm going with all of this. I came away to give it some thought."

"Well, you're young enough to change direction. Have you discussed it with your parents?"

Steph shook her head. "Ha! My parents aren't really the discussing type. They run things their way and I just have to fit in. They're not like your folks at all. I moved out as soon as I was old enough. I had to get away from that house, it's like a mausoleum. I suppose that fits in really well with the business."

"That's sad. What about your sister?"

"Much the same. She disapproves of my lifestyle."

Cori wondered what her sister found unacceptable. She briefly looked into Steph's eyes, then laughed. "Is it that bad?"

Steph puffed her cheeks out and blew. "Everything. My sexuality, because I'm a lesbian, not as though I've ever hidden it. Maybe I should have done."

Well, that answered one question. "I don't think it's something we should hide." She hesitated, wondering if she should tell Steph. Now was as good a time as any. "I wasn't sure about my sexuality, then I met someone and realised who I was. So, I didn't come out to my family until I was twenty-one."

Steph stared. "Really? And how did they react?"

"Perfectly accepting." Cori laughed. "I suppose with all the race issues they'd dealt with, me being lesbian wasn't such a big deal."

"Jeez, you're so lucky. And are you still with that same woman?"

Now wasn't the time to discuss her past. She'd dropped that titbit so they could discuss their lives openly another time. "No."

Steph's eyes seemed to sparkle at that statement.

Cori leaned back in her chair. "Anyway, we weren't talking about me. Is it only your sexuality they disapprove of?"

Steph's nose wrinkled. "They dislike my choice of women. Maybe they'd be more accepting if I found someone nice and settled down. I guess I have to sort myself out generally, you know, make some miraculous discovery about myself."

Cori felt bad that Steph looked so uncomfortable and decided to lighten the moment. "Maybe you will. That's what you came here for. You never know, it might just jump up and slap you upside the head."

Steph laughed. "It'll need to be a heavy blow."

"Tell you what, if I see it before you, I'll let you know." Cori glanced at her watch. "Gosh. Do you know what time it is?"

Steph shrugged. "Who cares?"

"Me. I need some sleep. We dock at eight and the trip's at eight thirty, so I've ordered breakfast in my room."

"I forgot. It's too late now. Guess I'll have to stick my alarm on bright and early." Steph drained the remains of her drink and pushed her chair back. "Okay, ready."

They made their way to the elevator, and Cori pressed floor seven.

She got out and held the door. "Thanks again for the brilliant evening. Don't be late. I'll sit at the back of the theatre and then we can hand our tickets in together."

Steph winked. "You bet." She leaned over and planted a kiss on Cori's cheek. "Thanks again. Sleep well."

Cori wasn't sure if she would and when she got back to her suite, she closed the door and leaned back. She couldn't remember the last time she'd had such a wonderful evening. Steph was terrific company. She was funny and entertaining, but above all she seemed to be genuinely sincere. She thought about the evening as she undressed and hung her clothes in the wardrobe. She was pleased they'd covered the subject of sexuality. It was out in the open now. Of course, it wasn't crucial to their friendship, but say things got deeper? No, they wouldn't, not on the cruise anyway. There wasn't enough time to get to know Steph properly. Hah! She thought she'd known Dusty well and look what happened there. People lured you in and gave you a false sense of security…and then they changed their colours. No, she couldn't let that happen again. She was trying hard to be her own person. She mustn't slip up and let someone in. All the same, it had been an exhilarating feeling because Steph made her feel alive again and somehow gave her that sensation of confidence back. She sighed, got under the duvet, plumped up her pillow and settled into the comfort of her bed. It had to be destiny that she and Steph were on the same trip together. The connection happened even though she wasn't looking for it, and there was something telling her that Steph was there for a reason. Right now, she didn't know what it was, but she wanted to embrace it and see where it took them.

Her last thoughts were that tonight her life had seemed normal. She closed her eyes and drifted into an uninterrupted sleep.

***

Cori stretched, opened the door to her balcony and stepped out. She'd missed the sunrise by about half an hour. One day, she'd get up that little bit earlier. Oh, what a bewitching sight to behold. Antigua, her dream island, was a lush, green, hilly place surrounded by tranquil teal waterways. As they sailed slowly into the beautiful port, they were greeted by a burst of charming colourful buildings. It was just as she imagined it would be from all the photos she'd seen. Unfortunately, her thoughts were interrupted by her doorbell signalling that breakfast had arrived. The waiter set it up and she tucked into her fresh fruit, followed by poached eggs with brown toast. This was luxury, there was no getting away from it. In all the years with Dusty, they'd never had breakfast in bed. Plus, she didn't have to wash up or load the dishwasher. Dusty would sneer and say it was pure decadence and excessive indulgence that made her selfish. The tea tasted bitter now. *Sod Dusty.* She so wished she'd leave her thoughts, but she feared she'd always be there.

She put her shorts and a T-shirt on and packed her small rucksack with essentials. Hat, light jacket, sun cream, and hand sanitiser. She'd pick up bottled water on her way out. She made her way to the theatre and was just about to take a seat at the back when Steph jumped up.

She grinned. "See? Made it before you. Give me your ticket and I'll go exchange them."

Cori handed it over, and Steph ran down to the front of the theatre. It made such a change to be greeted with a smile and she really liked Steph's attention. Platonically, of course.

"We're on coach two." Steph sat down beside her. "Did you sleep okay?"

Cori smiled. "Like a baby."

Steph laughed. "Yeah, me too. Fantastic sunrise this morning."

"I missed it." She was a little surprised that Steph had seen it. She seemed more like a sleep in whenever she could type of person.

"No worries, there's always tomorrow. You've got five sunrises before you jump ship." Steph raised her finger and cocked her head. "Hey, that's us, they've just called coaches one, two and three. Quick, let's get out of here before we get killed in the stampede."

They left the ship, walked down the gangway, and were greeted by a band playing beautiful metallic island tunes. As they passed, they swayed in time to the music. They entered a building and passed through security then made their way along the pier towards the coach park and found their transport. They handed their tickets over and found a seat halfway down the aisle.

Steph stood back. "You sit by the window. That'll be a better view."

Strangely touched by the simple gesture, she blinked back the unbidden tears. "Thanks. You can take the window seat on the way back."

"Okay."

Eventually, the coach filled, and they set off. Conversation was minimal as the guide was giving a running commentary on all the places they'd be visiting, but Cori was still aware of the way Steph's leg pressed against hers. Clearly it had been too long since she'd had some simple human contact. She shifted away and ignored the quick flash of disappointment.

Their first photo stop was the blockhouse which served as a lookout for the British in the eighteenth century. The views were spectacular, and Steph seemed to be taking hundreds of pictures.

The guide tapped Steph on her shoulder. "Can you see the house over there, right on the farthest point on that cliff?"

"Yeah, it's massive."

"It belongs to Eric Clapton."

"Wow. I'll have to see if I can get some shots. Thanks." Steph clicked away.

Cori tried but failed. "You must have a better camera than me."

"I just got a new phone and it's got a great zoom on it. I'll send them to you."

"Thanks. You're providing me with all my holiday snaps."

"Well, it's my pleasure."

Cori watched Steph taking all the pictures. She had such enthusiasm and energy…something Cori seemed to have lost, until now. It seemed to be rubbing off on her and she so wished it would. Where had her spirit gone? The truth was it had been killed off many years ago. She prayed inwardly that perhaps she could retrieve it, or maybe someone like Steph could help her salvage something of the person she had once been. But perhaps that was asking for too much.

Enough thinking. It was time to get back on the coach. They headed through many hilltop villages with breathtaking views until they reached Shirley Heights, the most southerly tip of Antigua.

Cori clasped her hands together. "This is the place I've so been looking forward to. It's the scene that depicts the iconic image of Antigua."

"So, what was it used for?"

"It's a restored military lookout and gun battery."

Steph nodded. "Right." She whispered to Cori, "I just want to see the views."

Cori laughed. "Me too."

They exited the coach and were given forty-five minutes to wander around. The main group followed the guide, but Cori and Steph headed straight for the best panoramic vista.

Steph jumped up onto the low wall which overlooked the seascape and spread her arms. "I have never seen anything to beat this in all my life. Oh my God!"

Cori joined her. "It's truly amazing."

"How high is it, and what are the two harbours down there?"

"About four hundred and ninety feet." Cori pointed. "That's English Harbour, and that one's Falmouth Harbour."

Steph waved her arms around. "It's awesome, and it has a three-sixty view." She jumped down. "Must take some pics. Can you sit on the wall, Cori?"

Cori did as requested, though it felt awkward. Whenever she'd suggested she and Dusty take photos of themselves someplace, she'd been accused of being egotistical.

Steph took several photos and sat beside her. "Look at these, they're brilliant."

Cori leaned in. "Hey, that's really wonderful. It captures absolutely everything. You will send me these, won't you?"

"Sure thing. Will you take some of me? I don't ever want to forget this trip."

"Of course." Cori took the phone and took three or four shots then went back to check them with Steph.

"Great, thanks. Can we have one together?"

Cori nodded. How lovely to feel noticed by someone like this. "That would be really nice."

Steph looked around for a victim. She eventually collared someone from the coach, explained what she wanted and handed her phone over, then went to sit next to Cori.

The man waved his hand. "C'mon, you two, move a bit closer."

Steph put her arm around Cori's shoulder, and for some reason, Cori naturally inclined her head towards Steph. Steph's hand on her shoulder not only made her go goose-pimply, but it also gave her a sense of security she'd never experienced before. She'd noticed, whenever she was with Steph, she no longer felt isolated or lonely. Something deep within her mind whispered that everything would be all right. It was illogical, of course. It was just that she hadn't been shown such gentle kindness in too long. She mustn't make it into something it wasn't.

The man handed the phone back to Steph. "Best check them out."

Steph went through them. "Absolutely brilliant. Thanks, mate."

He saluted and went back to join the group who were making their way back to the coach.

Steph pouted. "Guess we'd better go. Wouldn't it be brilliant to bring a picnic up here and watch the sunset?"

"Apparently, that's the best photo you can get."

Steph smiled. "Next time, eh?"

Cori punched her playfully on the shoulder. "Come on, you."

They travelled back to the town by a different route which was equally as awe-inspiring as their outward journey. The guide gave a running commentary telling everyone about his wonderful island and when they drove down the hill the coach stopped in the centre of town.

"Okay, folks. Shopping time. If you wanna browse, now's the time."

Cori looked at the brightly coloured line of shops along the red tarmac road. "Do you want to browse?"

Steph looked at her watch. "Generally, yes, but I've got a ship's tour booked this afternoon, and right now I need sustenance."

"I'm not bothered about shopping, but I do need to eat. What's the ship's tour about?"

"The Art. The décor. The everything. Apparently, we're even visiting their exclusive restaurant and will be taken around one of the top-notch staterooms."

"Why? Do they have a special restaurant?"

"You bet." Steph laughed. "You don't think they eat with the riff-raff, do you?"

"But what more could you possibly want to eat? We can order anything." She couldn't fathom being any more extravagant than she'd already been.

"Maybe they get the Beluga caviar instead of the cheaper ones. Not sure, but I guess if you can afford those suites, you want extra for your money. Anyway, I'll let you know later. Are we meeting in The Galaxy as usual?"

"Yes, we'd better. Will you have time to send me the photos from this morning?"

"Sure, I'll do them over lunch."

They got back to the ship and went straight up to the restaurant. They chatted about what they'd seen and how they'd both adored it. It was so nice to have things in common with someone, especially when they didn't disparage what they'd seen in some passive-aggressive way.

Steph tapped the table. "Nearly forgot." She rummaged in her rucksack and came out with her phone. She flicked through and tapped quickly. "I'll send you all the relevant ones."

Cori's phone pinged. She opened it and found the file of photos. "Thanks, Steph. Think I'll sit on my veranda and send a variety to my family and friends."

Steph momentarily looked a little sad, but then it was gone, and she gave a thumbs-up and grabbed her bag. "Best go now, see you later."

Cori waved and left shortly after. She changed into her bikini, took a bottle of Diet Coke from her fridge, and settled on her sun chair in the shade. She chose several photos and mailed them with a little note to her parents, grandparents, and brother. Then she sent the same to Liz. It was evening in the UK, but she guessed Liz would be right back to her unless she and Gem were out gallivanting. Just as she'd predicted, within minutes there was a reply.

Oh my God! Who is she? How did you meet? Arm around your shoulder...you leaning in...what else has happened? Yippee xxx

Predictable, but it tickled her pink. *Her name's Steph. She's in the singles group. Teamed up as friends. Trip together in Antigua. Closeness was for the photo. Nothing else has happened. Oh yes, we had dinner together last night. xx*

Wow. You sound like you're having fun...I'm impressed. The weather looks fabulous. It's snowing here!! What are you doing tomorrow on St. Bart's?

Ha ha. You'll never believe this. Going for an adventure on an ATV around the island.

You're not driving it, are you? Gawd help us.

No way. Going with Raf, the hostess.

Have you gone off the rails?

No. I nearly did in St Kitts though. She added a smiley emoji.

Very funny. Keep me posted...on everything. There was a pause as dots appeared and disappeared before the rest finally came through. *Be gentle with yourself, lovey. You're amazing.*

Tears filled Cori's eyes. Liz knew what she was going through, even this far away. *Will do. xx*

Cori put her phone down and moved into the sun. She closed her eyes and lapped up the warmth on her body. It helped her to collect her thoughts and ponder what would happen next. Everything appeared to be going well and she couldn't help but wonder if this might be a turning point in her life. Could she ever get back to the person she was before she'd met Dusty? She seemed to be gaining a little confidence but then doubts crept into her mind…or was it Dusty haunting her? Everything Dusty did stuck like tar to her soul. She was trying oh so hard to break away from the emotional cage she'd been in, but it wasn't easy. It was scary. And what next? These were small steps. She hadn't had any therapy yet, but somehow, Steph was helping her to heal. She made her feel brave, but what would happen when she was back on terra firma? There'd be nobody to lean on then.

Was it yet another calm before the storm as she'd become accustomed to, or was it an outlandish dream of achieving the impossible? She opened her eyes, focused on the sun shimmering on the rippling waves and took herself to a happy place with dreams of Jamaica and the family she loved.

Chapter Eight

STEPH DID A QUICK change and joined her tour, although she seriously considered cancelling it and suggesting that she and Cori sunbathe together instead. But she didn't want to miss a minute of the experience, since she'd probably never get the chance again. It lasted an hour and a half and when she got back to her room, she sat on her own balcony and whizzed through all the photos she'd taken. There were at least fifty and at some point, she'd delete a few, but not now. She leaned on her balcony rail and glanced up. Was Cori still up there sunbathing? She was on the seventh floor, but then she remembered they were on opposite sides of the ship. However, visions of Cori wearing a bikini flashed through her mind. She shook her head, attempting to remove the image. Must be the hot weather and the ambiance. Not many women had this effect on her. Not *any* to be precise. Flings were all she wanted, not something permanent where the people ended up as emotionless mannequins stuck together thanks to vows neither should have made in the first place. Fuck. The mere thought of her ending up like her mother and father scared her shitless. No, best not go there.

She sighed. Surely, once upon a time, they'd been in love. Or maybe they hadn't…maybe it was just a coming together of two people who had nothing else to do, or had it just been convenience? They certainly shared one passion which was their trade, but apart from that she hadn't witnessed any signs of romance or love between them. They were quiet and conservative, and come to think of it, they hardly ever talked about anything apart from their funeral business.

She chuckled. Maybe it turned them on. It hardly conjured up romantic feelings for her. Still, they'd had two children, so they must have had sex at least twice. She shuddered at the thought. Perhaps that's why she'd felt safer sticking with flings. There was no deep personal involvement, just the sex and a bit of attention. Yes, they were more her scene. A casual liaison without expectations of commitment worked for her, and she never promised anything she wasn't going to give or led anyone on. Fleeting and impersonal, maybe, but it had all the benefits of a relationship less the drama, and it wouldn't turn into stale bread that eventually crumbled to dust.

Of course, it didn't always work out well. She'd once turned up at a party with someone new and the woman she'd recently had a fling with had gone apeshit. They'd hooked up because they'd agreed they wanted a good time, and it was just a passing fancy for both. So, when they'd started to disagree and fight, they'd both known it was time to end it. At least, that's what she'd thought. On that occasion it hadn't gone according to plan.

Of course, she never introduced any of them to her family or close friends, the few that she had. That would somehow make it official. No, she wasn't ready for a real relationship, but a fling added spice to her life and made her feel alive.

In that case, why was she always thinking about Cori? She reckoned it was because of her chivalrous side. Cori seemed vulnerable and she wanted to wrap her in a cloud of cotton wool and protect her. There was nothing wrong with that, was there? Of course not. And normally, she'd have been all about a vacation fling. But there was something about Cori, something that had clearly been hurt, and she wasn't about to make that worse by trying it on with her. Not to mention, she had plenty of her own baggage to sort out, and she should be concentrating on that, not getting in bed with a hot woman.

Now get a grip and go get your shower. She picked out some smart casual clothes and headed up to the lounge. It was the first time she'd felt it, but there was a definite swell on the sea. As she made her way down the long corridor, she held on to the rails along the side. Now she knew what they were for.

Once in the lounge, she ordered a Black Russian with Diet Coke from the bar. Everybody was there, apart from Dorothy and Lena. Unfortunately, Raf was sitting next to Cori, but at least she'd had her company all day. Maybe she could jiggle things a bit when they got down to the restaurant.

Raf folded her arms across her chest. "You missed a great trip today, Cori. What happened?"

Cori slumped into her chair. "I'm sorry, Raf. I've been so looking forward to seeing Antigua and wanted to get a flavour of the island, so I swapped it for the highlights. How was it, anyway?"

"Awesome. You missed a treat." The warmth she usually put into her tone when she spoke to Cori was missing.

Steph looked at Cori's body language, at the way she seemed to shrink into herself, and got pissed off. Raf had no right to make her feel bad. "We had an awesome time, didn't we, Cori? She practically knew as much as the tour guide!" She smiled and was glad to see Cori take a deep breath and smile back. "Hey, didn't that Steve guy get killed by a stingray?"

"Sure did. Terrible accident." Raf chuckled. "Last one that stung me ended up in a coma."

Steph nodded. "I bet."

Raf looked at her watch. "I wonder where Dorothy and Lena are? Hope they're okay."

Just as she said it, in they walked. Lena had a firm grip on Dorothy's arm and toppled as she guided her towards their table.

Steph dashed over and took Dorothy's arm. "You two all right? Here, have my seat, Dorothy."

Dorothy sat down. She looked a little green around the gills, and Steph guessed she was suffering from a bit of seasickness. She turned to Lena. "Have you got pills?"

"Yes, thank you, Steph. We called in at reception to get some. That's why we're late."

Steph pulled out a chair for Lena and she gingerly sat down. "You'll soon feel better, they usually work very quickly." Steph looked over at Raf. "Is it going to be like this all night?"

"No, Captain says it'll ease up later. It's often a bit choppy around these waters. Weather forecast is good for tomorrow, though." Raf elbowed Mike playfully. "The aristocrats from the special staterooms were having dinner in their fancy restaurant. Captain comes down and interrupts. "I have some good news and some bad news. Which do you want to hear first?"

"The good!" Everyone said in unison.

The captain said, "We won eleven Oscars!"

Raf howled and Mike chuckled.

Dorothy grimaced. "I don't understand. Can you explain?"

"Not important, Dorothy," Steph mumbled quietly, but loud enough that Raf could hear. "Hardly appropriate under the circumstances." First, she'd made Cori feel bad, and now she was mocking Dorothy's sea sickness by talking about sinking ships.

Raf raised her eyebrows. "Anyway, folks, time for dinner."

Steph took Dorothy's arm and Cori quickly steadied Lena. They headed down to the dining room. This time Steph managed to get a seat next to Cori, although it didn't look like Raf cared at all, and everyone else spread around the large circular table.

Over dinner, they talked about their tours and how they'd loved Antigua. Cori showed Lena some of the photos they'd taken and Raf leaned over, looked, and sneered. Must have been the one where Steph had her arm around Cori. She smiled across at Raf, and Raf looked away.

When Cori had finished, she put her phone away and turned to Steph. "So how did your tour go this afternoon?"

"Absolutely brilliant. An hour and a half of sheer indulgence. You wouldn't believe how flashy the Caribbean stateroom is. Somebody says it costs ten thousand dollars a night to stay in that room. The veranda is huge, and you get a butler and chef and everything your heart desires."

"Do you think it's worth it?" Mike asked.

"Personally, no. But I guess if you have money to burn, it's nothing. And the artwork is out of this world. Do you know, there's a Picasso, a Monet, and a Van Gogh, all scattered around the ship."

"No kidding," Patti said. "Wish I'd taken the tour."

"Yeah, it was brilliant. I took loads of photos. I love to see other people's take on interior design. It's fascinating." Steph showed them a couple of pictures. "Then there's the private dining room. Now *that's* something else."

Cori shrugged. "I still say you can't beat all this." She waved her hand indicating the splendour before them.

Steph nodded. "I agree, but it's good to see. You know, how crazy it can get when you've got so much to spend."

Patti turned to Raf. "Are there any celebrities on board then?"

"Not this time. There is a lord and lady—" Raf lowered her voice, "but mostly it's new money and people who will never be able to do this more than once in their life." Her eyes flicked quickly to Steph and then away. "There's a lot of that around." Raf looked at her phone on the table. "'Scuse me, folks. I have to take this." She left the table.

In the meantime, they continued with desserts, followed by coffee and liqueurs. The atmosphere relaxed notably, and Steph was once again reminded of her family. How were people so unaware that their presence made people uncomfortable?

When Raf returned she didn't sit back down. She looked irritable and crabby. She looked at Cori. "I'm off for a smoke. I'll see you up there." Cori stood. "I'll join you. I've finished now." She placed her hand on Steph's shoulder. "Shall we meet for a drink in the Galaxy after?"

Steph smiled. She hadn't expected Cori to make that suggestion. Certainly not in front of Raf. She was pleased that Cori seemed to be getting some confidence back. "Great. See you there."

She said her farewells to the gang and when she left, she hovered by the casino. She spotted Annette, the croupier at the roulette table and gave a little wave. If Cori hadn't suggested a drink, she'd possibly have been in there. But she knew where she'd prefer to be.

She passed by the smoker's lounge and glanced in. She lingered a little and saw Raf and Cori by the window. They were deep in conversation. Raf still looked as jumpy as a cat and as cross as two sticks. She watched her stub her cigar out and immediately light another one. Steph would have liked to have hung around, but hopefully Cori would fill her in on all the gossip. At least Cori's body language was relaxed, and she didn't look upset. If she had, Steph had a feeling she wouldn't be able to help getting involved again.

As usual, everybody had grabbed all the tables by the stage, no doubt waiting for the band to come on. Steph saw that the table they'd had last night was free, far away from the maddening crowds.

Cori came into the lounge and when she spotted Steph she strode over and took the seat opposite.

"Drink?" Steph asked.

"I've had way too much, but I'd love a Diet Coke, please."

Steph called the waiter over and ordered a Sprite for herself. "What the hell's wrong with Raf?"

"She booked a tour for me tomorrow. Obviously the one that she was on."

"And?"

"Well, you know all those la-di-da people in the fancy suites?"

Steph nodded.

"Apparently she's been assigned to one of them who's in a wheelchair. She has to look after her most of the day and take her on the highlights tour of St. Barts."

Steph laughed. "Aw…what a shame and how sad."

Cori looked contemplative. "She'd booked that all-terrain vehicle around St. Barts for us. Anyway, she says one of the guys from the centre will drive me."

"You're joking. An ATV? I've driven one before. I drove all around one of the Greek islands. I love them."

Cori sat up straight. "If you want, you could come with me and drive, as long as you take it slow. To be honest, they scare me but I'm trying to get out of my comfort zone a little."

Steph bounced around in her chair. "Wow, I'd love to. And I promise I won't frighten you. What time do we leave?"

"Eleven. I think it takes about four hours. That includes a few stops and one at the beach for swimming and a packed lunch. So, take your swimsuit with you if you want."

"Yay! This is awesome. Thanks so much."

"Thank you too. I'll feel much safer with you than some local, or Raf."

Steph winked. "Particularly Raf."

Cori giggled. She finished her drink and stood. "Right. Need to get some sleep. See you in the theatre at ten-forty."

"You bet." Steph joined her and they made their way back to their rooms. She didn't want the night to end, but she'd come to understand that Cori seemed to like her sleep and wasn't much of a night owl. What an amazing surprise that they'd get to spend the day alone tomorrow. That same image of Cori in a bikini flashed in her mind and she couldn't help but grin.

***

Steph drew back the curtains and opened her balcony door. What a sight. She'd forgotten they were anchored today and the view of Gustavia's harbour was so picturesque. It didn't look crowded like a lot of the islands, just a scattering of little red brick houses nestled below the steep hillsides on either side of the small harbour town. There was only one other small cruise ship anchored nearby, along with half a dozen private yachts. She watched the crew lowering the tender boats that would take them into the port. One passed by her balcony. At least she got a good view of it. She took some photos and then went up for breakfast. She took nothing with her apart from her phone, key card, and passport which she slipped into her back pocket. She figured she'd pay for stuff if she needed it. No need to carry around a bag with a bunch of stuff in it.

When she got down to the theatre, Cori was waiting for her, and she fetched their coach tickets for the short ride to the ATV centre.

Cori sighed. "I couldn't believe it when I opened my curtains. It's so beautiful. It's like a postcard and so elegant."

"Yes, very French and chic. Apparently, it's the playground for the wealthy and sophisticated. Miles from Paris, but decidedly French." Granted, she was quoting something she'd read from an internet search, but it sounded good.

"I've heard. I can't wait to see it. Aren't we lucky?"

"Yeah, I keep having to pinch myself. Can't believe I'm here and seeing all these fantastic islands. I feel incredibly privileged." Steph looked towards the stage and listened to the announcement. "That's us. Let's go for our next adventure."

They piled into the tenders and chatted to their fellow passengers. The guy next to Steph nudged her. "See that yacht there?"

"Yup. Can hardly miss it. It's nearly as big as our ship."

"You know who owns it?"

Steph hated guessing games. "Please tell me."

"That Russian billionaire oligarch who owns the football club."

"Really." Steph stared goggle-eyed as the tender slowed down whilst passing the yacht. She got her phone out and snapped away. "Jeez, there's even a helicopter on it."

"Yep. Two helipads. It's twice the size of the pitch at Stamford Bridge. I've been reading up on it."

Steph shook her head. "Wait 'till I tell them back home. They're not gonna believe it. Do you think he's doing a bit of shopping in the port?"

"If he is, they'll close it to the public. He's got a luxury mansion here as well."

Steph googled it. "Bloody hell, it even has a three-person submarine. It's like a James Bond movie."

"What's that?" Cori asked.

Steph related the story and Cori leaned forward to get a view of the yacht they were passing. "Wow. Hope you can send me some pics."

"Along with all the others we're going to take today. Mind you, you'll have to do the photography. I'm driving."

Cori grimaced. "Oh hell!"

When they got into the port, they joined their small group. There were a couple of minivans waiting for them which took them to their starting point.

Steph jiggled around when she saw the ATV.

The boss of the outfit was called Beau. He approached her. "Have you driven one of these babies before?"

"Yes. I've had about six hours on them."

"Okay, let's do a little test drive then."

All the other drivers did the same and Steph passed with flying colours. They put their helmets on and Cori sat beside her. Steph handed Cori her phone. "Your job."

Steph could sense that Cori was scared, but they took a steady pace from the port and up into the hillside villages. They sped up a little once they were out of the town and zipped through the countryside at a decent pace, but they took loads of stops from the highest points to get some great shots of the scenery. Every so often they'd go over some bumpier tracks and Cori's body would graze against hers. Steph sighed and glanced at Cori. She was so happy to be sharing this adventure with her. Things had really turned out well, thanks to Raf's forced withdrawal, and life couldn't get much sweeter than this. It was surprising, really, how not trying to get with someone eased the pressure. She could enjoy Cori's company for what it was, without any expectation or tension. Maybe she'd give real dating a try once she was back home. The thought made her laugh. As if. Once they were out of this idyllic bubble, she'd still be the person she'd always been.

They traversed slowly along the hilltops and the route took them through tiny villages and along the spectacular coastline. Eventually, they headed back up north and ended up at their final destination, Saint-Jean beach.

Beau dismounted his ATV. "Okay, folks, there are sun chairs provided and if you just follow me, I'll hand out your packed lunches. Sorry it's a bit late, but I thought it was more comfortable to eat here than on a roadside somewhere." Beau handed them all a box plus water or Coke. "Go relax, take a swim, whatever you want."

Steph raised her hand. "How long have we got?"

"About an hour. I'll call you when it's time to leave. If you want though, you can stay, as long as you don't miss the last tender at five. It's only a couple of minutes' walk into Gustavia. You can make your mind up later."

Steph nodded, slung her rucksack over her shoulder, and passed Cori hers. "C'mon. let's go bag our beds. I saw there were a few right on the water's edge."

They made a quick dash and threw their bags onto the beds. Steph stretched and took in the horizon. "Wow, this is brilliant, isn't it?"

"You're not kidding. The whole day has been perfect, and thanks so much for driving me."

Steph smiled. "It was my pleasure." She unpacked her bag and spread the towel on the bed. "I put my bikini on underneath, thought it would be less embarrassing."

"Yes, me too."

They pulled their T-shirts and shorts off and lay on their beds.

Steph had a quick peek at Cori in her bikini. She looked gorgeous. Her figure without clothes on was crazy sexy, and just as fantastic as she'd imagined. The yellow bikini was certainly her colour, though she imagined Cori would look sexy in any shade. She thought about suggesting they take their bikini tops off. After all, they were in Little France, as she called it, though she imagined Cori would be too shy. Shame, because she'd have loved to get a glimpse of her naked breasts. She felt her clit twitch at the mere thought, and she was sure she'd find it impossible to keep her hands off Cori's body. She took a deep breath, lay back and tried to erase the erotic thoughts from her mind. It didn't work. Instead, she shot up, grabbed Cori's hand, and pulled her to the water's edge. She desperately needed to cool off. They ran hand in hand until the water covered their waists.

Cori turned around and took in the surroundings. "It's a different world, isn't it? Mind you, I feel like I've had a taste of it on this cruise."

"One hundred percent. Best holiday I've ever had." She nudged Cori. "Bet you always take luxury holidays."

Cori looked down and kicked at the water. "No way. We—" She stopped, frowning. "I've hardly been out of the UK apart from a long weekend in Paris and Rome, and it wasn't luxury, and it was many years ago."

Steph didn't question her any further, but one day she'd like to know who the "we" was. Cori looked so sad, and she hated to see that. She pulled her further in. "Let's swim."

Cori looked reluctant, even though the water was a beautiful temperature. Steph scooped up handfuls of water and threw them over Cori.

She screamed, "You just wait!" She scooped water herself, but Steph swam off.

She turned around out of reach and laughed. "You'll have to catch me first."

Cori dived in and Steph swam away, but slowly. This was one time she wanted to be caught. Where was Cori though? She stood and glanced around but couldn't see her. Then, she felt something grasping her ankles. She lost balance and went under.

By the time she'd got up, Cori was several yards away giggling and pointing. "You're too slow."

Steph grinned, dived in and swam as fast as she could, following Cori who was doing the same. She caught her easily and grabbed her legs. Cori shrieked again and tried to kick free, but Steph had a firm hold. She let go and they surfaced together. Cori splashed water at her, but Steph managed to grip Cori's wrists and pulled her close to her body. She held her momentarily and their breasts touched. Steph's nipples hardened, and she was sure Cori's did too. Their eyes met and Steph bit her lower lip. Should she kiss her?

"Hey, you two. Time to leave."

They both looked around to see Beau on the edge of the water. The moment was broken.

Steph coughed and slowly let Cori's hands slide from her own. Cori's gaze was intense before she looked back to the shore. The awkward moment stretched, and Steph wished she could rewind time.

"Do you fancy walking back through the port?"

Cori hesitated. "Err, I'd love to."

"Best go tell Beau then." They swam back to shore.

"We're staying, if that's okay. Thanks for the great day, buddy."

Beau winked. "Come see us again one day." He waved as he left.

It was a nice idea, but once Cori hopped off in Jamaica, they may never see each other again. But something had happened between them, and she was sure Cori sensed it too. They stood for a while, silent. Steph couldn't think of a thing to say that wouldn't potentially make things even more awkward.

Cori kicked at the sand. "I guess we'd better get dry."

Steph nodded. "Looking forward to seeing the village. It looked kinda quaint. Interesting décor."

Cori pushed her arm playfully. "Hey, can we glance in the shops too?"

"You bet." It had taken a few minutes, but they now seemed relaxed with each other. However, Steph couldn't help thinking about what had happened in the sea. Something had changed and it warmed her to the core of her heart. But how to see where it might lead without destroying the little they'd built so far?

They put their clothes on and strolled along the beach towards the port. "Christ. Look at all those private yachts. Hey, look at this one, do you think they want a washer-up?"

Cori shook her head slowly. "I think they'll have every appliance you can think of."

"Sometimes I get a bit envious."

Cori rubbed her forehead. "It doesn't matter how much money one has…it can't guarantee happiness."

"Very true. Let's go wander around some shops. See if we can afford anything?"

Cori smiled. "Thought you'd never ask."

They ambled through the winding streets and went into a craft shop. Steph picked up a necklace which was made from tiny shells. She put it back down again. She whispered to Cori, "Do you know how much that is?"

"Arm? Leg?"

"Fucking stupid." She put her hand over her mouth. "Sorry about the language."

Cori laughed. "I think we'd better stick with some postcards instead. And they're bloody expensive too. Are they Monet's?"

"No, Ripoffs. Another famous French artist."

Cori giggled. They linked arms and strolled back to the quayside towards the tender. The closeness felt so natural, and Steph couldn't help but think the dynamics of their relationship as friends had moved on to something more. There was an intimacy that she'd never felt before.

They boarded and as they passed the yacht anchored by their ship, Steph turned to Cori. "You know what? Even with all their money I doubt they'd have a better day than us."

"You're absolutely right. It's been fabulous."

The day may have come to end, but she knew deep down it was just the beginning. She wanted more than brilliant memories and loads of photos. She wanted real love. Whatever that was.

When they got back, Cori looked at her watch. "Heck, I didn't realise that was the time. I need to shower and things."

"Me too. I hope we can have a change tonight and eat in The Brindisi. It's such a beautiful evening and I'd love to sit outside."

"Well, let's hope Raf reads our minds. And I hope she's in a better mood."

Steph shrugged. She wished they could eat alone again tonight, but that was out of the question. Perhaps she'd see if she could book something different for tomorrow night. Maybe *she* was feeling all romancy and stuff, but what if Cori wasn't? Perhaps it wasn't the greatest idea she'd had, but as far as she was concerned, it felt pretty damn good.

They walked up the couple of flights of stairs to their deck and when Cori had left, Steph planned. She'd go down a floor and check out the Pacific Coast restaurant. Nothing ventured, nothing gained.

Chapter Nine

CORI PUT THE FINISHING touches to her hair then made her way up to the lounge. They were just about to set sail and she spotted Steph, Patti, and Mike standing by the window, so she waved to the others as she passed by to join them. She stood at Steph's side, and they waved to Beau, and it almost felt as though they were saying farewell to a friend. She didn't know if she'd return, but she had happy memories, and nobody could take those away…not even Dusty.

Steph tapped her on the shoulder. "What do you want to drink? Your usual."

"Oh, please. I guess I'm boring ordering the same thing all the time. Still, it's only for another few days and then it'll be rum, rum, and rum."

Steph pushed her bottom lip forward. "Don't remind me."

Cori punched her playfully. "Stop it. We've got three more days left yet."

That news seemed to cheer Steph up and they went back to their seats and joined in the conversation about their trips on St. Barts.

Cori slid into the seat next to Raf. "Hope your day wasn't too bad."

Raf looked up to the ceiling. "It's part of the job." She pressed her hand to Cori's knee. "I was just so looking forward to driving you around St. Barts. I hope they looked after you?"

Cori cleared her throat several times. "Actually, Steph drove me." She felt a flush creep up her neck. "It seemed like a good idea, since she had experience." It frustrated her that she felt the need to excuse the fact that she'd had Steph with her. Would she ever stop apologizing for what she wanted?

Raf's mouth smiled, but her eyes held all the warmth of a viper. "Absolutely. As long as you enjoyed it."

Cori hugged herself and could feel a sense of shrinking into oblivion. "Yes, it was lovely." Her throat constricted. She had to get out of here if only for a minute. She pushed her chair back. "Will you excuse me? Be back shortly."

She saw the look of concern on Steph's face.

She exited as quickly as her wobbly legs would allow. Once in the Ladies, she took lots of deep breaths until her breathing returned to near normal. It seemed stupid really, reacting to Raf's response in that way, but at the time, it came flooding back. It could have been Dusty sitting there uttering those words. It was exactly the behaviour she was trying to escape from, and yet here it was, back to bite her. She looked at herself in the mirror. That wasn't Dusty out there. She wasn't the same person she'd been when she was with Dusty. She was moving forward, and Raf would be gone from her life soon enough.

After composing herself, she returned to the table.

Steph got up immediately and let Cori in. "Come join me." She took Cori's hand and squeezed it tightly. Immediately, Cori felt the tension slipping from her body and squeezed Steph's hand back.

Raf looked uncomfortable and tapped her hand on the table. "It's such a lovely evening, I thought we'd dine in The Brindisi this evening."

Patti eyes widened. "Oh, how thoughtful. Did you manage to get a table outside?"

"Of course. I pulled some strings."

Patti clapped her hands. "You're so good to us, Raf."

Raf waved her hand. "You're all so worth it."

It was hardly sincere, and Cori saw Steph looking down as she covered her mouth with her other hand.

Raf tipped the contents of her glass into her mouth and set it down on the table. "Okay, guys, let's move our asses."

Everybody finished their drinks and obeyed.

When they arrived at the restaurant, it was full, and they were even queueing outside the doors. They followed Raf to the veranda and found they'd been allocated the same table as before which was in a prime position. Raf certainly had her uses.

Steph turned to Lena and Dorothy. "Would you ladies like the same chairs as before?"

"Please. That's so kind of you."

"No problem." Steph slid in and Cori followed her onto the leather seating. She whispered, "Are you okay?"

Cori smiled. "I am now. Thank you." It was good to have Steph around. She was so thoughtful and seemed to pick up on her every mood. Just that small gesture had brought her back to the land of the living.

Mike and Patti joined them on the other side and Raf took the chair next to Cori.

Raf picked up the menu. "Awesome. They have foie gras tonight."
She turned to Steph. "Will you be joining me?"

Steph shook her head. "No, I don't like it."

Raf raised her eyebrows. "What's not to like, Steph?"

Steph flushed and her body seemed to freeze.

Cori answered. "Personally, I hate it when they force-feed a duck
or a goose, just to get some rich liver. Call it a delicacy, but I call it
inhumane."

Steph visibly relaxed. "My sentiments entirely."

Raf shrugged. "Everyone to their own. I certainly won't be missing
out."

During the course of their meal, Steph paused. "I can't remember
what's happening tomorrow. What's everyone doing?"

They all laughed, but Raf kept a straight face. "Swimming with the
dolphins."

Steph's eyes sparkled. "No kidding?"

"No kidding. You can take my place, if you like?"

Steph's eyes narrowed. "What's the catch?"

"It's an expensive tour and will possibly cost you an arm and a leg."
Raf hooted. "'Cos there's mostly sharks out there."

Everyone chuckled. Cori nudged Steph. "It's a sea day tomorrow."

Steph didn't blush or retaliate, she simply laughed along with the
group. "Hey, that's a good one, Raf. You had me going there." She
winked. "Anyway, I've already swum with dolphins. I didn't like it
much 'cos they were too cliquey."

There were titters of laughter from around the table and then Dorothy
turned to Lena. "Are we on the dolphin trip tomorrow, Sis?"

Lena patted Dorothy's hand. "No, darling. We're going to play cards
instead."

Dorothy smiled. "I prefer that."

There was a lot of chatter during the meal and when they'd finished,
their plates were cleared away.

Raf leaned her elbow on the table and turned her attention to Cori. "I
only heard today that you're leaving us in Jamaica."

Cori smiled. "I'm afraid so." Her smile developed into a grin. "I'm
going to spend some time with my family there."

"Well, that's wonderful, hun. Do your parents live there?"

"No, they're in England. My grandparents and brother live there. I really can't wait to see them. It's been such a long time."

Patti leaned forward. "Well, I think that's just delightful. Do you have some photos?"

Cori smiled and nodded. She pulled her phone out of her bag, flicked through some pictures, and passed her phone to Patti. "My grandparents and brother."

Patti held the phone at arm's length. "They're a fine-looking family." She looked over at Cori as if she'd never seen her before or as if she was double-checking something. "So, were you adopted?"

Cori winced. "No. They're my natural family."

Patti gave a little laugh. "But they're coloureds."

Cori saw Steph's clenched fists as she jumped to her defence. "They're Black. In fact, Cori and her brother are both mixed-race."

"Well, that must be a throw-back then. I mean, it's so unusual for col—, I mean Blacks to produce a white—especially one so pretty as you, Cori."

Cori grimaced. "My mum is white. Not as though that makes any difference to my feelings, because they're the best family a woman could ever wish for."

Patti smiled, but she continued to look confused.

Raf held her arm out. "May I have a look?" Raf took the phone and shook her head. "Well, that's the nicest looking family and I bet you're gonna have yerself a ball, honey."

Cori smiled. "Thanks, Raf." Raf seemed genuine on that score. Maybe she'd suffered a bit of bullying herself. People were so bigoted. Luckily, being at ease with her ethnicity had never been an issue. If only she'd met someone like Steph and not Dusty, things could have been different all around. Then again, as Dusty always told her, she'd brought it all on herself. She supposed she had.

After dessert and coffee, the gang left Cori, Steph, and Raf and went off to the show. Tonight, it was songs from Seven Brides for Seven Brothers, and they seemed to be excited about it.

Raf laughed. "You giving that one a miss?"

Cori smiled. "I'm sure it'll be wonderful, but it's not one of my favourites."

Steph chipped in. "Now if it was Mamma Mia or Bohemian Rhapsody—"

Raf nodded. "I agree. They do tend to cater for the more, err, let's say mature traveller." Raf held her hand up. "However, on New Year's Eve, we're doing a tribute to Abba in the central lobby atrium. I hope you'll come and support it."

Steph put her thumbs up. "Sure thing. What time?"

"Ten thirty. Then it'll take us right up to midnight. I'm gonna be one hell of a busy lady tomorrow, and on New Year's Eve."

Steph grinned. "Sea days are Raf days. We always look forward to those."

Cori kicked her leg, hoping she'd not say any more. At least Raf and Steph didn't seem so hostile now. She hoped they'd drawn a line under their conflict. Cori hated disputes of any kind. That's why she always gave in to Dusty. What was the point in arguing, especially when she could never win?

Raf slapped her thigh. "Well done, Steph. You got it." Raf clicked her fingers. "Time for a smoke."

Cori stood. "Yes, me too."

They made their way to the smoker's lounge and Steph tapped Cori on the shoulder. She tilted her hand to her mouth, as if to say drink.

Cori wasn't going to hide anymore. It was silly to hide something she was enjoying because of a stranger's attitude. "Thanks, Steph. I'd love a Tia Maria."

Steph turned to Raf. "Can I get you a drink?"

Raf gave a half-smile. "Thanks. Got to be up early tomorrow."

Cori would have been fine with Raf joining them and was pleased that Steph had good manners and hadn't excluded her.

Raf got her cigar out and lit it. "So, are you two an item?"

Cori nearly choked on her cigarette. She could feel the heat rising from her neck. "Steph and I are just good friends. Nothing more." She wasn't sure about that anymore. After their time on the beach in St. Barts, her emotions had changed. She could hardly wait to be alone with Steph and almost felt a mystical bonding. She'd jumped to her defence earlier, just like Steph did whenever she became low. Yes, there was now something deeper. But she couldn't be utterly certain she was ready to trust again. The need to run from the table and Raf's behaviour suggested she wasn't as far along in her healing as she wanted to be.

Raf patted Cori's leg. "Just checking. And by the way, ignore that asshole, Patti. Some of them from the south are like that. Luckily, most aren't."

"Thanks for your support, Raf." Cori took a deep breath and tried to forget the racist comments from Patti, as well as the fact that Raf was still touching her. "So, what have you got lined up for us tomorrow?"

"Team events over the morning and afternoon. Putting, paddle tennis, bocce, and shuffleboard."

Cori shrugged. "Never played any of those, apart from the putting, but I'll join in."

Raf seemed to take that as an invitation to stroke her leg again. "Thanks, sweetie. You'll love them all." She stubbed her cigar out, stroked Cori's hair lightly, and hesitated, as though waiting for an invitation to do more. When she didn't receive one, she tilted her head slightly, and then left.

Cori waited for a moment before leaving. Raf had her good and bad moments, but there was no question she had zero attraction to her. When she thought of attraction, she thought of Steph. She headed to the lounge, spotted Steph at their usual table, and took a seat opposite.

Steph gave her a beautiful smile and passed a glass to Cori. "Chin-chin." She clinked her glass. "Are you okay?"

Cori nodded. "Yes, thanks, but I'm glad you suggested this."

Steph growled. "That fucking Patti...I could have killed her."

Cori put her hand on top of Steph's. "I was taken aback at what she said. Somehow, I didn't expect it and I really appreciated what you did."

"I felt like ripping her head off."

Cori laughed. "I could see."

"Tell you something, I'll be avoiding her for the rest of the trip, otherwise I'll say something."

"I won't be seeking out her company either. Still, there's only a couple more nights."

Steph flinched. "Don't remind me. Wish I was coming with you."

Cori crossed her arms. "You don't. You're just saying that. You must have an exciting life to get back to, not that you talk about it much."

"I'm not kidding. I said I'd love to visit Jamaica. I'd love to meet your family. I'd like to spend time with you and get to know you better." Steph sighed. "I bet you'll forget all about me when you hop off the ship."

Cori shook her head. "Not true. I'd like to keep in touch." Although, was that a good idea? There was chemistry, there was no denying that now. She still wasn't sure she was ready for anything more than friendship.

Steph furrowed her brow. "I don't even know where you live."

"Market Harborough."

Steph slapped her thigh. "You're kidding me! I live in Coventry. We're like forty-five minutes away from each other."

Cori shook her head. "That's amazing. Do you know, I've never been to Coventry?" She laughed. "Mind you, I've been sent there many times." She wasn't joking either. The British idiom apparently originated during the English Civil War when Royalist soldiers were stationed there. They were ostracised and nobody spoke to them, and now "being sent to Coventry" had come to mean you'd become an outcast of sorts. A regular occurrence with Dusty.

Steph chuckled. "Well, I'll give you the grand tour one day."

"That's a deal. Likewise with Market Harborough."

"I've passed through it once or twice. It's a beautiful town, full of history."

Cori nodded. "Yes, I really love it." That much was true. She just hated living in the house that she and Dusty had bought together. Well, mostly with her money. She could have paid off the remaining mortgage, but whilst Dusty was alive, something lurking in the grey matter told her to resist. Now it didn't matter, she could do what she liked and come Spring, she hoped she'd have the courage to put it on the market.

Steph rubbed her finger around the edge of her glass then looked across. "I don't suppose you'd have dinner with me tomorrow?"

Cori inclined her head. Dinner alone with Steph sounded perfect. And potentially dangerous. "I'd love to. I suppose the gang will be in the main restaurant so we could go to Brindisi."

Steph grinned. "I managed to get a table in Pacific Coast at seven forty-five."

"Brilliant. How come?"

"The manager in Island Prime told me they always hold a few tables in reserve for special guests. If they're not taken, anyone can book them. So, I popped up and hey presto. I'm not special, but I can act like I am for a night."

"Great, I love Asian food."

"Me too. Shall we meet in the Caribbean Dream lounge again...say seven fifteen?"

Cori smiled. "Terrific. Anyway, we'll see each other during the day, unless you have other plans."

"No way. It's a sea day, and that means it's —"

They said it together and laughed. "Raf day."

Cori raised her eyebrows. "She's got it all planned. Competitions over the course of the day. Putting, paddle tennis, bocce, and shuffleboard."

"Hey, that's great. I love sporty stuff. Can we try and get on the same team together?"

"Let's do that. We'll have the timings in the magazine tonight, so we can meet up in the Café, go along together, and be the first there. She can't split us up then." She bit her lip. Why did that sound so…so… She sighed. Emotions hadn't been her friends in a long time, and now she couldn't even recognize what she was feeling.

"Great idea." Steph put her hand to her mouth and yawned. "Whoops, sorry. Best go get some sleep."

When they stood, Steph opened the crook of her arm and Cori slipped her hand through. When the elevator arrived at Cori's floor, Steph held the door, but when Cori went to leave, Steph put her hand on Cori's arm. "Thank you, for today. It really was amazing."

They stared into one another's eyes, and Steph's gaze moved to Cori's lips. Just as she was about to lean in, laughter from the couple coming around the corner made them jump apart. Cori flushed and held her hand to her racing heart.

"It was amazing. See you tomorrow." She backed away, then practically ran down the corridor to her room.

When she got to her suite, she quickly hung her clothes up and slipped into bed. She closed her eyes and realised she was pleasantly tired. She sighed. Another wonderful evening and brilliant company and tomorrow she'd be in Steph's company most of the day and evening. As she tried to fall asleep, questions kept intruding. What would be the harm in a dalliance? Something to make her feel good again. Something to remind her that she was attractive and wanted? She flipped onto her back. It didn't need to mean anything, right? But then, if they did stay in touch and saw one another back home, then it would be awkward. She turned onto her side again and pictured Steph lying there beside her.

It didn't help her sleep.

***

As arranged, Cori and Steph met up and went straight up to the paddle tennis court. Raf was standing there, clipboard in hand. She gave that tilt of the head, as if she somehow knew they'd arrive together.

"Teams of four, so whoever turns up next will be with you."

Cori nodded. She hoped that it wouldn't be Patti and Mike. Somehow, she thought there'd be a bit of an atmosphere and she was almost certain Steph wouldn't be able to hide her anger. As for Cori, she was concerned about what people thought, and Patti had certainly overstepped the mark regarding the comments about her family.

Luckily the couple she'd met on the ziplining trip, Nyall and Jess, rolled up.

They greeted her like a long-lost friend. Nyall kissed her on the cheek. "Hey, Cori. We wondered where you'd got to."

"Great to see you two." She turned to Raf. "Can they join us?"

Raf turned her palms up. "Sure thing, hun."

Cori introduced them to Steph, who then got a big hug also.

Patti passed by and smiled but gave them a wide berth.

Raf clapped her hands together. "Okay, folks. I know the court isn't supposed to be for four players, but let's have a bit of fun."

Cori had played tennis in her teens, but frankly, she wasn't really a sports person, whereas Steph said she was. Steph tried to cover the court, but they collided on many occasions. Their teammates didn't do much better either. Things tended to get worse after lunch when Nyall and Jess downed a bottle of wine between them. There was plenty of laughter, very little point-scoring, and relief when it was over.

When they'd done with the games, Cori nudged Steph. "I think we'd better tell Raf that we won't be there tonight. To be polite."

Steph shrugged. "Okay."

Cori tapped Raf on the shoulder. "We're eating elsewhere tonight. Thought we'd better let you know."

"No problem. And don't forget, Friday is barbeque night on deck. The biggest feast you will ever see. I know it's your last night, so it'll be like a farewell party. There's a terrific steel band on after."

Cori beamed. "Sounds brilliant. Might see you later in the smoker's lounge."

Raf smiled then stared at Steph. "Just thought I'd let you know, because apart from the main restaurant, none of the others will be open."

Steph grinned. "Love barbeques, love steel bands." She kicked a stray golf ball. "Shit. I was hoping we could spend your last night together."

"We will be together. And we'll meet up when we get back home." Cori knew full well what Steph meant, but after tossing and turning all night, she couldn't acknowledge what was between them. It was too complicated.

Steph's shoulders slumped. "Of course we will. I'm being stupid."

Cori checked her watch, uncomfortable with what was being left unsaid between them. "Think I'm going to grab some afternoon sun and catch up on emails."

"Sounds good. I'm gonna grab my bikini, take a swim, and sit by the pool." She winked at Cori. "See you as arranged."

"Definitely."

Back in her room, Cori checked her phone texts and saw there was one from Liz, checking up on her.

Where are you? Haven't heard for ages.

Sorry, busy, busy, busy. Cori gave her a brief catch-up on everything that had happened over the last few days. She told her a little about the closeness she'd developed but left a lot out. She wasn't ready to share the moments of desire, of longing, that she'd had. Not yet.

So, it's going well with Steph. Shame you'll be parting company on Friday. Can't you take her with you? She sent a smiley face.

We're keeping in touch when we get back. She lives in Coventry. Actually, she said she wished she was getting off in Jamaica... That thought, in particular, had been running through her mind all night.

So why don't you ask her?

Don't be silly. Anyway, got to dash now. Shower, dress and off to Asian tonight.

I can take a hint. Keep me posted. xxxx

Will do. xxxx

Cori laughed out loud. What a crazy idea to invite Steph. She had a job to get back to, and she was sure it was busy at this time of the year, what with the 'flu epidemic and everything. And a woman like Steph must be in demand by all kinds of friends. And women who wanted to be more than friends.

But Steph had said she'd jump at the opportunity and Cori knew her family would welcome her with open arms. Ridiculous. What if she made the offer and Steph declined? But if she didn't make the offer, she'd never know and she'd lose the opportunity to find out if there could be more between them. Did she want more? She hadn't thought so, but after those intimate moments they'd shared, she could hardly stop thinking about Steph. But what if they took it further and Steph only wanted a holiday affair? She'd been broken before, so how could she cope with a broken heart yet again?

Tomorrow they were in Punta Cana, Dominican Republic. They weren't anchoring until mid-day, so it was another highlights coach trip. It was an afternoon jaunt, so if Steph said yes, they could deal with it.

She opened her balcony and got out her writing materials. Distracting herself with her children's writing had always worked in the past, and this time was no different. She lost herself in creating the adventures she would have loved as a child, and soon, it was time to get ready. Cori opened the cubicle, turned the water on full blast and let the rainfall shower cascade over her body. It was invigorating and left her full of vitality. She slipped her robe on, dried her hair, and wandered into the wardrobe. She wanted to look elegant tonight, so she chose a pair of black satin trousers and paired them with a sparkly cream top. She liked the way Steph looked at her, like she was the only person worth noticing in the world. She'd looked at her much that way during their ocean swim, and it had felt almost magical. She added the finishing touches and made her way down to the Dream lounge where Steph was waiting for her with a drink in hand.

Steph whistled. "Wow, you look fabulous."

Cori looked down and fiddled with one of her buttons. "Thank you. Likewise." And she wasn't lying. The tight white trousers really showed off Steph's great legs. She stopped staring and looked up. "Love that waistcoat."

"Thanks. I think we complement each other."

Steph nodded in the direction of a table nearby and told her all about her afternoon. "You won't believe this, but I had to prevent a punch-up on deck."

Cori looked skyward. "No, I don't believe you."

"I'm serious." She lowered her voice. "Two nationalities were involved. Let's just say they've never liked each other. One left a towel on their sunbed during lunch. The other one moved it off and put it on a chair and settled in. Man returns and the argument begins. You wouldn't believe the names they called each other. Anyway, the one with the artificial leg—"

Cori interrupted. "No way." She laughed.

"I'm not kidding. He sidled up to the one with a walking stick, puffed up his chest, and started pushing him back with his belly. Then the other one retaliated and did the same. They looked like two fat frogs. So, walking stick man raised his stick…and that's when I intervened."

"Thank God. How come nobody else did anything?"

"They all kept their heads down. So, I got up and said, 'Enough, gentlemen.' Not as though either behaved like one. I removed my towel and proffered my bed to artificial leg man. They both went beetroot red and apologised to me. Not to each other, however."

"Good for you. Were they young?"

"Gawd, no. They were ancient. Possibly in their late hundreds. Anyway, they should know better." Steph flipped her hand over and looked at her watch. "Hey, we'd best move our asses."

They finished their drinks and made their way to the restaurant which was tucked away at the back of the ship. Cori's jaw dropped as they entered the room. "Gosh, this is stunning. Look at this bronze, what is it?"

"An interpretation of a Tibetan prayer wheel. Do you know, this piece of sculpture is the single most expensive piece of art on the ship? It's so heavy that the deck had to be reinforced with extra steel."

Cori laughed, strangely pleased at how easily Steph assimilated information and enjoyed sharing it. "How come you know so much?"

"It was part of my tour the other day. I really love looking at different decors. Got hundreds of photos of the interior of the ship. It's fascinating."

"I'm impressed." Cori turned to see a young lady walking up the steps to greet them. She had a beautiful smile and bowed her head as she approached.

"Good evening, Ms Steph. Good evening, Ms Cori. Welcome to Pacific Coast. My name is Trang and I'm here to make sure you have an unrivalled culinary experience tonight."

Trang looked about sixteen, but Cori imagined she must be much older because her name badge said she was the maître d. Cori gazed around. It was much bigger than she'd expected and although there were lots of tables, they weren't too close to each other and allowed privacy of conversation. The intimate atmosphere was certainly more date-like than any others they'd enjoyed so far. She tugged at her blouse.

Trang pointed to a table. "You have a choice, ladies, either the one at the back or the one by the window."

Steph smiled. "Window anytime. Do you agree?"

Cori nodded and turned to Steph. "Gosh, this is exotic."

"Isn't it just. Great ocean view too."

They took their seats and Trang spread a napkin on each of their laps. She said their waitress, Nila, would be along shortly. Nila showed up and placed a signature cocktail on each plate together with a menu each.

Steph sipped her drink. "That's refreshing. The menu is pretty good too, and you can mix and match dishes from Vietnamese, Thai, Korean, Chinese and Japanese cuisines."

Cori laughed. "You may have to help me on that one."

Nila returned and they ordered their meals, along with a bottle of Oyster Bay. Shortly the food was served. They picked up their glasses, wished each other bon appétit, and tucked in.

Cori bit into her duck spring roll. "Haven't had this for years. It's delicious." She stared at Steph's appetizer. "What did you have?"

"The soft-shell crab in tempura batter." She picked out a small piece and passed it over to Cori with her chopsticks.

Cori wasn't sure what to do.

"It's okay, just pop it into your mouth."

It seemed an intimate thing to do and not something that had ever happened with Dusty. Whatever she ordered, she ate. There was no sharing. She took the morsel and sighed. "That's beautiful. Would you like some of mine?"

"No, thanks. There's loads here."

They both followed with the Miso soup and then Cori had the Miso Black Cod and Steph chose the Curried Seafood Laksa.

Cori unwrapped her hoba leaf and the aroma from the spices poured out. She helped herself to Jasmine rice and put a few of the mushrooms on her plate. Halfway through she pulled a face. "Only thing I'm not keen on are the mushrooms."

Steph laughed. "Shitake happens."

"Ha ha, very funny. What's your curry like?"

"Fantastic." She put her chopsticks down. "So, what's happening tomorrow in Punta Cana?"

"We don't get there until midday, and we're anchoring, so we'll be taking the tenders into the port. I don't think there are many excursions.

Mine's highlights again which suits me."

"I think mine is too. I can't remember. Should be a great evening though."

"Yes, it sounds promising." *Come on woman, ask her.* Cori took a deep breath. "I was wondering if—no, forget it." There didn't seem any point. She most likely would say no then she'd feel an idiot. And what was she thinking, inviting a virtual stranger to meet her family?

Steph placed her palms together as if praying. "Please don't do that. You know, begin a question and not finish. What did you want to say?"

"It's silly really. I mean, I don't think you'll want to, or I don't think you'll be able to."

Steph raised her eyebrows.

Cori held her hand up. "Okay, okay. You know you said you'd like to go to Jamaica…would you like to join me?"

Steph's mouth gaped. "You're asking me if I want to go with you?"

Cori nodded.

"Are you serious?"

"I wouldn't ask otherwise."

Steph raised her arms in the air. "Yay! I'd love to. I mean, are you sure it'll be okay with your family?"

"Positive. They love entertaining. Don't worry, I shall let them know." Her heart fluttered in her chest. God, what was she thinking?

"How long are you staying there?"

Cori checked her phone diary. "Flying back on the twelfth of January. A daytime flight from Kingston to Miami and then I'll be on the evening flight from Miami." Cori grimaced. "I don't want you to get your hopes up too much in case it's not possible. Did you arrange everything through the company?"

Steph nodded. She slapped her hand on the table. "I'm going to have a damn good try. I shall be down at the destinations desk at nine forty-five. I don't suppose you'd join me? You know, to explain and stuff."

"Of course I will. Anyway, you'll need all the flight times and such." Cori ran a finger over her bottom lip. "What about your mum and dad, and your job? Aren't you a big part of the organisation?"

Steph shook her head. "No way. I think they'll be pleased."

"Pleased?"

Steph seemed to hesitate. "I got involved with someone who turned out to be emotionally disturbed. Long story. Let's just say I caused some embarrassment for them and they're not super excited to have me around."

Cori shrugged. She wondered what the heck that could be about. Whatever it was, it must have been quite serious. Now she began to wonder if she'd made the right decision.

Steph seemed to notice Cori's discomfort and laughed. "I can see you need to know. Okay…I'll tell you." Steph shook her head. "It was a bad mistake. I got semi-involved with this woman who was a friend of someone who was a client. It all happened so quickly. One minute we were sharing a kiss, and the next minute…well, we're having sex on the floor in the funeral parlour."

Cori raised her eyebrows. "Right. Is that normal for you?"

"Christ, no." Steph snorted. "She was hot, though. Anyway, we did the usual stuff like going out for meals a few times, then she invited me back to her place. After some heavy snogging etcetera, we ended up more or less naked. She pulled out some handcuffs and blindfolded me, then guided me to a room. I assumed it was her bedroom. I thought we were just going to have sex with a little kink thrown in, and I was up for that. I heard her kick the door shut. It was quiet and I wasn't sure what she was doing. Then she removed my blindfold. The room was dimly lit by hundreds of candles…and there in the centre was a wooden coffin."

Cori covered her mouth. It seemed serious, but she couldn't help a giggle escaping.

"Not only that, but when I'd oriented myself, there she was, clad in leather with a whip in her hand."

"You're joking?"

"Nope. Boots and all." Steph coughed. "Anyway, she was obviously into BDSM. I wasn't. I like a bit of fun when I know someone well…but believe me, this was *not* what I wanted with her. She cracked the whip several times and told me to get into the coffin. Of course, I objected strongly, in fact I told her to fuck off. Then she whipped my arse. I can tell you, it bloody hurt like hell, so I climbed into the coffin, naked as a new-born and freezing my tits off. I won't go into any more detail, but let's say she attempted to have her wicked way with me. However, I kicked out at her and told her I'd scream the place down if she didn't release me." Steph took a sip of her drink, her cheeks pink. "I'd heard about people who get off on stuff having to do with death, but this was a new one for me."

"Do these people really exist?"

Steph laughed. "Yes, I had one of my very own."

"Then what?"

"She let me go, I put my clothes on quickly and I ran the hell out of there." Steph rubbed the back of her neck. "The rest is history. She made a complaint that showed we'd done the dirty, or at least suggested we had, thanks to the CCTV cameras, and here I am."

Cori reached and took Steph's hand. She gave a small giggle. "Thanks for telling me. It couldn't have been easy."

"You're damn right it wasn't. I haven't told anyone else. I felt such a twat."

Steph had been upfront and although the story was quite bizarre, she must have been terrified. Steph was not only a caring person, but an honest one, and she was really beginning to have faith in her. It gave her a feeling of satisfaction, because for the first time in eight years she'd let herself trust her instincts. It was scary, true, but she couldn't help but hope they'd make it work.

During dessert, they chatted about their favourite highlights of the trip so far. They agreed it was St. Bart's, but really Cori had loved it all. However, it had been a special day on the beach and the mutual chemistry between them could not be denied. On that day she found that she was not only infatuated with Steph but captivated by her. Suddenly her world had begun to shine.

Cori patted her tummy. "That meal was brilliant. I'm so glad you booked it. Thank you for asking me to join you."

"Yes, it was fantastic, and the company was pretty damn good too." Steph winked. "Bet you could murder a ciggie now?"

Cori laughed, relieved that the usual guilt she felt about admitting to her vice was absent. "Yes, I wouldn't mind one."

They thanked their waitress and as they left, they heaped praise on Trang for giving them such a remarkable experience.

Cori chuckled. "It always makes me laugh when we leave any of the restaurants. Almost like we're running out without paying the bill."

Steph raised her eyebrows. "Believe me, we've paid for it. I worked out how much it cost per day, but you know what, it's been worth every penny."

"I totally agree."

When they got in the elevator, Steph pressed the next floor up and then the eleventh. "I'm going to sort all my flight details out, so I'm prepared for the morning." The elevator door opened, and that same air of unnameable tension flared. Then Steph smiled and stepped back. "See you at Destinations in the morning."

"I'll be there." She smiled when Steph waited until the elevator door closed, keeping eye contact. The twinge of disappointment was interesting. Had she really wanted Steph to try to kiss her again? She put her hand to her chest, over her heart which felt stronger than it had in a long time. Yes, maybe she had.

When she got into the smoker's lounge, there was very little room. The group of Texans that she'd become familiar with had spread themselves around and were incredibly rowdy. Still, they were having fun and that's what Christmas and New Year were all about. Luckily, Raf wasn't there so she'd be able to make a quick escape. She perched on a spare chair by the door, had her ciggie, and left quickly.

As soon as she got to her room, she texted her family in Jamaica. *How would you feel about me bringing a friend with me? Her name's Steph and she's really nice, and I like her.*

The reply came back within seconds. *Wonderful! We'll welcome her with open arms. Plenty of room here and we love entertaining. Not as young as we used to be, so she'll be good company for you. Thrilled!*

Relieved, she replied quickly. *Thank you. See you soon. Not long now. xxx*

She got into bed and grinned from ear to ear. She drifted into a slumber, happier than she'd been for many years. She could draw out this holiday dream just a little longer, and with a beautiful, intelligent, kind woman at her side. For the moment, anyway.

Chapter Ten

STEPH DID A LITTLE dance along the corridor to her room. As soon as she got in, she sorted through all her documents and put them into an envelope, ready for tomorrow. She began a list. Change flight. Hopefully she'd get on the same one as Cori. If that succeeded, she'd make arrangements to disembark in Jamaica. Extend her parking at Heathrow, otherwise she'd be clamped. Drop a note to her parents. If she was extending her holiday, she'd need to get some laundry done. She'd eked her clothes out perfectly but if it went according to plan, she'd need a fresh supply of shorts and tees.

Yay! She could hardly believe it. Like a dream come true. The more she thought about it, the more she was convinced that coming on this cruise and meeting Cori was meant to be.

She didn't think she'd be able to sleep, but it wasn't long before she felt herself relax as she drifted to thoughts of Cori's pretty pink lips, and the way she blushed and fiddled with something when she was paid a compliment. The way her curves looked in her bikini, and the way her eyes lit up when she talked about writing. She listened the way few people did these days, and it made Steph feel heard, something that hadn't happened in a long time. With Cori, she didn't feel like such a disappointment. At that thought, her mother's perma-grimace flashed up, as well as her sister's perpetual look of drab disappointment. Cori didn't see her that way now, but what would she see when they were back in the real world? She punched her pillow and started counting backwards, a trick that always worked to put her to sleep.

Suddenly Steph shot up from her bed, her heart racing as she looked around. She squinted to make out her surroundings. Once she'd oriented herself, she sighed with relief. It wasn't that her dream was bad, it was just that she was on a deserted beach, miles of it, and she was calling Cori's name, but she wasn't there. She'd ached and there'd been tears, but no Cori.

She had no idea what it meant. Right now, she had no time to ponder the answer, because today she was on a mission. She hoped it didn't end in impossible.

She showered, put some clothes on and headed for the restaurant. After a hearty breakfast, she contemplated finishing with cinnamon buns topped with cream cheese icing but resisted. Tomorrow she'd do that. Or would she have the pancakes? Such decisions.

It was only nine thirty, but all the same, she made her way down the stairs, early for probably the first time in her life. Bugger, there was already someone waiting by the desk. When she got closer, she could see it was Cori. That really lifted her spirits, not as though they needed any elevation. And Cori being there early sort of proved that she was as eager as her to spend more time together.

Steph bounced up to the desk. "Jeez, from up there, I thought I'd be second in the queue."

"Well, I'd finished my breakfast, so I thought, why not." Cori tapped the desk with an envelope. "Got everything here."

Steph waved hers. "Me too." She placed her palms together as if praying and looked skyward. "Please, baby Jesus, make this happen for us."

Cori touched her arm. "If it's meant to be, it'll happen."

Eventually, a man came from the office behind and smiled at them. "How can I help you ladies?"

Cori looked at Steph. "Shall I explain?"

"Please."

"Good morning, Charles. We need your expert help." Cori filled him in and handed over her flight details.

Charles disappeared into the office to fetch his paperwork. "Well, the disembarkation isn't a problem. All we have to do is inform the port authorities in Port Antonio. So really, it's just changing the flight in Miami and getting you on one from Kingston to Miami. I'll call them now."

Steph crossed her fingers and held them up. Cori followed suit.

They couldn't hear what was being said on the other end, but Charles kept repeating, "Uh-huh. Uh-huh. I see. Okey-dokey, I'll check." He covered the phone piece with his hand and looked up. "No problem with the flight to Miami. On the flight back to Heathrow, do you want to sit together? If so, you'll have to upgrade, or Ms Cori will have to downgrade."

It sounded so demeaning. Of course, Cori would be travelling business class. She was a successful writer.

Cori punched Steph's arm. "I'm only in World Traveller plus. It's well worth it, and it's only a few hundred extra."

Only a few hundred! She'd way extended her budget to pay for this trip. Still, she'd put it on her credit card and deal with it later. She wasn't about to prove that she wasn't able to keep up with Cori. She'd figure that out eventually herself. "Phew. Thought you were in business. In that case, most definitely."

Charles nodded. "That's an affirmative." He chatted a little more then put the phone down. "Okay, I'll print this out and send it to your room. Won't be there until later as I have to go organise the excursions. Don't worry, it's all taken care of. I'll send baggage tags as well. There'll be instructions, but you need to have your luggage outside your door by ten p.m. tomorrow night. Disembarkation will be approximately eight thirty a.m., before the other passengers depart for their excursions."

Steph nearly jumped over the desk and hugged him. "Yay, I'm going to Jamaica." She grabbed Cori, picked her up, and swung her around. "Thank you. A million times, thank you."

Cori was splitting her sides laughing. "Put me down, you crazy woman."

Steph put her down and kissed Cori's forehead, then flinched a little but didn't stop smiling. "Sorry. Just so excited. Anyways, best get on with my next job, amending the car parking and a couple of emails. It shouldn't take long. Do you want to meet for lunch before we take the trip?"

"Yes, great. Where?"

"By the pool, say eleven thirtyish. We could watch the sights from the front of the ship."

"Good idea. See you there." Cori waved as she left, and there certainly seemed to be a spring in her step too.

Steph went back to her room and amended her car booking, then emailed her mum and dad.

Hi there, folks. Well, it's New Year's Eve, so firstly, I'll wish you a Happy New Year. Today we're anchoring in Punta Cana, Dominican Republic. The weather is beautiful, and I'm booked on a highlights trip. Tonight, yet another lovely dining experience, followed by an Abba tribute band to see in the New Year. I feel this time-out has really done me a lot of good. I've had time to think and assess my past and my future. Talking of which, a friend I've met on board has asked me to join her on an extended holiday with her family in Jamaica. I've accepted. Perhaps it's best I stay away for a while longer. Returning thirteenth January. Speak to you when I get back. Love and best wishes, Steph xx

She didn't expect a reply immediately, and quite frankly she didn't want to hang around for their response. Even just sending them an email was a reminder how she'd so often disappointed them over the years. Maybe she was one of those changeling babies, a fairy child swapped out with a human child. It would explain why she fit into the family like a branch glued to the genetic tree.

She changed into shorts, gathered her belongings together, and put them in her rucksack ready for the trip. She didn't usually take one, but it looked a bit overcast, so she threw in her rain jacket. She made her way to the pool area and searched for Cori. She found her sitting in a quiet spot on the deck looking out to sea. She had her earbuds in, and her phone rested on the arm of her chair. She was no doubt listening to music as she tapped away on her thigh in time with the beat. Steph didn't disturb her immediately but took in the lovely sight before her. Cori was beautiful, but there was more to it than that. She was one of those people who made the world a better place and her kindness and modesty always shone through. A breeze blew and Cori brushed away a strand of hair from her forehead. She must have been aware of someone's presence and turned her head slightly and looked up at Steph.

Cori pulled the earbuds out and smiled. "Sorry, I was miles away. I was just floating on a boat going up and down with the waves."

"And why not? You are allowed to relax and just *be*."

Cori nodded. "Thank you. I don't usually allow myself such indulgences."

"Why ever not?"

Cori shrugged. "Force of habit."

It was tempting to dig deeper, but she'd leave that kind of discussion for Jamaica. Right now, she wanted Cori to continue in her happy mood. Steph looked up to the deck above. "Looks like we're heading in. Shall we go look?"

Cori packed her things away and they made their way up the steps. Steph leaned on the wooden rail. "Not the prettiest arrival. Guess we've been spoilt after Antigua and St. Barts." The blocks of three and four storey buildings were squished together side by side, bland in their beige-white sameness. There was no personality, no vibrant colours, like there'd been in the other islands. This looked like a tourist port and nothing more.

"Absolutely. If we'd come here first, we'd be oohing and aahing. It's pleasant enough."

That was typical of Cori. Seeing the good. "You're right. I'm looking forward to getting a better look on the tour." They watched the ship anchor and the lowering of the bright orange tenders that would take them into port, then headed to get some lunch. They stood close, their shoulders touching, and Cori's shy smile made Steph's breathing quicken. God, she was so pretty.

During the meal, Cori seemed to be miles away. Possibly thinking of Jamaica and her family. Hopefully she wasn't regretting her offer for Steph to join her. Steph threw a piece of bread roll at her. "Wakey, wakey."

Cori looked confused. "What?"

"Just thinking. I can't believe it's New Year's Eve. A new year on the horizon and I'm so optimistic. I usually dread the same old year coming at me."

Cori smiled. "Funny you say that; I feel exactly the same."

Steph winked at Cori and clicked her tongue. She couldn't quite bring herself to say it, but she really thought that Cori was going to play a big part in her future. It was something she'd never felt before. Relationships had been so uncomplicated in the past, in fact they'd never meant anything to her, but maybe it was time to grow a little and form something deeper than casual sex. It scared her, and yet the anticipation was exciting. She felt totally present, something she'd never really experienced in her life. However, she wasn't stupid, and she reminded herself again that cruise life was like being trapped in one of those romantic bubbles where everything seemed sugar-coated. It was all sweet and made everyone's brain go mushy. She smiled to herself. Nice though, as long as she didn't lose touch with reality.

They made their way down to the theatre and went through the normal procedures. It wasn't long before they were called, and they headed to the tenders that took them to the port. As per usual, it was a new port, so the normal security checks applied. Just a question of scanning their belongings, that was all. Steph's came out first, and she headed for the exit. She felt something heavy on her back, like she was being dragged down. She instinctively tried to brush it off. At first, she thought it was Cori, or someone messing around.

Someone shouted. "Señora, deténgase ahora!"

What the fuck was happening? She turned to find the weight on her back was that of a dog. A strange-looking thing; something like a cross between an Alsatian and a hound of some description. Attached to the dog was a guard.

Cori shouted. "Steph! Stop!" The next minute, Cori was by her side, and so was one of the crew from the ship.

The guard held her arm. "Señora, por favor venga conmigo ahora!"

She understood Señora, but that was it.

"You have to go with the guard." The man from the ship said. "My name is Juan, I'm Spanish. I'll translate."

Steph held her chest which was about to burst. "I don't understand. What have I done wrong?"

They all followed the guard. The dog seemed calm now and the guard directed them to a small room. He spoke and Juan translated. She emptied the contents of her rucksack onto the table. All that came out was her rain jacket and a couple of bananas.

"No está permitido traer vegetación a República Dominicana," the guard shouted.

Steph shrugged.

Juan shook his head. "Didn't you read that? You're not allowed to bring vegetation into the Dominican Republic."

Steph rubbed her brow. "Christ, it's only a couple of bananas. I thought we may need them...you know, just as a snack."

Juan grimaced. "There is a fine up to two thousand dollars for smuggling illegal substances."

"Bananas?" Suddenly, Steph's credit card was reaching its maximum. Either that, or she'd be locked up.

Juan took the guard to one side, and they had a long chat. He returned. "They have looked upon this incident leniently. Fortunately, our cruise ship has a very good reputation. In future, I suggest you read all your literature before you leave the ship."

Steph breathed a sigh of relief and she saw the colour come back into Cori's face. She turned to the guard and smiled. "Muchas gracias, Señor."

They left the building pronto and boarded their coach. It was the only one there and they'd waited for them. They climbed up the stairs and everyone laughed and applauded. Would she ever live this one down? She doubted it.

They found a seat at the back, sat down and then Cori burst into fits of laughter.

"You are something else!"

Now that Steph was free, she saw the funny side and joined in. When they'd stopped giggling, Steph placed her hand on Cori's leg. "I bet you think I'm a right asshole?"

Cori chuckled again and covered Steph's hand with her own. "An asshole, no. A liability, yes."

Steph shook her head. "Shit. I'm gonna get so ribbed tonight."

Cori nodded. "It's going to make a great story though." Then they fell about laughing again, and their hands stayed right where they were.

Whilst they headed out of town, which wasn't very exciting, a young guy called Yared gave a bit of a commentary on the Dominican Republic in general.

A passenger raised her hand. "Is it safe to go out at night?"

Yared stroked his cheek. "Overall, the Dominican Republic is safe to visit, but has danger and crime also," he said with a clipped accent.

"So, it's not safe?"

"Like anywhere, some places best not visited. Most thefts occur in the hotspots, like restaurants, shops, and public transportation. And you must be careful on the beach too." He looked around the coach. "Ladies, please not venture out alone, especially in the evenings."

Steph elbowed Cori. "I wasn't planning to, and I don't think we'll be extending our stay."

"No way."

An elderly American leaned into the aisle. "Hey, Yared. We wanna look around after the trip. Is it okay to get an Uber?"

Steph and Cori looked at each other and raised their eyebrows.

"Is he for real?" Steph whispered.

"Nope."

Yared seemed to consider this question. "Uber is sometimes safe, and sometimes not. There is still a bit of risk involved. The roads are a little dangerous." He frowned. "Especially at night."

The man nodded and started a conversation with his wife, or whoever she was.

After about half an hour, they'd covered quite an area. Steph leaned across and pointed to Cori. "Look, there's another gated community. Are all the resorts gated?"

Cori nodded. "They've all got beautiful beaches though."

Steph laughed. "No wonder they're all luxurious. Not much else to do."

Cori grimaced. "I'm sure there is, but it is basically a tourist island. I suppose it's much like Jamaica. It has a high crime rate, and there are no-go areas there too. I hope that doesn't put you off."

Steph shook her head slowly. "No bloody way."

They were obviously nearing their first destination and Yared walked down the aisle. He spoke very quietly. "When we get off the bus, please be careful." He looked at one of the passengers. "Can you put rings and necklaces away, please. And keep electronic devices out of sight. Don't keep wallets in back pocket and keep handbags close by or leave on coach."

Cori shook her head. "Stupid people. They told us not to wear jewellery and things on the information page." Cori giggled. "Mind you, they also told us not to smuggle vegetation in."

"Alright. Message received. Anyway, I don't flash any bling around." Possibly because she had none. She bought odd bits of jewellery from the market and was always happy with her purchases.

Unfortunately, the coach didn't have a very good air-conditioning system, and everyone seemed relieved when it came to a standstill. Yared took his mic. "We are now making visit to Altos de Chavon. It is Italian style village located above Chavon River Valley. We will visit a Roman amphitheatre, archaeological museum, and cultural centre. After, you may go for stroll through village where they are plenty artisan workshops and art galleries, plus souvenir shops. They all take dollars. You can also enjoy views of the river valley below. Now, please follow me and keep together."

Once they'd got out, it was an altogether different picture. Steph pointed at the quaint church. "Hey, it's really pretty. Must get some shots." She took her phone out and saw a reply from her mum and dad. Why ruin her day? She'd save that little gem for later. They moved closer. "Hey, why are all those people outside? Must be something going on." Everybody was dressed in their Sunday best and suddenly, out came the bride and groom.

Cori tilted her head. "Aww, don't they look wonderful. So happy."

"Ha! Wait until the honeymoon's over."

Cori put her hands on her hips. "Oh, aren't we the pessimist?"

"Well, when you have parents like mine it doesn't exactly inspire one to look for happy-ever-after."

"Wait until you meet my grandparents. They've had a wonderful marriage and my mum and dad are still blissing."

Cori had obviously been through some hard times and yet her family had set her some fine examples of perfect marriages. The last thing she wanted to do was put a damper on Cori's ideals. She put her arm around her. "I'm sorry. That's awesome to hear. Maybe I'll view it in a different light one day."

Cori slipped her arm in the crook of Steph's. "C'mon, let's go."

They continued through the twisty village streets until they reached the amphitheatre. "Pretty impressive, eh?"

"It's wonderful and it's more picturesque than I'd imagined."

"I'm really glad we came. Worth seeing."

After a wander around the museum and the cultural centre, Yared let them loose and told them to be back at the coach in half an hour, so they wandered back to the main square and found a bench to sit on.

Steph stared at a half-starved dog laying on the pavement looking forlorn. "Have you noticed how many stray dogs there are in this village?"

Cori grimaced. "I know. I noticed a few hanging around the church."

Steph shook her head. "Obviously their piety doesn't run to feeding their own animals." She looked around. "Be back in a few minutes." It took a while to orient herself in the shop, but she found everything she wanted. She bought water, half a dozen plastic bowls and pouches of dog food. She emptied the food out into one and filled another with water. The dog shot up and saliva dripped from his jaws, but he was wary and hung back until Steph moved away. He gobbled it up then drank some water. Within minutes, more dogs appeared just as Steph had imagined. She did the same with the other bowls. The dog who'd already feasted made a dash for them, but she shooed him away. "Hey, give your mates a chance too. I'll give you some more in a minute, greedy guts." The dog stepped back, almost as if he understood, and Steph laughed. When she'd finished, she returned to the bench. "Shall we go?"

Cori was staring at her. She took a tissue out and dabbed her eyes. She didn't say anything, but when she stood, she took Steph's hand, squeezed it, and they wandered off hand in hand back to the coach.

Overall, it wasn't a bad trip, but not one of the best. Holding Cori's hand was the best part, for sure.

Once back on board, they agreed to meet up in The Galaxy at their usual time.

Steph picked out her outfit for the evening. A cream suit with a black T-shirt underneath. She knew it was a good combination and tonight she wanted to look stunning. Normally, she wasn't that bothered, but yes, she wanted to impress Cori. Before showering, she sat on her own balcony and opened her mail to read the one from her parents.

Dear Stephanie,
So pleased to hear you're enjoying your life on board. Of course, January is going to be our busy period and we could have done with your help in the business. Your sister, Hillary, suggested you reflect on your life and where it's taking you. It appears that once again, you are only focusing on yourself. And now you're taking off to Jamaica with some stranger you've met. No doubt a woman with some dubious background. When you return, your mother and I think it's time we had a long and in-depth discussion. Best wishes, from your mother and father.

Oh fuck! And a Happy New Year to you too. Were these people really her parents? Once again, she was certain she'd been accidentally swapped at birth. Or was she adopted, and they'd never told her? Or did they just find her in the graveyard and thought it their duty to look after her? She was tempted to reply and tell them to stuff it and look for someone else to walk ahead of the cars, and work in the flower shop, and do any other menial task they could find for her. But she had no clue what she wanted to do, and bills didn't pay themselves.

She felt like throwing her phone overboard, but instead, she put it away. *Come on, girl, it's New Year's! Forget about all that crap and live in the present.* The thought of meeting up with Cori cheered her, so she showered, got ready for the celebrations, and made her way to The Galaxy.

Dorothy and Lena waved as she entered, and on the way over, she ordered her usual drink from the bar.

She smiled at them both. "You ladies are looking incredibly

glamorous this evening."

Dorothy smiled coyly and Lena brushed one of the tassels hanging from her dress. "Oh, thank you so much, Steph. We put the same dresses on every New Year, but of course it doesn't matter because they're all different passengers." Lena looked Steph up and down. "I must say you look very with it. A little like one of those celebrities."

Steph bowed dramatically. "Well, thank you kindly, Lena."

Next to join them was Mike, Patti, and Raf. They greeted each other and as they took their seats, Lena tapped Raf on the arm. "Everyone looks so delightful. I was just saying to Steph, she looks a bit like a celebrity."

Raf looked Steph up and down and smirked. "You up for an Oscar award tonight?"

Steph chuckled. "Yeah, right. I'm sure you've been nominated for Best Original Score on many occasions."

Raf roared. "Good one. And I've won them."

"I bet." But at least she hadn't scored with Cori.

"Speaking of which, where *is* Cori?"

Steph shrugged. She could have punched her, but at the end of the day, she knew the truth. Raf hadn't got anywhere near Cori, even though she may have tried.

And then she walked through the door, looking like a film star. Steph would be so happy if she was on her arm. She must have made it obvious because her mouth gaped as she walked towards them.

Both Raf and Mike whistled at the same time. Cori blushed like crazy. Steph knew she'd be self-conscious and that's why she hadn't joined them in the whistle. Cori tugged at her dress as though she was trying to lengthen it, but it didn't work. The dress was stunning and encrusted with sequins in black, ivory, and gold. It was sleeveless and revealed just the right amount of cleavage, and she wore a matching see-through cape shawl. The whole outfit was a bit art deco in design and looked vintage and luxurious. Her heeled shoes were gold and matched beautifully. Cori carried it off well, but it was obvious she felt uncomfortable with all the attention.

Steph stood. "Come and sit, Cori. I'll go order you a drink." She made room for her and whispered in her ear as she got closer. "You look awesome."

Cori straightened her cape and looked up, her feelings clear in her eyes. "Thanks."

Steph waved to a waiter, ordered Cori's drink, and sat down beside her. When he brought the drink, Cori nearly downed all the contents in one go. Then she sat back and relaxed.

Raf stroked Cori's bare arm. "You look sensational, honey." She leaned forward and looked at Mike. "Hey, Mike, what did the horny guy say to his date?"

Mike stroked his chin. "No idea. C'mon, Raf, tell me?"

"If my right leg was Christmas and my left leg was New Year's, would you like to spend some time between the holidays?" Raf slapped her thigh and laughed.

Mike laughed and shook his head. "You are a hoot, Raf."

Steph smiled tightly at Raf. "You're a barrel of laughs, aren't you? Sure gonna miss you."

Raf smirked. "Yeah, I hear we're losing you in Jamaica too?"

"Wow, good news certainly travels fast."

Patti looked skyward. "Isn't Jamaica full of drug addicts?" She laughed. "Or do you like the odd spliff yourself, Steph?"

Steph wanted to jump up and smack her, but she remained calm and didn't reply. She hadn't realised how bigoted and bitchy the woman was. It just went to show, sometimes you never knew someone.

Raf shook her finger at Patti. "Jamaica is a beautiful island, full of beautiful people. There's no more trouble there than there is anywhere else in the world." She waved her arms. "And the music is amazing. I love reggae."

Patti didn't comment. Was she surprised that Raf came to her defence, or was she defending Cori?

Cori smiled. "My dad plays a lot of reggae. We grew up with so many different types of music in our household." She laughed. "My mum loves classical music and opera. So often she put one thing on, and my dad would switch it to reggae. It went back and forth and became a huge joke."

Steph nodded. "That must have been fun. I think it's great to have eclectic tastes and we should always be open to new ideas."

Raf winked. "Yes. I like variety. It's the spice of life."

Dorothy frowned. "I don't like spices, especially late at night."

The comment brought a smile to their faces, but at least nobody commented.

Raf polished off her drink and stood. "If you'll excuse me, folks, duty calls. Your usual table is booked in the Magnetic Arc, and I hope to see you all later for the Abba tribute."

"Is it in the theatre?" Lena asked.

"No, honey, in the atrium. We're rolling back the carpets, so get ya singin' and dancing' boots on." Raf touched Cori's shoulder. It was more like a massage. "Might see you later for a smoke before we get going."

"Absolutely. See you there."

When Raf left, after giving Steph a sly smile, they all agreed it was time to go down to dinner. There was a party atmosphere in the restaurant and on every table, there were an assortment of hats, tiaras, masks, party horns, and poppers.

Steph squeezed her hands together tightly. "Party time. Isn't this just great? They really go to a lot of trouble."

Lena beamed. "It's wonderful, isn't it? They're so good to us."

Steph agreed in principle. But they were paying megabucks for this. Well, most were. All the same, throughout the whole trip they'd had the best of everything, and she'd willingly have paid full price, if only she could have afforded it. She'd started with lobster bisque, then had egg and truffles, filet mignon with an assortment of vegetables, and followed it with dark chocolate mousse. And then there were petit fours. Cori chose the consommé, salmon mousse, quail, and crème brûlée. When Steph saw the quail, she thought there was barely enough meat for a sandwich. Cori made a fair job of dissecting it, but it was painful to watch, and Steph wanted to shout, *pick the bloody thing up!* But of course, Cori was way too classy to do that.

Steph wiped her mouth with her napkin after the dessert. "That has to go down as one of the best meals I've ever had."

Cori nodded. "Delicious. There was so much to choose from. I'm not used to making decisions."

So, who made the decisions for Cori? There was so much to find out and she wondered if their time in Jamaica would be sufficient.

Lena stood up and took hold of Dorothy's arm. "We noticed there were some seats in the atrium, so we're going to grab ourselves a couple before the masses start arriving."

Cori got up too. "I'll walk with you." She turned to Steph. "Sorry, just going you know where."

Steph shot up. "I'll come with you."

Patti screwed her nose up. "Of course, you're going into that smelly room."

Steph tightened her fists. Good job they were by her side. "I don't partake, but it's a fab room and the people are so friendly and accepting. Anyway, I'll tell Raf you said that."

Patti touched her face with her hand. "I didn't realise Raf smoked. Everyone to their own."

"Absolutely. Raf loves her cigars."

Patti's smile looked forced.

Right now, Steph knew where she'd like to shove a cigar. She was going to be happy to see the back of Patti. She'd seemed to be such a better person than she'd turned out to be, but that was obviously for show.

Steph took a seat outside the lounge and waited for Cori. She could see Raf standing by the window puffing away and Cori went to join her. She settled into one of the armchairs. She'd have gone in tonight if it hadn't been for all the cigar smokers. That smell tended to cling to your clothes more than cigarette smoke, and it hung in the air too. It was funny because she hardly ever smelt smoke on Cori. It wouldn't have bothered her that much anyway because quite a few of her exes had smoked.

Raf strode out of the room. "See you later. Got to go change into my costume."

"See you soon, Raf." Steph smiled and wondered how often Raf didn't get the woman she pursued on the cruise.

Cori joined her outside. "Thanks for waiting. Are we going downstairs for a drink?"

"Yes, let's go mingle." Steph took Cori's arm. "Raf said she was going to change into her costume. What do you reckon she'll be wearing?"

"Something outrageous, no doubt."

"I bet."

When they got down to the atrium there were huge crowds gathered around an area that was obviously set up for the Abba Tribute. Steph managed to collar one of the waiters who brought their drinks over to them. It wasn't long before the band arrived from a door at the side of the bar. The Bjorn and Benny lookalikes wore white shiny suits with bell bottoms and black shirts and enormous platform heels. Frida had a black jumpsuit with leg flares and platforms. They received massive applause, and then Agnetha, alias Raf, finally made her entrance. She glided down the spiral staircase dressed like a disco queen in a white jumpsuit boasting bell drape sleeves with gold fabric trim and the traditional seventies style flared trousers, along with the platform boots, complete with blond wig, giving her the authentic dancing queen look. She held her head high and tossed her head dramatically as everyone clapped, cheered, and whistled. No doubt her debut would be the talk of the ship tomorrow.

She took one of the mics. "Welcome to the world of Abba. From now until midnight we're gonna hit you with all those groovy timeless songs. So, dance, sing, and enjoy. And don't forget to put your masks and tiaras on."

Steph took her mask from her pocket and put it on. "Do you recognise me?"

Cori giggled. "I suppose I'd better put my tiara on."

She did, and it looked perfect. Steph reached over and straightened it for her. It was only a gold replica of course, but the coloured jewels certainly matched Cori's eyes. "You definitely look like a princess. Good way to end and start a new year."

Raf certainly meant what she'd said. For the next one and a half hours they covered all the favourite tracks, starting with "Super Trouper." The drinks flowed and the party began. It was jovial and festive, and it wasn't long before Steph grabbed Cori's arm and pulled her onto the dancefloor.

Cori leaned in. "I can't dance. Haven't danced for years."

Steph laughed. "Pardon? Can't hear you. Dance? You can hardly swing a cat around. Just move and sing."

After that, Cori seemed to relax and join in with all the songs. When they sang "Dancing Queen," Cori lifted her arms and waved them in the air along with everyone else So far, this was turning out to be one of the best New Year's parties Steph could remember, although perhaps when tomorrow came, she wouldn't remember much. Usually, she was pissed by ten thirty and rolled back home with someone she'd met and regretted it when she awoke the following day. She was sure she wouldn't be going to bed with anyone tonight, but for once she wasn't bothered. She was having fun of a different kind and somehow it threw a unique perspective on her old life and how meaningless it had been. Or was this just euphoria?

She smiled to herself. *Who cares? Live for the moment.* Watching

Cori dancing at a distance in that hot dress was driving her nuts, so when Raf sang "The Winner Takes It All," Steph took the opportunity to pull her close. Luckily, it was a tight squeeze on the dance floor, made tighter by the couple who kept pushing them together. Steph wasn't complaining. She wanted to increase the intensity without rushing into it and placed her hands just below Cori's waist. She let them slide down, just above her bum. Cori didn't pull away. The closer they got, the more connection she felt. Cori's eyes met hers. She saw desire…just the way she felt. Then Cori leaned on her shoulder, and every part of their bodies touched. She nearly cracked under the pressure and kissed her. She resisted. There'd be time enough for that. She didn't want an audience, she wanted privacy.

The time sped by quickly as they danced and sang the night away. Then the music stopped. Raf dabbed her face with a tissue. Perspiration was trickling down her cheeks. Steph wasn't surprised. Their performance had been amazing, and they'd thrown their hearts and souls into it.

Someone handed Raf a plastic bottle of water and she drank it down in one go. "Phew! Thanks, I needed that. Grab yourself a glass of champagne, the waiters are on their way around. And then it's countdown!"

Cori covered her mouth with her hand. "Oh my God! Are we really about to head into the New Year?"

Steph grinned. "Sure are. And what an end to this year." She reached out and took two glasses and gave one to Cori.

Raf had a glass in her hand too. "Count with me. Ten, nine, eight, seven, six, five, four, three, two, one!"

The ship's horn blew signalling midnight. Raf shouted. "Happy New Year, everyone."

Balloons dropped from the ceiling, party horns hooted, and poppers popped and scattered all over the place.

"Happy New Year," they all shouted.

They drank and put their glasses down on a nearby tray. Their eyes met. Steph's heart was beating so fast, she could hardly get her breath. Her head was buzzing with anticipation as she saw Cori's eyelids flutter, then close. She felt her breath on her cheek. And then their lips met. Feeling her lips pressed against hers sent shivers throughout her entire body. She shuddered as their bodies swayed and everything faded into oblivion. It was good. So, so good. Cori felt perfect in her arms, held against her where she could keep her safe. The thought was startling. She'd never felt that way about anyone before. She looked down into Cori's eyes and was about to go for another kiss, but the moment was broken when Raf ran over.

Steph was sure Raf wouldn't want to kiss her, and the feeling was most certainly mutual, but she headed straight for Cori. It was funny, because Cori seemed to be prepared and turned her face just slightly as Raf went for her lips. The kiss missed the intended spot and caught Cori an inch past her mouth. It gave Steph a warm feeling, but Raf's smile was icy.

Cori touched Raf's arm and stepped back. "Happy New Year. I have to say you've put the best show ever on tonight. It's been a fantastic evening."

Raf winked and gave a little shrug. "Still plenty more to go. We're playing until one a.m. Best get back to my duties." She backed into the crowd and gave Steph the slightest nod. Back on stage, she picked up the mic. "Okay, folks, there's plenty more champagne and dancing and if you're a bit peckish, there's snacks in all the bars. Let's party!"

Steph saw Cori yawn. "Tired?"

Cori giggled. "I am, but I hardly dare let this night go."

"There's always tomorrow. And guess what, we're already there." Steph took Cori's hand. "C'mon, time to sleep. It's our last day tomorrow, but at least you can have a lie-in."

Cori tilted her head. "I think I ordered breakfast in my room. I'm sure it was ten o'clock."

"Should give you plenty of time for sleep then."

Steph steered Cori towards the elevators and pressed seven. She walked her along the corridor to her door, wondering what might happen next. That kiss had been something else, and if Cori invited her in, she damn well wasn't going to turn that invitation down.

Cori scanned the card, pushed the door open and placed it into the holder. The lights came on. She hesitated in the doorway, as if she wasn't sure what to do. Then she gave her head a little shake, as though talking to herself, and pecked Steph on the cheek. "Thanks for making this holiday so special. You'll never know what it means to me, or how important it was." She shook her head and waved her hand. "Sorry, ignore me. I think I'm slightly inebriated. See you tomorrow."

Steph cupped Cori's face with her hand and ran her thumb over her cheekbone. "Likewise. Only it'll be later today."

"Oh yes, of course," Cori said, gently taking Steph's hand from her face and squeezing it before letting it go. She smiled and softly closed her door.

Steph leaned against the wall for a minute and caught her breath. There was no question in her mind, there was something hot between them. Something unusual and intense. With any other woman, she would have gone in for the kiss and let her hands wander freely. But she didn't want to mess things up with Cori, and what that meant, she didn't know yet. She hummed quietly as she strolled along the corridor and ran down the stairs to her suite. Tomorrow! Their last day on board and the beginning of a new adventure. Where it would lead, she had no clue, but that was the exciting part. A journey through uncharted territory was exactly what she needed before she returned to a life she couldn't imagine going back to anymore.

Chapter Eleven

WHEN CORI LAY HER head on her pillow, the room spun a little. Yes, she had consumed too much alcohol, but it was different than just being tipsy. It was more of a giddy sensation. The kiss? She hadn't given any thought to sharing a kiss at midnight, and yet it was so natural and unpremeditated. It was a precious moment and exactly the way it should happen, as spontaneous as a lightning strike, a link of energy being shared between the two of them. Her body had felt alive, sensual. The feel of Steph pressed against her and the desire in her eyes had been electrifying. She'd seriously considered inviting her in and letting things take their course. But then common sense had taken over. They were about to spend more time together in Jamaica, and she didn't need it to be complicated. But oh, what a wonderful feeling running through her body as she replayed the night. She sighed happily and closed her eyes.

Oh hell. What was that ringing in her ears? Was it the phone? She lifted her head off her pillow and glanced around. Then it hit her. It was the doorbell. She looked at the clock. It was ten. Shit, her breakfast! She shot out of bed, grabbed her robe, and opened the door. "I'm so sorry. I must have overslept."

The young waitress smiled. "Don't apologise. Everybody is the same today. Happy New Year, Ms Cori."

"Oh, of course. And a Happy New Year to you, Rosanna."

"Shall I set it up on the balcony? It's such a beautiful morning."

"Please, that would be lovely."

When Rosanna left, the first thing Cori did was pour herself a cup of tea. She was so thirsty, but at least she didn't have a massive hangover. In fact, she'd had yet another peaceful night's sleep. She smiled as she remembered the kiss she'd shared with Steph. She touched her lips with her fingertip, still recalling the softness of Steph's lips on hers.

After breakfast, she lay her head back on her chair and stared out to sea, dreaming. It was so peaceful, and it would be a shame to come back to reality. But in fact, reality was good now. She had so many things to look forward to. Talking of which, she had to get some laundry done and then pack and prepare for her departure tomorrow.

She sorted through her washing for the clothes she'd need in Jamaica. Mostly T-shirts and shorts. She knew her grandmother would do them, but she wanted to arrive without giving her any hassle. She placed them in the bag provided and went in search of the laundry room. She found it on another corridor and pushed the door open. It was a hive of activity. There were three washers and three dryers and all of them were full. She guessed everyone had the same idea.

She wasn't sure what to do. Should she wait or leave it?

In walked Steph. "Hey, fancy seeing you here."

Cori crossed her arms, but in truth, she was happy to see her. "This is floor seven's laundry room."

Steph laughed. "Yeah, I know. Floor six was full. I used my initiative." Steph held her hands up. "Don't worry, my washing is finished. I'll just transfer it into the dryer."

Cori bunged her washing in as soon as Steph had hers out. "What do I do now?" It didn't look like any machine she'd used at home.

Steph came to her assistance and put the load on for her.

"Should be finished in about forty-five minutes." She laughed. "Then you can have my dryer."

Cori laughed in return, that same giddy feeling from the night before suffusing her. "See you then. Going to do some packing."

Steph grinned. "Me too. Shall we have lunch together?"

"Good plan. If I don't see you before, I'll catch you by the pool about one."

Steph put her thumbs up and left. Cori tilted her head. Somehow, everything was so light with Steph. She wasn't pretentious and seemed so honest. Then again, she wasn't really a very good judge of character, was she? Look at how Dusty turned out. She wished she could stop comparing them, but she couldn't let herself fall into another Dusty trap.

The laundry seemed to take an age. She was in and out of the little room every fifteen minutes, and the dryers were empty, so she didn't need to wait for Steph's. Then of course she had to iron everything. She hated creased up clothes, even though she was packing them all.

She didn't see Steph again until lunch time. She was propping up a post by the jacuzzi. "The jazz band is just warming up. Bit noisy here, shall we see if we can get a seat on the veranda?"

"Great idea."

Steph took Cori's hand and led her through to the outside seating. It was an intimate gesture, and Cori couldn't deny she rather liked it. Steph pointed. "There's one over there."

They left their bags, drifted back to the food area, loaded their plates with goodies and returned. They chatted about the celebrations last night and how wonderful the evening had been, but there was no mention of the kiss. There was certainly tension in the air, but it was filled with warm vibes and happiness. Steph leaned her elbow on the table and stared into her eyes. She opened her mouth as if to say something, then stopped. For once, she seemed lost for words and Cori was plain confused. Neither seemed to know what to say, but perhaps it wasn't necessary.

When she'd finished, Cori placed her knife and fork on the plate. "Have you finished your packing?"

"Ha, you jest. Not started yet."

Cori shrugged, unsurprised. "I've got everything folded and ready to go on the bed, I just haven't finished yet. Still, I've got all afternoon. What time does the deck party start?"

"Six thirty. I'm only doing casual."

"Me too. And don't forget we have to put our luggage out by ten. Then I'm going to have an early night."

"You bet." Steph eyed the king prawn left on Cori's plate. "Can I have that?"

Cori giggled. "Of course you can. Help yourself. You can always go back and have as many as you like."

Steph stabbed her fork into the prawn and popped it into her mouth. When she'd finished, she looked up. "But this one tastes so much better. Probably because it was yours."

Cori looked down at her hands on her lap. It was a lovely thing to say. She wondered if Steph really meant it or was it just part of her clever patter?

Steph leaned in. "You okay?"

Cori looked up. "Yes, of course. Just thinking I ought to get back to my packing. So much to do and we have to be down early."

Steph smiled. "Okay. Let's make a move." Steph put her arm around Cori's shoulder. "Do you know, for once I'm really looking forward to packing. Going into the unknown. It's like an odyssey. How will I return to my native land? Same as before, but changed by the people and experiences on my journey?" She smiled at Cori, her eyes soft. "I have a feeling I know which it will be."

Cori nodded. "For me too."

Steph chuckled. "Then we'll be sharing it together, just like I share your food."

Cori punched her on the arm playfully. "C'mon, you, let's go." When they parted company, Cori couldn't help but think how Steph always made things so carefree. Nothing seemed to faze her, and she always seemed to be in good humour. It was such a novelty, and one she thought she could get used to.

Cori finished most of her packing and sat on her balcony writing and sketching for a while. She'd left out clothes for this evening and some for tomorrow. She'd finish everything later.

After showering, she put on some jeans and a blouse and made her way to the pool area. It was jam-packed. She thought she'd arrived early, but all the tables were taken, and people had already started queueing for their food. She had a feeling of claustrophobia and almost turned around and headed out, but she saw Raf waving from a table on her right. She took a deep breath and walked over. Raf got up, took her hand, and guided her around to a seat at the back. All the gang were there apart from Steph.

Raf pouted. "You have to come sit with me tonight, honey. I'm so gonna miss you."

"Yes, it seems really strange. I can't believe it's come to an end." She grinned. "Although for me, it's a new beginning."

"Me too," Steph said as she joined the party, taking a seat next to Dorothy.

Wow, to think they'd be spending the next eleven days together. It was a long time considering she didn't really know Steph. She was sure she would by the end of the vacation. For better or for worse. Hopefully the former, if she didn't go and screw things up as she had in the past.

It was a beautiful balmy evening and perfect for their last night onboard. All the food looked amazing, and the atmosphere was upbeat. The only downside being the queues, and by the time you got back to your table, the food that was hot was now tepid.

The wine flowed, although neither Steph nor herself were knocking it back. She wanted a clear head for tomorrow, and it looked like Steph did too.

Cori looked at her watch. It was nine p.m. She still had to finish some packing and prepare her rucksack. "I'm afraid I'm going to be a party pooper. Still have some last-minute things to do."

Raf scowled. "Aww. You're going to miss the steel band. Mind you, guess you're gonna see a lot of those in Jamaica."

"I hope so. I love the sound and I'm sure my brother will take us to see loads." Cori stood. Steph got up too. "Well, folks, it's been great meeting you." She kissed Lena, Dorothy and Mike on the cheek and touched Patti's shoulder. That was as much as she was prepared to do, and she noticed the tense smile Patti gave her in return. Steph followed suit, without the shoulder touching.

Raf opened her arms. "Come and give me a big hug, honey."

Cori reciprocated and kissed her cheek. All in all, Raf had done her job and she'd always made her feel welcome. However, she'd also made her feel pain, the pain that she was trying to forget. "Thanks, Raf, for everything, and for giving me those wonderful experiences on all those trips." Cori suspected she may have wanted to provide more memorable experiences, but luckily, she'd been thwarted.

Raf handed her a card. "Let's keep in touch. We've exchanged emails when I sent the ziplining videos, but just in case." She kissed Cori on the cheek. "It's been a pleasure meeting you and have an absolutely fabulous time with your family. And you never know, our paths may cross again one day."

"Thanks, Raf. You just never know." She crumpled the card in her pocket. That kind of aggressive energy was no longer welcome in her life.

Raf pecked Steph on the cheek. "Look after her."

Steph winked. "I'll do my very best. And thanks for being the hostess with the mostess."

Raf laughed and waved them off.

When they'd left, Cori tilted her head. "It's sort of sad, really. Apart from Patti, they've been a great bunch of people."

"Yeah, it's been really terrific. It's funny how in such a short time they become like a regular crazy family." She put her arm around Cori's shoulder. "But now you're going to see your real family."

Cori beamed. "Absolutely." She got out at the seventh floor, and she couldn't help but wonder, for a split second, if she should invite Steph to her room. Just to chat and hang out for a while. But when the primary seating was a bed, that seemed like a bad idea. She wasn't ready for that yet, though her body was telling her otherwise. "See you in the atrium bright and early."

"You bet!"

Cori finished packing and popped her cases outside the door. She slipped into bed and stared at the ceiling. She was sure she'd never get any sleep. She was wide awake so picked up her Kindle and started a new book. She mostly went for crime thrillers, but instead, she'd picked one that her mum had recommended called Away with the Penguins. Apparently, it was one of those feel-good kinds of books. As soon as she started it, she understood why.

She must have dropped off for a while and when she looked at the clock, she blinked several times. It said six o'clock. She couldn't remember dozing off, but her Kindle was laying on the floor, so she must have fallen asleep. Dreams of Steph's laugh, her smile, her lips, had swept through her all night, and it left her unsettled. She showered and then her breakfast arrived, but she could hardly eat anything. Her stomach churned so she just ate a bit of cereal and fruit, washed down with a few cups of tea.

She stepped onto her balcony for the last time. It was seven thirty, the sun had risen over an hour ago, and it was another beautiful day. A warm glow engulfed her. At last, she'd be seeing her family in their own surroundings. It was quite melancholic to think that if Dusty hadn't died, Cori wouldn't be here. What a terrible thought.

She took a deep breath, said goodbye to her room, threw her rucksack over her shoulder and left.

There weren't many people in the reception area. She doubted if many were leaving the ship permanently in Jamaica, so it was hardly surprising. She took a seat in a comfy wingback chair, leaned back, and closed her eyes momentarily. When she opened them, Steph was sitting opposite her with a silly grin on her face. "Hello, you."

"And hello to you too." Steph squinted. "You okay?"

Cori rubbed her tummy. "An attack of nerves."

Steph wiped her brow. "How do you think I feel? I'm gate-crashing your vacation."

Cori sat up straight. "No, you're not. Get that notion out of your head. You're here because I hate mosquitos and I hope you're going to be chief swatter."

Steph laughed. "Jeez, you found out about my other profession."

They covered their ears as the ship's horn blew, signalling they were docking. They looked wide-eyed at each other, at a loss for words.

Charles from Destinations strode towards them. "Okay, folks. We're a bit later than anticipated, but it shouldn't be long now. When you've cleared security, you'll need to find bay seven. That's where your luggage will be. If it isn't, there will be a ship's representative in the building. I'll give you a thumbs up when you can leave."

Steph stood and shook Charles' hand. "Thanks for everything."

"My pleasure." He saluted and went back to his desk.

They waited in silence, glancing at Charles every so often until he gave a wave. "Okay, ladies, off you go. Have a great trip."

They jumped up, headed for the entrance, and crossed the bridge to the port authority building. After security, they found the bay and their cases were ready and waiting.

Cori took a deep breath. "Here goes."

Steph pumped her fist. "Yay!"

They walked out into the car park and Cori took a quick look around. She couldn't see her family. Perhaps they were somewhere else? Suddenly, out of nowhere they appeared. They threw themselves at Cori, and she was crushed under a wave of loving hugs.

Josh swung Cori around in his arms. His grin stretched from ear to ear. "Welcome, big sis."

Cori couldn't focus through her tears. She couldn't say anything, either. Then she felt her grandparents' arms around her too. They huddled, swayed, and cried.

Her grandma held her at arm's length. "You need some weight on you, sweet pea. You're all skin and bone." Then she burst into tears again. She sniffed and wiped her eyes with the back of her hand. "I can't believe you're here."

Her grandpa moved her gently out of the way. "Give the girl some space. My turn now. Come here."

He hugged her like there was no tomorrow. "You been missing from our lives too long."

Cori still couldn't say a word. She wept and couldn't catch her breath. She pulled them all into her arms. "I love you all so much."

Josh pulled away and laughed. "This is getting too much for me. Can't you catch up with all this when we get home?"

Her grandma slapped his arm. "Don't be so cheeky." She slapped her forehead with the palm of her hand. "We're being so inhospitable. Introduce us to your friend."

"Oh my God, I'm so sorry." She took hold of Steph's arm and pulled her forward from where she'd been standing and watching the reunion. "This is Steph. She looked after me all through the cruise."

They turned their attention to Steph. "Welcome to Jamaica, honey. We're so happy to meet you," her grandma said.

Within seconds, they took her into a group hug.

Eventually she was allowed to come up for breath. "Thank you so much for letting me come stay with you. It was my dream to visit Jamaica, but I never thought for one moment that I'd be here. Thank you so much, Mr and Mrs Lewis."

"Cut the Mr and Mrs. You can either call us Grandma and Grandpa or Errol and Tianna." Cori's grandpa stroked Steph's face. "And any friend of our granddaughter is a friend of ours too."

Josh passed her grandpa his walking stick which he'd dropped as he'd rushed over. "Come on, I missed breakfast for you. I'm bloody starving and Grandma's making us hundreds of pancakes when we get back." He picked up their suitcases and turned to Steph. "Come on, Steph, you take the smaller ones, and we'll get them loaded. Those three will be ages."

Cori stood in the middle and put her arms around her grandparents. "This is surreal." She laughed. "Are we really having pancakes? Because I couldn't eat a thing this morning."

Her grandma leaned her head on Cori's shoulder. "You can have anything you like, my little sweet pea."

Cori's smile was off the radar. She followed Josh to the car and got in the back with her grandparents, whilst Steph jumped in beside Josh.

Josh switched the engine on. "Let's get this show on the road. If the traffic's not too bad, we should be there in about thirty minutes."

"Is it in Port Antonio?" Steph asked.

"On the outskirts. It's set in the hills and has great views of the bay. Best of both worlds because it's cooler up there and really quiet and yet close enough to the port."

"Sounds fantastic. You work there, don't you?"

"Yes, and at the new office in Ocho Rios. Sorry to say, but I have to work for the next few days. It's busy right now with the tourists. Luckily, I've got good staff in both places, so I'm taking some time off so we can all go out together and show you the sights. Thought it would give you a chance to settle in. I'll leave the car if you want."

Cori shouted from the back to be heard over the traffic noise. "That's great. And you drive on the left."

Josh laughed loudly. "In theory. In practice, you'll see most drive in the middle, or anywhere not occupied by another vehicle."

"Oh. I'll let Steph drive then."

Steph nodded. "I'm good with that. I think."

Josh blasted his horn. "As long as you keep one hand on the horn permanently, you're okay. Like anywhere, we have good drivers, bad drivers, and crazy drivers. The main roads are fine, but if you're going to take the secondary roads, you need to be extra aware. There's lots of blind corners and twists."

Cori looked at her grandparents. "Do you still drive?"

They both shook their heads vigorously. "Why would we, when we have family to chauffer us around?"

"Huh. Well, thanks for all that, little brother."

Josh slowed down and indicated. "Almost there now."

He turned up a long gravel driveway. There were a few potholes which he steered around and then they came to some tall iron gates which were open and looked a little rusty.

Josh laughed. "Don't worry, we never close them. Too heavy and I don't think they've been shut for decades."

The plaque on the wall at the side said Devon House.

Cori leaned forward. "Hey, that's my dad's name."

Her grandfather nudged her. "Sure is. We named it after him. Bought it when we'd got the business going. Was going cheap. Quite a ramshackle place back then, but we fell in love with it, didn't we, Tianna?"

"Sure did."

"Done it up over the years. Dare say it'll be too old fashioned for you two kids, but we like it just the way it is."

Josh turned his head briefly. "Don't worry, Sis, the annexe has been modernised this millennium."

As they drew up to the house, Steph covered her mouth with her hand. "Wow, it's like one of those enormous houses you see on the telly."

Josh nodded. "Yeah, it was. Belonged to some rich white family years ago."

Steph seemed enthralled. "Hey, that's a great colour scheme. The light terracotta really goes well with the darker pan tiles, and the white around the window frames and pillars make it really stand out."

Cori recalled Steph's love of interior and exterior design and it was lovely to hear how she was praising her family's home. "Steph's really into all this. She's quite the expert."

Steph shook her head. "No. I just like to see good taste, that's all."

Both Cori's grandparents looked happy with Steph's enthusiasm.

"Of course, I've seen lots of photographs, but they really don't do it justice," Cori said.

Her grandfather smiled broadly. "Well, thank you both. Pleased it meets with your approval."

Josh pulled up in front of the house. "Right, let's get you two settled in then we can have pancakes."

Cori waited for her grandparents, but they waved her on. "Go with Josh, then we'll eat. After that, we'll give you the grand tour," her grandma said.

They followed Josh into the annexe. The cool inside was a blessing after the heat of the sun, although it was only just after eleven. "What a lovely temperature," Cori said.

"I installed air-con here." He laughed. "In the main house, they still only have the ceiling fans. Guess it's what they're used to." He opened one of the doors. "The sitting room."

Steph strode ahead. "Oh my God, this is amazing. I love this style of furniture, and yet it's not dark because of the white ceiling." She turned in a circle, taking it all in. "And it's so airy."

"Hardly use it, really. We're mostly outdoors. Although technically this is our winter, we still have eleven hours of daylight and seven hours of sunshine, and it's the busiest time of the year."

Steph walked towards the French windows, but Josh took her arm and pulled her back. He chuckled. "You can see all that later. Grandma will kill us if we don't hurry up."

Steph grinned. "Okay. As long as you allow me to take some photos later?"

"You'll have plenty of time. Take as many as you like." He carried the luggage upstairs and put it down. He opened one door. "Your room, Sis, and the other is Steph's. Have a quick look in, no more. You both have balconies."

Steph closed her eyes tightly. "Jeez. I've taken your room, haven't I?"

Josh shook his head. "Nah. It's better if I stay in the main house. There's a back door straight up to my room. I often work late—" he laughed, "or play late, so this way I won't disturb you."

They had a quick peek into Cori's room. "This is better than my suite on board. Thanks so much, Bro."

"My pleasure, Sis…as long as you don't visit too often."

Cori tried to punch him, but he ran downstairs.

They followed him to the main house. It was just as Cori imagined. The furniture was a lot older and darker, and the ceiling fans whirred in the background. All the same, it was homely and unpretentious.

Cori's grandma pulled out a chair. "Sit yourselves down, and help yourself to juice or coffee."

Steph sat down and looked across at Josh. "Shouldn't we go and help?"

"No. Definitely not."

The dining table was full to overflowing with fruits of every description. Within minutes Cori's grandparents walked in carrying plates stacked high with pancakes and crispy bacon.

They sat themselves down. "Tuck in," Cori's grandpa said.

Cori led the way. She helped herself to a few pancakes and bacon, then drizzled maple syrup over them. "I'm going to save the fruit until after. Hope you don't mind."

"Sweet Pea, you do it exactly as you want."

Steph followed, and then Josh. Then Cori's grandparents loaded their plates.

Cori's grandma picked up her knife and fork. "Now you can tell us all about your cruise."

For the next hour, in between eating, Cori and Steph related some of their adventures on board the *Caribbean Dreams*. They all seemed to be captivated by their stories and both Cori and Steph kept interrupting each other and laughing, especially when they talked about Raf.

When they'd finished, Cori's grandpa leaned back in his chair. "And how are your mum and dad?"

Cori beamed. "Honestly, they're great. Busy as hell." Cori quickly covered her mouth with her hand. "Sorry, I didn't mean to swear."

They laughed and turned their attention to Steph. "So, what do you do for a living, Steph?"

Steph looked at Cori, and Cori smiled. "Go on. Tell them."

So, Steph told them about their family's business as undertakers. They were surprisingly impressed.

"In Jamaica, it's a big thing. On the ninth night after the deceased has passed away, we celebrate with food, white rum, dancing, music and sharing stories," Cori's grandma informed them.

Steph nodded. "I wish we did the same in England. It should be a celebration of that person's life. Not some dire thing where everyone looks like they're about to follow the person into the grave."

Cori's grandfather leaned forward. "You must come to our church if you have time. There's lots of singing and it's quite an experience. Then we all have Sunday dinner together."

Cori's father had told her about this family tradition, though it wasn't exactly dinner, it was brunch.

Steph grinned. "I'd love to. Thank you."

Josh stood and pushed his chair back. "Has everyone finished?"

Cori and Steph both rubbed their tummies.

"I'll take that as a yes. Shall the three of us clear up? And then we'll show you around."

When they'd finished, Cori's grandparents took them on the tour of the house, followed by a walk around the gardens. There were a few acres of land set in stepped terraces attached to the house, and each had a spectacular view down to the bay. They admired the vista and took a different route back to the house. When they got to the top, Cori and Steph gasped. "I didn't know you had a pool!"

"Well, sweet pea, we were saving that as a surprise," her grandpa said.

Cori gave a cheer. "Now I know where we'll be spending all our time."

Josh nodded. "That was the plan until I have my days off. Then we'll all take off to some of the sights. Grandma and Grandpa want to be there on a few, but they won't be coming with us in the evenings." Josh laughed. He looked at his watch. "Anyway. Hope you two can occupy your day. The fridge is full of snacks and I'm sure Grandma will be feeding you tonight. In the meantime, I have to go over to the office in Ocho Rios and check everything is running well." He kissed everyone before disappearing.

Her grandma gave Cori a big cuddle. "You two gals go settle in. When you've done, you'll find towels in the cupboard plus inflatable loungers for the pool. Josh pumped them up last night." She laughed. "Even have those doodahs for holding your drinks, so be sure to bring some with you. If you need anything, you know where to find us, sweet pea."

"Brilliant. Thanks for everything."

Cori watched as her grandparents walked back into the house. She tilted her head. "They're both looking frail. Guess it doesn't come over when you FaceTime."

"How old are they?"

"Grandma's eighty-two and Grandpa's eighty-six. They had my dad late in life."

"Well, to me, they look good, especially when you see some people of their age back home. And how they managed to produce that wonderful brunch, beats me. Jeez, I so wish I had a family like yours."

Cori kicked a pebble back into the garden. "Yes, I'm lucky. Mostly."

Steph took her arm. "C'mon, the quicker we unpack, the quicker we can get on those lilos. I'm taking the lime green one."

"I want that one. Race you upstairs. Whoever wins gets the choice." Cori pushed Steph out of the way, sped up the stairs, and giggled all the way.

Chapter Twelve

WITHIN THE HOUR THEY were back down and lounging in the pool, with cans of Coke beside them. Steph honoured their bet and even if she'd won, she'd have offered the lime one to Cori. They sunbathed, swam, lazed in the shade, and whiled away the afternoon. All of this felt like a dream, and Cori had made it possible. She had dreams of another kind too, like that there'd only been one bedroom and they'd have to share. It was going to be hell knowing Cori was only next door to her. It wasn't just the sex angle, it was so much more, but she hadn't quite figured out what the *more* was. Sadly, this was just a fantasy and when it was over, they'd go back to living their very different lives.

Steph opened her eyes, and Cori's grandma was standing beside the pool. "Okay, you two. Dinner in an hour. That okay with you?"

Cori leapt up and splashed off the lilo. "Perfect. Do we have to dress for dinner?"

"No. Just don't be late." Her grandma waved her finger warningly and then walked away, humming softly.

Steph stood. "I need to shower and change into shorts and T-shirt." She noticed the quick glance Cori stole at her as she stood there in her bikini. Her nipples hardened and Cori quickly looked away, her cheeks flaring.

"Let's go then." They put the inflatables away and took the towels with them. When they got to their rooms, Cori opened her door. "See you soon."

Steph gave a little wave, taking a last look at Cori's backside in the small bikini bottoms. That was a sight she'd never tire of. After showering, Steph put some clothes on and went out on the balcony. She leaned on the wooden handrail and sighed. The bay was a sight to behold.

"Idyllic, isn't it?"

Steph looked over, and there was Cori doing the same. Her hair was loosely tied back, the wisps moving a little in the light breeze, and her sun-kissed skin glowed. She was breathtaking. "You're not kidding."

Cori smiled and jerked her head. "Come on, let's go."

Cori's grandpa beckoned them into the house. "We've set the table in the conservatory. Sorry, we don't stand on ceremony here." He placed a bottle of sorrel on the table along with a bucket of ice and mixer drinks. "Have you ever had sorrel, Steph? There's beer if you like."

"It's good with me, Grandpa. I've read about the spices used in it and I've always wanted to try it. Thank you." It seemed overly familiar calling Cori's grandparents by a familial name, but she didn't feel comfortable calling them Errol and Tianna, and she didn't have any grandparents herself, so it felt kind of warm and fuzzy.

Cori's grandma scooted by them with a massive bowl of salad. The chicken was on the table together with a dish of sweet potato mash.

"Yummy." Steph said. "Is this jerk chicken?"

Cori's grandma nodded her head. "Sure is. Thought it was a good choice on your first night."

Steph and Cori helped themselves as ordered.

"Wow, this is fantastic. What are the spices?" Steph asked.

"Cinnamon, cloves, ginger, thyme, garlic pepper and nutmeg." Cori's grandma winked. "And maybe something secret that I never let on to Cori's mum."

Cori slapped the table with her hand. "Well, that was mean. I hope you're going to tell me."

Cori's grandma smirked. "Well, that just depends. I may, or I may not. Guess I have to pass it on to someone, and Josh sure as heck doesn't know how to cook."

"You'd better trust me then. I could really get around my dad with this recipe. Mum's is great, but whatever you've added to the normal spices sure makes a difference." Cori shook her finger at her grandma. "That's a mean trick to play on my mum."

Her grandma snickered. "Well, you know that sons always say their mom's food is the best. I ain't letting go of that one."

Cori laughed. "You're very naughty. But your secret is safe, long as you pass it on to me."

"That's a deal, sweet pea."

They ended their meal with pineapple and home-made ice cream, and when they'd finished, Steph collapsed in her chair and held her stomach. "Tell you something, that was better than on board."

"Thank you, Steph."

Steph put her elbow on her chair arm and rested her chin on her hand. "I can't for one minute think why Cori's dad would want to leave

Jamaica." Shit, she should never have said that. Too much sorrel. God, it was strong. She rubbed her brow. "Sorry, I'm out of order. That's none of my business."

Cori's grandpa chuckled. "If anything offends us, we'll find you a hostel. Anyway, I think Tianna can answer that one."

"Easy-peasy." Cori's grandma laughed. "It wasn't, at the time. See, Devon was twenty-three. He looked a lot like Josh in those days. Handsome boy. All the girls after him. As you youngsters say, he was putting it about a bit. 'Specially as he was managing our car hire in Port Antonio. Oh, looking back, he was havin' himself a ball. All those female tourists hiring cars. Groups of them from all over Europe. And then along comes Alice. Hired a car for her and her friend whilst they were on vacation." Her eyes gleamed. "See, she was a couple of years older than Devon. More mature. Just what Devon needed. Course, we didn't know much then, but they'd gotten together and had themselves a fling." Her grandma took a sip of her drink. "Then she went back to England. Oh, he was so down. Couldn't eat or sleep and just wandered around in a dream." She jerked her head towards her husband. "Errol says to him, 'Now listen, son, get over to England. See how you feel then.' So that's what he did…took himself a holiday. Long and short of it, he came back, got all his papers and within the year he'd moved to England. Our Alice was a driving instructor, had her own business at twenty-five. A canny lass. Devon got his qualifications, they got married and he joined her in the business. Done well for themselves, haven't they, sweet pea?"

"Sure have, Grandma."

"Wow, what a lovely story," Steph said.

Cori's grandma laughed. "Got a good swap in the end with our Josh." She nudged her husband. "Hey, Errol. Show Steph the old photos while Cori and I tidy up."

Steph smiled widely. "I'd love that."

Cori and her grandma cleared the debris and disappeared into the kitchen. Steph waited patiently whilst Cori's grandpa vanished into another room. She noticed they'd left the remnants of the salad on the table, so she picked it up and headed towards the kitchen. She hung back when she realised the two of them were having what seemed like a private conversation. She knew she should walk away and not eavesdrop…but then again—

"I'm so sorry about Dusty. I wish we could have been there for you. I know we never cared for her much, but all we ever wanted was for our little sweet pea to be happy." She held Cori at arm's length. "She kept you away from us. From your mum and dad. We never saw you happy… and believe me, that's all we ever wanted." She sighed. "All the same, we're sorry it happened that way."

What way? Who was Dusty? Why hadn't she made Cori happy? Why had she kept them all apart? Steph's mind was going ten to the dozen. Was this why Cori had lost confidence? Was it because she'd lost Dusty? Had they parted…or something worse? Shit! She wanted to burst into the kitchen and ask all those questions, but she knew she'd have to wait for the right time. But she realized how little she really knew about Cori, and it made her a little sad. Had what they shared on the cruise been just surface stuff?

"Honest, Grandma, I'm okay now. I've just had a lot of stuff to deal with. I still have some things to work on, but I'll get there."

"Steph's lovely."

"I know. So was Dusty…to begin with."

Jeez, was she comparing her to this Dusty woman? She knew nothing about her but from what she'd detected over the course of the cruise, this woman had destroyed Cori's self-esteem. And now she knew Cori had been kept from her wonderful family, too. She had to find out more, but now wasn't the time. She went back to the table and put the salad bowl down. Cori's grandpa was sitting on the sofa with the photo album.

"Let's see those photos. I love looking back." That was a complete and utter lie. She had no happy memories of childhood to look back on. Her life was a sham. She'd manufactured happiness in her mind, but none of it was true. She just cruised through life waiting for something to happen. It never did, and now she was in a complete and utter rut. Somehow, she had to change her life. If only she had a magic wand.

Steph could still hear Cori and her grandma talking in the other room. Unfortunately, her good hearing didn't stretch as far as the kitchen. She looked at the photos Cori's grandpa showed her and laughed as he told her stories to go with those photos. They looked so happy, these people in their dated outfits and big smiles. She was fairly certain her family didn't even own a photo album.

He closed the album and yawned. "Excuse me, Steph. It's been a long day." He laughed. "Way too much excitement for me."

Steph smiled. "Me too. And thanks again for your wonderful hospitality."

"You're more than welcome."

Steph stood there uncertainly. She didn't want to intrude, but she didn't want to just leave, either. Then Cori and her grandma came out, and it looked as though Cori had been crying. She wanted desperately to take her in her arms, but of course she couldn't…well, not yet. But it was beginning to feel like there would come a time when it would happen.

They gave their thanks and headed back to the annexe. When they got to their rooms, Cori rubbed her eyes and yawned. "I'm done in. Must be too much sun."

"Yeah, me too," Steph lied, wishing she could ask Cori the questions she was burning to have answers to.

"Great day though. See you tomorrow." She blew a kiss before she shut the door.

Steph stared at the closed door and shook her head. Curiosity was eating at her, but right now she was powerless. Instead, she went to bed and dreamed about the terrific day they'd spent together. Cori was kind, sweet, gentle, and funny. She was so smart, and she had this great family. She was someone you wanted to treat well and spend your life with. But what would she get in return if she chose Steph? A woman with a career she didn't like and a family who were as warm as ice cubes at the North Pole. She had nothing to offer except a shoulder to cry on and someone who would stand up for her. Not exactly a stellar recommendation. She sighed and stared out at the swaying palms, letting them lull her to sleep.

The following day, they breakfasted with Cori's grandparents. Luckily, it was just fruit, cereal, and toast. Steph really didn't think she could continue eating to the extent she'd been doing for much longer. Her shorts were getting tighter and tighter by the day. After breakfast, Cori's grandparents sat in the shade reading their newspapers whilst Steph and Cori floated on their lilos. After a while, they dried off and transferred to their sunbeds.

Cori's phone pinged. She picked it up, looked at it for a while and smiled.

Steph leaned on her elbow. "Good news?"

"Hmm?"

"You were smiling."

Cori seemed to be giving some thought before replying.

"My fourth book was launched today."

Steph sprang up from her bed and grabbed hold of Cori's hand. "Congratulations. Why didn't you say?"

Cori turned around as if to check her grandparents weren't listening, but they'd left the terrace.

Cori shrugged. "It's no big deal."

"Shit, Cori, this is fantastic news. I've wanted to ask you about your writing since you mentioned it, but you always seemed to shy away from the subject. What's it called?"

"*The Adventures of Scatty the Rat.*"

"Catchy title. Is it a sequel or what?"

"No. It's the first in a series. I had another three before featuring *The Dancing Pig.*" Cori cleared her throat and seemed to almost brace herself. "They were bestsellers."

"Wow, that's amazing. You should have said. Christ, you'd have been the star of the ship."

"I don't want to be any star. It's just something that's my passion. My life. You see, it kept me going. It was all I had to look forward to most days." Cori looked down and wrung her hands in her lap.

Steph placed her finger underneath Cori's chin and lifted her head. "Why are you so ashamed? Fuck, I'm thrilled for you. I feel proud to know you. It's *such* an achievement." Steph shook her head. "What the hell happened to you?"

"I suppose I got too big for my boots."

Steph punched her on the arm playfully and laughed. "You...big for your boots? You're the most modest person I've ever met. If it were me, I'd be telling the world. On a megaphone. From the Empire State Building." Steph stared at Cori, waiting for an explanation.

"I was a librarian."

Steph waited patiently, though patience wasn't her middle name.

"I've always written stories. Ever since I can remember. It was just for my own amusement, that's all. Then I did an online writing course. I wrote a whole book, *The Dancing Pig.* At first, she'd encouraged me."

This was it. The answers she'd hoped for. "Can I ask who?"

"Dusty."

Cori briefly explained how they'd met and how long they'd been together. "I finished the book and stupidly showed it to an agent who was giving a talk in the library. She loved it and said she knew a publisher who would be interested. I didn't tell Dusty. God, how arrogant I was. Looking back, I can't imagine how pretentious it must have seemed."

Steph wanted to interrupt but she listened instead, not wanting to stop Cori's flow.

"It was ages, and to be honest, I'd forgotten about it. Well, let's say I'd dismissed the idea." Cori held her head in her hands. "Such egotism." She removed her hands but didn't make eye contact with Steph. "Then I heard from the agent. A publishing company were interested, and they wanted to meet up."

"Wow, how awesome."

Cori shook her head. "Dusty went ballistic. She said she'd been humouring me, waiting for the novelty to wear off, and that it was just for fun." Cori swallowed. "Of course, I'd gone behind her back, which was terrible. She was justified in her annoyance. She'd never thought I was actively seeking out an agent and a publisher. It was all a pipe dream, and of course it took the edge off my elation. Still, eventually she agreed for us all to meet up. Her included."

I bet she did! This Dusty woman sounded like a shit and a half. "So, what happened next?"

"My first book was published. It was a great success."

Steph took a deep breath. Really, she wanted to swear extensively, but she kept her cool as best she could. "And obviously the second and the third did the same?"

Cori nodded. "The publishers wanted me to attend all sorts of events. Readings, book signings, etcetera. After all, they'd invested a lot of time and money into all the various aspects of getting the books onto the bookshelves and marketing them. I tried to skip as many as I could. Tried to keep it low-key."

"Why? You'd earned it, and as you said, that's what's expected."

"I know, but it wasn't fair on Dusty. She worked hard and had to get time off."

Why couldn't you go on your own? Steph wanted to throttle this Dusty.

"Anyway, she managed it. I mean, I needed her there by my side, and she attended all the functions."

"But?"

"Understandably, there were always massive arguments before and after. It took all the pleasure away. It wasn't as though I was an egomaniac. I didn't crave stardom, and I certainly didn't wish to become a celebrity, as she said. But I know it looked that way to her."

Steph took hold of Cori's hand. "Cori, you're not the boastful type. I can't understand why you think you are…or was it because Dusty told you that?"

"No. She was very supportive. It was my fault."

"Don't be ridiculous."

Cori collapsed in a heap and sobbed, and Steph wrapped her arms around her and let her cry. Eventually, she sniffed and wiped her eyes. "All I ever wanted to do was write books for children. I look back to my childhood and how my mum and dad used to read to me at night, and how I got lost in my fantasy world, and that's the place it took me to when I wrote them…but Dusty died because of my selfish behaviour."

Steph kept her arm around her shoulder. "Trust me. Tell me what happened?"

"The publishers had organised a big do. They were taking me out for a celebratory meal in a super-duper restaurant in London that included an overnight stay in a plush hotel. Dusty said it was out of the question. Actually, she wasn't invited. They'd suggested I come alone. I know they didn't like her much. She had this way about her, sometimes. She could be charming, but there was often a bite to her words that could make people uncomfortable." Cori coughed. "It always took a while before people understood Dusty. She'd had a hard life."

Steph rubbed Cori's arm. The more she heard the more evident it became that Cori had suffered domestic abuse. She needed help, desperately.

Cori blew her nose on the tissue that Steph had given her. "Dusty said that if I went, she wouldn't be there when I returned."

Thank God! She'd keep her opinions to herself, though.

Cori looked around again. "I haven't told anybody the details…my parents, my grandparents, my brother, or my best friend. But I'm telling you. It's crazy. Please don't repeat it."

"I promise you, whatever you say stays with me."

"I don't know why, but I told Dusty I was going anyway. I told her it didn't matter if she wasn't there when I got home."

Steph raised her thumbs. "Good for you."

Cori took a deep breath. "She picked up her helmet, and as she left, she slammed the door." She shook her head slowly. "I knew I shouldn't have done it. I don't know what came over me. I thought about chasing after her and apologising, but it was too late. I heard her motorbike rev up and off she went."

"Why should you have apologised? It was a celebration, and she should have been pleased for you."

Cori rubbed her hand across her forehead. "No. I was getting carried away with my own self-importance." She looked down. She began to shiver and weep again. "I never saw her again."

"What? She left you?"

"In a way. She had an accident on the motorcycle. She died when she collided with another car, while I was out celebrating. And it was all my fault."

Steph wasn't quite sure what to say. She'd have liked to have said, "Karma," but that wouldn't have been appropriate, even though she was thinking it. "It wasn't your fault, Cori. Shit. It was an *accident*. They happen, and you can't blame yourself for something you had no control over."

"No! It was because of my actions. If I hadn't made her so angry, she wouldn't have left. She wasn't paying attention to what she was doing on the road, and that was my fault."

She needed to convince Cori otherwise. She was blaming herself because she'd been indoctrinated. The more she heard about Dusty, the more she despised her, even though she'd never met her and was never going to. "That's not true. Trust me, Cori, you need to talk this over with a professional. There are loads out there who deal with exactly the kind of abuse you went through."

"No, there aren't. I tried, but I didn't have the courage to follow through and find anywhere to help me."

"Then I'll help you. I promise."

Cori leaned her head on Steph's shoulder. "Thank you. I know you're right, it's just that I've lost my confidence. Some days I feel like a child wandering city streets alone."

"I'm here for you, and I'm not going away." Steph kissed Cori's forehead. It was a promise she knew she could make, no matter what happened between them.

Cori's grandma shouted from the doorway, "Come on, you two chicks. I've prepared some sandwiches. You must be starving."

Steph stood, took hold of Cori's hands, and pulled her up. "Be brave,

Cori. Good times are ahead of you. You just have to believe it."

Cori gave a half smile and nodded. She was sure Cori didn't feel like celebrating right now, but Steph would make a point of taking her out for a special evening.

***

Over the course of the next few days, their routine was much the same, but at least Cori seemed to have cheered up. Perhaps because she'd lightened her load by sharing what she'd been through. Steph knew there was so much more to come out, but Cori had to do it in her own time, and there was no way she was going to push her.

Josh took a few days off and they all went off to see some sights. A lot of the attractions seemed to be centred around Montego Bay, like rafting on the Martha Brae River, and visiting the Rastafari Indigenous Village, so he'd booked all of them into a small hotel, otherwise their grandparents wouldn't have been able to cope with the trip. Steph took pictures galore. She wanted these memories to stay in her mind forever. If she was honest, she wanted Cori to be in her life just as long. As the days passed by, they seemed to be growing closer and closer. She took as many photos of Cori as she could, many of them when Cori was unaware of the camera, and she looked so soft, so beautiful, that it made Steph melt more than any Jamaican sunshine ever could.

When they returned, both grandparents looked worn out.

Josh took them both to one side. "I think we need to give them some space. Let them rest and recuperate." He laughed. "They're not used to all this excitement. I know they want to take you to their favourite restaurant, but I think we'll leave that until later. In the meantime, do you fancy going to a beach bar with me tonight? They've got a reggae band on. We could grab something to eat first?"

Cori whacked Josh on the shoulder. "Thought you'd never ask. I want to see your life. I want to see your friends, too."

Steph winked. "Wah time we a touch road?" Her Jamaican accent was abysmal, and it was good when the others laughed.

"Be ready by eight." Josh waved and left them.

"Hey, that was really good, Steph." Cori took her hand and swung it as they left the house and walked back to the annexe. She didn't let go.

They walked in silence, as though it was a moment to pay attention to, one to cherish, and when they got back to their rooms, she lifted Cori's hand and kissed it gently. "See you soon, Cori."

Steph took a shower. The physical tension between her and Cori was undeniable and driving her a little crazy. What she wouldn't give to have Cori in the shower with her, covered in soapy bubbles, their skin pressed together... She banged her head gently on the tiles, trying to knock some sense into herself. Cori had a lot of healing to do and getting into some romantic thing with Steph wasn't going to help her do that. She needed to be patient and see where things went naturally, without putting any pressure on Cori at all. She got out and dressed hurriedly, shaking out the wrinkles in her shorts as best she could.

She knocked on Cori's door. "You ready?" Cori came out looking as splendid as ever in some white jeans and a tight black tee that hugged her breasts perfectly. She looked good enough to kiss, so Steph did exactly that. It was only a light kiss on the lips, but it sent tingles throughout her body. She'd dearly love a long lingering kiss, but that would have to wait. She was sure she'd know when the time was right.

Chapter Thirteen

CORI SAT WITH JOSH in the front of the car. "Where we going, bro?"

"It's a surprise. Hope you'll like it." He drove through Port Antonio and pulled up in front of a hotel called the GeeJam which was nestled in the rainforest at the foot of the Blue Mountains.

Steph whistled. "Wow, this looks awesome."

"Thanks, I think so." Josh got out. "Follow me." They went through the hotel and into a small restaurant called Bushbar. They were shown to their table overlooking the azure seas of Port Antonio.

Cori stared at the view. "This is spectacular." She glanced around the bustling restaurant. "It's got a brilliant ambiance. So chilled."

A waiter came over with a bottle, uncorked it and filled three glasses. "Enjoy."

Josh picked up his glass. "Congratulations, Sis."

Cori shrugged. "On what?"

"A little bird told me your new book has been released."

Cori stared at Steph.

Steph held her palms up. "Sorry. Couldn't let this go by without a celebration."

"Well, thank you both. It's nothing, really."

Josh shook his head. "It bloody is, so stop protesting. That woman treated you like shit. She was jealous of everything you achieved. Well, it's not gonna happen anymore. So, get used to it. We're celebrating your accomplishments from here on out."

Cori grimaced. Josh was right, but she'd found that out way too late. Could she really put all that on one side and start afresh? She didn't think she could. Not without help, as Steph had suggested, and that seemed a long way off. However, for now, she was going to try and enjoy it. She raised her glass. "Thank you again."

They drank, feasted on lamb chops followed by flambéed bananas drenched in liquor, and chatted about the beaches and places they still wanted to visit with Josh. When they'd finished, they headed back to Port Antonio to a rustic bamboo bar by the side of the beach.

Josh found them a table. "Are you two going to try the local beer, Red Stripe? It's more like a lager."

Steph rubbed her hands together. "Oh yeah. Bring it on."

Cori nodded. "Yes, me too."

The beers arrived and two young guys came up behind Josh and flung their arms around him.

Josh shoved them away playfully. "Not sure why, but these two crazy guys are my best friends, Agwe and Sanka."

Cori and Steph smiled and nodded to them. "Hi, guys."

"This here is my sister, Cori and her friend, Steph."

Sanka punched Josh's arm. "So, you weren't joking when you said your sister was white? I always thought you were messing with us."

"Nah. Just the family genes getting crazy." He looked at Cori fondly. "Cori looks just like Mom, and I look just like Dad. People used to argue with Mom and Dad, saying we couldn't possibly have the same parents. I think Mom nearly decked someone over it once."

Everyone laughed. Agwe and Sanka joined them for a quick beer and when the musicians arrived, they said their goodbyes. Agwe shouted, "See you at football practice tomorrow."

Cori laughed. "Football? You hated football!"

Josh put his head down. "I loved football. Still do."

"Never. You opted out. You found any excuse to get out of sports, especially football."

"Sis, you of all people should know that people change." He squeezed her hand.

"And I'm glad you've changed too. It's good to see you happy. Hey, before I get too pissed, here's the number of a reliable taxi driver if you two want to go out alone sometime. There are a few good restaurants nearby and Dan will look after you. He'll take you to beaches also." He leaned closer, his expression turning serious. "But you need to be careful, okay? Being gay here is still illegal, and people aren't exactly accepting." He waited until they both nodded their understanding before he smiled and leaned back again. "Unfortunately, I have to go back to work. But I'm taking a couple of nights off at the end of your vacation, and of course I'll be taking you to the airport." He passed a slip of paper over to Steph and she put it in her bag.

The reggae music started, and from then on, there was no conversation.

Steph raised her voice. "Hey, Kingston Town. One of my favourites."

Steph stood and took Cori's hand. "Let's dance."

Cori hated making an idiot of herself. But Steph was insistent, and she didn't put up much of a fight. Taking Josh's warning into account, she watched every move Steph made but didn't reach out to touch her or hold her the way she wanted to. They'd save that kind of dancing for when they were alone. Still, Steph's moved her body so sensually made Cori crazy with desire.

Josh nudged her and winked. He was dancing with a woman right next to her. Normally, she'd feel self-conscious at how transparent her desire was, but between the alcohol and the music than ran in her veins, she lost herself in the feeling of being home.

They danced, drank, and sang their way into the early hours of the morning, and when they got back, she and Steph made their way to the annexe. Steph's arm was around Cori's waist, and when they got to Cori's room, Steph pressed her against the door and kissed her. This kiss wasn't hesitant, or sweet. It was hot, passionate, and it made Cori's knees weak. She hung on and moaned softly when Steph kissed her neck and lightly bit her earlobe. Her nipples grew painfully hard, and she pressed into Steph as she returned the kiss.

But then Steph pulled back, breathing hard, and rested her forehead against Cori's. She whispered, "Goodnight, beautiful," and reached around Cori to open the bedroom door. She shut it softly once Cori was in her room, and then all Cori remembered was falling into bed. Clothes and everything. She kept thinking of the way Steph's body felt as it brushed against hers, and her body ached with the heavy sensation of desire she hadn't felt in so, so long. She smiled and drifted off into the stars.

When Cori eventually surfaced the next day, she went and knocked on Steph's door. Steph appeared looking as bleary-eyed as her.

"I need coffee, and lots of it," Steph said with a smile.

"Me too. Let's go see our grandparents."

Steph tilted her head. "I like that. Ours. I've never had any and they really do feel like mine, even if I've only known them for about a minute."

Cori took Steph's hand. "They are yours." She led her down the stairs, not letting go of her hand. It had become common for them to be touching all the time, and there was no expectation to it. It was just… nice.

Although it was eleven thirty in the morning, Cori's grandparents had everything ready for them, as if they knew exactly when they'd arrive. "Help yourself, chicks. Your grandpa and I are just going down to the supermarket."

"How are you getting there?" Cori asked.

"Dan's taking us. Always does."

Cori nodded and smiled. "See you later."

It was a cloudy day and slightly cooler than the norm, so they took off for a walk instead of going to the pool.

Steph was chewing at her fingernail.

Cori nudged her. "What's up?"

"Wondered if you fancied going out for dinner tomorrow night?"

"I'd love to. Are we going to ask Josh's friend to take us?"

"Definitely."

"So where to?"

"I googled restaurants and there's one that's recommended not far from here. Thought we could go for an early meal."

"Great. Book him." They quickened their pace up the hill to a spot that had even better views over the bay. Of course, Steph took stacks of photos and selfies of the two of them with the view in the background. She looked so intent, and her usual interest in just about everything around her always made Cori smile. "Tell me if I'm out of order, but you haven't talked much about your parents. Do they know you're here?" She gently caressed Steph's arm. "Will you tell me more about your life?"

Steph put her phone away and sat on a wall. She took a deep breath. "They didn't approve of me coming here, no. On the one hand, they wanted me to stay away. But deep down, they want me back so that they can punish me some more. They'd prefer that I stay in my room in self-imposed flagellation mode." Steph shrugged. "Frankly, I don't want to go back. We have nothing in common, and I'm always a disappointment. I'm not happy in my work, but I don't know what to do. I'm bored. A robot could do my job, and at least a robot wouldn't feel like a total screw-up all the time."

Cori shook her head. "So, what are your main interests? What do you want to get from a job, apart from a pay cheque at the end of the month? Make a list."

Steph shrugged. "Don't know where to start. It's all I've ever known, but there's no new skills to learn. I underperform and lose focus."

"You're in the wrong job, Steph. You need a challenge."

"I'm at a dead end. 'Scuse the pun. There's no scope for development, but it's the family business, and for all that they don't like me, I'm still family."

Cori crossed her arms. "Steph, all you've done this holiday is take photos. Views, the ship, the rooms, us. So why don't you develop your hobby?"

Steph grimaced. "I don't want to become a photographer. So much competition."

"So, what else are you passionate about?"

Steph grinned. "That'd be telling. I could show instead…"

It was a tempting offer. "I shall ignore that for the moment. All I'm saying is that you need to look for something that'll make you light up with pride. I may be on the wrong track, but you seem to love architecture."

Steph stared out at the water for a few minutes. "I guess my passion is architectural design, you're right. But that's a whole new ball game."

"So? Pursuing a new career path is a great idea. Just take that step."

Steph continued to stare out at the horizon for a moment, then she opened her phone and flipped onto photos. "When I bought my apartment, it was a shambles. I virtually stripped it and rebuilt it myself." She showed Cori the before and after photos.

Cori stared at the transformation. "That is unbelievable. *This* is what you should be doing."

"I'm too old to change professions."

Cori giggled. "You're thirty-one, and that's too old? Heck, you're a go-getter. Surely you're not going to waste the rest of your life being unhappy?" It seemed a stupid thing to say. After all, Cori had wasted many years of her own life, but Steph wasn't like her. "That doesn't seem like the woman I've come to know at all."

Steph frowned. "You think I could really do it?"

"Of course I do. You'd be perfect for that profession. You have flair and confidence. You could look into it, at least."

"I don't know. My family…" She groaned. "They'll be glad to be rid of me, and they'll also say I'm making a huge mistake and being irresponsible. I can't win."

"In that case, what do you have to lose?" The words echoed in her heart. "We only have the lives we make for ourselves, right?"

Steph perked up and began to nod slowly, and then more emphatically. "You're right. When I get home, I'll do just that. Thanks, Cori." Steph put her arm around Cori and kissed her on the cheek. She lingered there, and when Cori turned her face, the kiss came again, this time longer, sweeter. She pressed herself to Steph, liking the way they fit together. Steph pulled away, the sweetness of emotion in her eyes making Cori feel gooey inside. They rested their foreheads together for a moment, then turned and walked back in an easy silence.

They spent the rest of the day talking to her grandparents and dipping in and out of the water to keep cool. They hadn't discussed what was happening between them. It felt like it might spoil it, somehow, dissecting it. She wanted to let it be what it was. For now, anyway.

After dinner with her grandparents, they agreed on an early night. Cori was still shattered from the previous evening and her hangover seemed to linger with her all day, whereas Steph looked bright and chirpy as though she could go off clubbing again tonight. She imagined Steph was used to this kind of life. Hers was dull in comparison and she wondered how that would work if they took this relationship further. She smiled at the notion there would be a chance at something later. Perhaps they'd find a compromise. She knew the secret to a happy relationship was compromise, but it was something she'd never experienced before. Dusty had been totally inflexible. But, as she so often reminded herself lately, that was before. She could choose who she wanted to be, and who she wanted to be with, now.

The following day they caught the local bus to the village with her grandma to buy all her special spices, and Cori took the opportunity to buy some for her mum, but there was no way Grandma would share her mystery ingredients. She guessed she'd have to wait. In the meantime, she was enjoying showing Steph around and sharing family memories with her. They managed to spend an hour in the sun before they prepared for their early evening dinner.

Dan arrived at five and took them to their restaurant. It was called Pearl Root and it certainly was a little gem. Dan pulled up outside. "Buzz me when you're ready. Be sure to try the oxtail. It's the best in Jamaica. And try their ginger beer."

Steph gave him a wink and a wave.

They walked up the steps and into the restaurant which overlooked the picturesque Pearl Bay.

Cori's jaw dropped. "This is awesome. It's so quaint and the atmosphere is so serene."

Steph wiggled her eyebrows. "Romantic, too."

Cori gave her a sweet smile. "Sure is. You did good." She looked through to the back of the restaurant. "I don't suppose—"

Steph grinned. "Yes, I booked the veranda."

Just then, the waiter came over, greeted them, and showed them to their table. Before he left, Steph said, "Do you fancy the ginger beer?"

Cori nodded. "You bet."

He returned with their drinks along with the menus. "You've made it just in time, ladies. Pass me your camera, 'cos here it comes."

Cori looked over her shoulder at the streaks of pink and orange slicing through the sky. She reckoned Steph had planned for exactly this moment. Her breath caught at the sweet, simple gesture that meant so much. She put her arm around Cori and pulled her close as they leaned on the balcony overlooking the Caribbean Sea as the sun set in the background.

Cori leaned on her shoulder. "Thank you for this. You think of everything." Moments like these were once-in-a-lifetime, and they'd certainly had their fair share of those on this holiday. How could it get better? Or would it be like a fairy tale? They'd ride off together, but the mundanity of real life would settle in, and the bubble would burst once they were back? She didn't voice her doubts. She simply enjoyed the feeling of Steph beside her as they watched the sun go down in companionable silence. After they'd watched the sun set, they looked at their menus.

Steph chuckled. "No contest, I'm going for the oxtail."

"On this occasion I'll join you. I don't want to miss out on the speciality."

The oxtail arrived and was a hearty meat stew served with rice and peas. Cori looked across at Steph. "Wow, this is delicious." She giggled. "The ginger beer is fantastic. I think I prefer it to regular beer. All the taste without the hangover."

Steph grinned. "I like the rum and sorrel mixture your grandfather introduced me to. And I have to admit that I like the occasional whiff of pot I catch."

Cori nodded. "I'll stick with the ginger beer, and I've never taken drugs."

Steph shrugged. "No harm in a bit of ganja. Been there, done it, but like you, I'll stick with ginger beer when we're out. Having said that, I think we should legalise pot, especially for people with medical issues."

Cori nodded and stared down at her napkin. Should she tell Steph? What would be the harm, she'd confided in her with almost everything else. "Dusty smoked marijuana."

"Really. Medical purposes?"

"No, she was a hypocrite and a compulsive liar. I could smell it on her clothes. When I asked her about it, she said she didn't use it, but worked with people who did, and apparently a lot of her friends indulged. After her accident, I found a big stash hidden away in the drawer she kept locked in another bedroom." Cori took a big swallow of her ginger beer in hopes it would take away the acrid taste in her mouth brought about by her bad memories of Dusty. The thoughts enraged her. "And I wouldn't have cared. If she'd been honest about it, maybe I wouldn't have been keen on it, but I'd have respected her choice to use it. Like I said, she was a liar. In many ways. I found other things, too."

Steph wiped away the condensation on her glass and tilted her head, as if waiting for Cori to continue.

Cori continued because she needed to get it off her chest. She had learned to trust Steph. She trusted her friend Liz, but Liz was too close. She knew her well and all Liz would say was that she'd been manipulated from day one. She'd been controlled and abused. Thing was though, she'd let it happen and there was an element of truth in everything Dusty had said to her. She *was* a loser.

Cori took a deep breath. "Dusty told me she'd spent most of her life in care. That she'd been farmed out to foster parents who were only taking her in for the money. She painted the picture of a terrible childhood. I made allowances for all of her insecurities."

Steph grimaced. "But?"

"When she died, I thought, that was it. She had nobody. But then, in the locked drawer I found a tin with photos. Family photos. At first, I thought they must have been her foster parents. Then I found letters. They were sent to a PO Box and were addressed to Jane Watson. They were from someone in Manchester, a woman called Beryl Watson. At first, I couldn't figure it out. Why did Dusty have these letters? They had nothing to do with her, and Dusty's surname was Granger." Cori sighed.

"Then I found the paperwork with a name change. Jane Watson to Dusty Granger. God, I felt so sick, Steph."

Steph reached over and took her hand. "Christ, what a shock. What did you do?"

"You mean after I was physically sick? I sat and put them in order and read through each one. It seemed that Dusty had been asking Beryl for money. She also wanted to see her. It was obvious from all the brief replies that Beryl didn't feel the same and had no money to give. There was also an address book. It had a few contact numbers with a landline and mobile number for Beryl Watson. I gave it a couple of days and then plucked up the courage and phoned the landline."

Steph's eyes widened. "And?"

"It was difficult, but I briefly explained who I was and who I'd been living with for the last eight years. All she said was, 'That's 'er and I don't want anything to do with 'er.' Then came what I thought would be the painful part, telling her about Dusty or Jane's accident. There was hardly any reaction. She said she was sorry, but there was no emotion in her voice. I told her about the funeral arrangements, and she said she wouldn't be coming."

"Just like that! Must have been some bad history between them."

"Yes. I wanted to know so I asked why Jane would have changed her name. She laughed. 'To forget 'er past of course." I asked her if Dusty had been in care and fostered. She laughed so loud I had to hold the phone a mile away. "Is that what she told you? Well, love, I can assure you she lived with me until I 'ad the guts to kick her out. I 'ate to say it but I raised a bad un there. She stole from me, bullied me, and she 'ad nothing of a conscience whatsoever. She was one of them psychopaths. I coulda ratted on her to the police, but she was blood. Just glad I only 'ad the one. Course, she came back for money, and I told 'er I'd get one of them injunctions. She kept trying though with the beggin' letters. Bet she fleeced you, too.'"

Cori remembered hanging on to something to stop herself from passing out. She felt the same way now as she repeated it. However, she was determined to finish her story. "I came off the phone completely devastated. When I'd recovered, I searched the bedroom again and found—" Cori looked down, hardly able to look Steph in the eye. She was so ashamed. Steph poured her a glass of water and handed it to her. She took a large gulp. "Thanks." She took a deep breath. "I found a credit and debit card in the name of Jane Watson. I took them to the bank, along with the paperwork for change of name and the death certificate. Eventually, after talking to the right person, they found she'd set up a regular direct debit from my account to hers. I'd never noticed because she handled all the finances, but it added up to thousands after all our years together. It took a while, but I got it back." Cori shrugged. "I even sent some money to her mum. Poor woman." Cori wiped her brow. "Dusty was right. She always said everything was beyond my understanding. She said everybody knew how dumb I was."

Steph got up and pushed her chair back. She took both hands in hers. "You are far from dumb, Cori. Dusty, or whatever she wished to call herself, was an abuser. You are a kind, caring, tender and big-hearted person. You were taken in by this con-woman. You're not alone. There are lots more people out there in the same position. I'm sorry that she had to die before you knew the truth."

Cori shook her head. "She was kind to me once. I think I was responsible for everything that went wrong in the relationship. If only I'd have helped her more."

"She was beyond help. But you're not. And that's a discussion for another time. Right now, I think we should call Dan, pay the bill, and go. We can have a nightcap when we get back."

Cori smiled, feeling hollowed out after everything she'd shared. "Yes, I'd like that."

Dan dropped them off and Steph quizzed him about him taking them to Reach Falls the next day.

"You don't wanna be with all those tourists. I can take you to a much better place. Give me a call when you're ready."

Steph grinned. "Great plan, Dan. Hey, that rhymes."

Dan laughed and drove away. Steph took Cori's arm. "C'mon. I'm going to make us some hot chocolate and a nice liqueur and we'll go sit on my balcony."

Cori waited whilst Steph made the hot drinks. Back at the restaurant, just for a while, the clouds had closed in, and the darkness had descended. Steph seemed to have a way of bringing in the light and dispersing the clouds, though, and her melancholy began to lift.

Steph passed Cori two small glasses, and she carried the mugs. "Follow me." Steph opened her balcony door and placed the mugs on the table. "Make yourself comfortable. Be back in a minute." She returned with a bottle of Grand Marnier. "Compliments of *Caribbean Dreams*. I ordered it, I didn't drink it, and I thought it was a shame to let it go to waste." She poured a little into the glasses and raised hers. "To a different future…for both of us."

Cori raised hers too. "I really do hope so. And thanks for being such a great listener. It means a lot to me."

"You can always talk to me, Cori. I'd like to think we'll be there for each other in the future too." She almost looked like she was holding her breath, and her gaze searched Cori's.

Cori smiled. "I think that's a definite."

Steph stood and leaned against the balcony rail. "You may think I'm crazy, but this is the best vacation I've ever had."

Cori joined her. "For me too. When I set off on the cruise, I was apprehensive. I suppose it didn't really matter because at the end of it I'd get to see my grandparents and brother. But then we met, and frankly, you've made my holiday better than I could have imagined."

Steph reached over and stroked Cori's neck. She ran her fingers through Cori's hair and drew her closer so that they were facing each other. She placed tiny kisses on Cori's mouth, then kissed her harder. Cori didn't shy away. Somehow it seemed natural. Because she had faith in Steph.

Steph gently parted Cori's lips and her tongue touched hers. She closed her eyes and let the tingling sensation continue. It felt like a bonding. They'd shared their past, their interests and life experiences, and now it was time to share something more.

Steph took Cori's hand and led her to the bed. She unfastened the buttons on Cori's shirt, folded it, and placed it on the chair. After unzipping Cori's jeans, she did the same to her own. She kissed her then spread little kisses down and across her neck. Steph folded the duvet back and Cori lay down on the bed. Steph removed all her own clothes, lay beside her, and smiled as she ran her fingers down Cori's cheek.

Laying like this was a new sensation for Cori. For once, she wasn't ashamed of her nakedness because all she saw was desire in Steph's eyes. They stared at each other and kissed. It was more passionate this time, more lingering, and it set Cori alight. It awoke something in her that she'd never experienced. It was a craving for sexual pleasure, but it was more of a whole physical need for love and affection.

Steph studied Cori's body admiringly and kissed her again. Her mouth was warm, and her tongue explored deeply. When her hand skimmed her breast, Cori's heart bounced frantically. She squeezed her breast gently, then ran her finger across her nipple. Cori gasped. She caressed it softly, then harder. She kissed her ear and worked her way from her neck to her breast. She flicked her tongue across her nipple, then nibbled it gently. Her hand travelled down her body, stroking her skin, right down to the inside of her thigh. Cori's breathing became heavy with anticipation as Steph removed her panties. She parted Cori's legs and gently stroked her clit. Cori caught her breath as she slid a finger in and then another. Cori moaned with pleasure as she pressed against Steph's fingers. She increased the pace and drove deeper and harder.

Cori moaned. "Yes. Now." The aching for release was unbearable and she couldn't hold out any longer. She clenched, arched her back and released. Her juices flowed freely over Steph's fingers and her body relaxed. It was a while before she said anything, but she was aware that Steph's arms were wrapped around her, strong, yet tender.

Steph kissed her forehead. "It's right, you know? I felt it. I hope you wanted this as much as I did."

Cori relaxed in her arms and rested her head on Steph's shoulder. "Absolutely. It was perfect."

They fell to sleep in each other's arms. It seemed so natural, and the lovemaking had been spontaneous, not something contrived. Steph was tender and considerate. Something she'd dreamt of all her life, and yet, until this day, she'd never known how it was supposed to feel. There was something more though, and she had no idea what it was.

Chapter Fourteen

THERE WAS A LIGHT tap on Steph's door. She was going to ignore it but then she heard the words. "Brunch is almost ready, chicks."

She'd forgotten where she was and shot up, realising it was Cori's grandma. She coughed. "Thanks. Be down in ten minutes." Cori was still fast asleep. To be honest, she'd liked to have woken her with some more lovemaking, but that was out of the question. She kissed Cori on the lips, and her eyelids fluttered.

She smiled back at her. "Hmm. What a lovely way to be woken."

"Err, yes. I'd like to do more, but your grandma has just announced brunch."

Cori slapped her forehead. "Shit. You're kidding. Do you think she knows?"

Steph giggled. "Without a doubt. We have ten minutes, so we'd better move our asses."

They arrived at the main house, and Cori looked a little coy and sheepish, and Steph certainly felt that way. They sat down at the table and Cori's grandparents came in with plates of scrambled food.

Cori pressed her hands together. "Ooh, this looks delicious. Ackee and saltfish?"

"That's right. Used to be your dad's favourite when he was a child."

Steph took a big bite. "This is so tasty, what's in it?"

"Saltfish and ackees." Cori's grandma laughed. "Well, there's a few other ingredients like onions, tomatoes, peppers and garlic."

Cori loaded her fork. "Another recipe I want." She didn't look up. "We had a great meal last night. Dan took us to Pearl Root."

Cori's grandpa wiped his mouth with the back of his hand. "Did you have the oxtail?"

"Sure did. And the ginger beer. Both fantabulous."

"Yeah, we've not been there for years, have we, Grandpa?"

"Nah, don't get out as much as we used to. Glad it's still good, though." He laid his fork down and held his stomach. "That was mighty good, Grandma, just like always. Anyway, what you chicks got planned for today?"

"We wanted to go to Reach Falls, but Dan said it'd be full of tourists. Said he knew a much better place that's equally impressive," Steph said.

He winked at his wife. "Bet that's Shanelle Falls. We used to go there when we were young to do our courting." They shared a glinting smile that lit up the room. "Take your swimsuits." He chuckled. "Or not. Make sure you take surf shoes. It can be a bit slippery and rocky in places. There's plenty in the cupboard."

Cori's grandma stroked her chin. "And I'd best pack you some food too."

Cori giggled. "What, after all this? I think we're only going for a swim."

"I'll make a sandwich and put some fruit in too. You may want to stay there longer. Trust me, sweet pea."

Cori blushed. Steph didn't, but she understood exactly what Cori's grandma was implying, and it sounded promising.

Steph made a move. "We'll help clear the dishes."

Cori's grandma waved her hand furiously. "You two chicks go off and enjoy yourselves. And don't forget, you're only young once."

Steph and Cori left the table. Steph put her arm around Cori's grandma. "That was absolutely wonderful."

She got on her tiptoes, kissed Steph on the cheek, and whispered in her ear, "Make sure you take care of my little sweet pea, eh? She needs someone like you."

Steph kissed her back. "I promise. From the bottom of my heart." She meant it too. The affection she held for Cori wasn't the usual way of things. It made her feel as if she wanted to move on to an actual relationship. Granted, it was new territory, and it was a tad scary, but she felt comfortable with it, and although the sex was different, there was a feeling of wholeness and harmony, and she liked it. In fact, it made her go all gooey just thinking about it.

Steph took Cori's hand. "Let's go on our next adventure."

When Dan pulled up on the side of the track, Steph and Cori stared at each other. It was in the middle of nowhere and all that surrounded them were tall trees.

Dan opened the door and they slid out. He handed Steph the rucksack. "If you don't get a phone signal, just walk back up the track."

Steph nodded and coughed. "Is this it, then?"

Dan cackled. "Nah." He pointed down the path. "Can't take the car any further. See that clearing?"

Steph nodded.

"Well, take the trail down. It's about a fifteen-minute walk. Give me a call when you're ready to come back." Dan got into his car, waved, and reversed back up the track.

Cori grimaced. "Looks like the back of beyond."

Steph took Cori's hand. Cori lowered her eyes and smiled sweetly. It was funny because Steph had never been into romantic stuff before but as soon as she touched Cori's hand, there was a connection, like a bond of unspoken closeness and reassurance. It gave her that feel-good buzz. She hummed and swung their arms playfully. Given how isolated the trail was, it felt safe enough to do.

The trail was only wide enough for one, so Steph let go of Cori's hand and led the way. She spotted the crest of Shanelle Falls about ten minutes into their journey. "Look at that!"

Cori gasped. Steph quickened her pace, unable to control her excitement. She reached the bottom and stretched her arms out as she stood by the pool. "Oh wow. This is awesome." The waterfall cascaded over the crest and bounced off a rocky ledge where it fell into the plunge pool. There was a slight earthy scent, possibly because it was nestled in the middle of a rain forest. They were the only people there.

Cori shook her head. "This place is a hidden gem. I feel so privileged."

"Me too. I can't wait to jump into that pristine water." Steph walked to the other side of the pool and found a secluded grassy spot. She took their towels out and laid them on the bank, together with their surf shoes. "C'mon. Race you."

They both threw their clothes off, and Steph headed towards the side of the pool in nothing but her swim shoes.

"Aren't you putting your swimsuit on?" Cori stared at her in a way that made Steph glad she was butt naked.

Steph laughed and turned her palms up. "No way. We've got the whole place to ourselves." She'd have liked to have dived in, but she had no idea of the depth. Instead, she slid from the bank and into the water. She waded out to the centre. There were a few rocks underfoot, but she could still reach the bottom. She went back and held her hand out to Cori, who still had her bikini on. She took Steph's hand and tentatively eased herself in.

"It's freezing," Cori yelped.

Steph took her in her arms and kissed her tenderly. "You'll soon warm up. Let's swim, baby." She plunged in and swam towards the waterfall. "It's okay, you can still touch the bottom here."

Cori swam towards her. "I want to go under the waterfall. I wonder if we can sit on the ledge behind."

Steph entered from the side, investigated, and came back out. "It's green and slimy." She stuck her hand out. "Come stand under with me."

"It's way too fierce."

"Not at the side. Come on, how many chances do you get to do this? Bet your grandparents did."

That seemed to convince Cori and she joined Steph.

"Brr…it's icy cold."

Steph grinned. "I'll soon warm you up when we get out." She slid her hands along Cori's back to her butt and squeezed.

Cori pushed Steph under the falls, giggled and swam back to their spot. She climbed out and folded a towel around herself. Steph made her way back and Cori passed her towel over. When they'd dried off, they lay in the sun staring up at the blue sky.

Steph turned towards Cori and propped her chin on her elbow. "I can't remember ever being so contented."

Cori tilted her head. "I suppose it's because you're on holiday. You've put all your problems to the back of your mind and we're in tranquil surroundings."

Steph leaned down and kissed Cori. "Is that what you think? Because this is much more than a holiday romance for me. I want this to continue when we're back home."

Cori smiled. "Do you? Really?"

"Yes, really." Steph kissed her. It was a soft kiss which became more intense. She traced her hand down to Cori's breast, but Cori turned and pushed Steph onto her back.

"I'm in control this time." Cori kissed her hard and slid her tongue between Steph's lips.

She savoured the taste of Cori's tongue and the feel of their warm skin pressed together. She felt the gentle touch of Cori's hand on her breast, stroking and caressing. Cori moved and nibbled her ear, skimming the surface with her tongue. Steph groaned. "Oh, yes."

Cori swept her tongue across Steph's neck, teasing her. Steph shuffled, yearning for more. Cori seemed to know exactly what she wanted and took her nipple in her mouth and sucked hard.

Cori ran her hand slowly down Steph's body, resting it between Steph's thighs. Steph parted her legs, trying to draw her in, but Cori made her wait. She held her breath as Cori's fingertips teased the skin of her inner thigh. It was unbearable and she was as wet as the falls.

At last, Cori's fingers swept over her pussy.

"My, you are wet, aren't you?"

Steph breath quickened. "Getting wetter by the second. I want you inside me."

Cori slid two fingers inside her, and Steph's body shook with pleasure. Cori pushed another finger in.

"Oh, God," Steph cried. She bucked forward. "Christ, woman. What are you doing to me?"

Steph pushed hard against Cori's perfect rhythm and met her tempo. She upped the pace until Steph could stand it no more. She dug her nails into Cori's back. "Now. Please, Cori."

Cori drove higher, harder, and quicker until Steph could stand no more. Her clit pulsated and tingled with pleasure as she clamped her muscles, curved her back, and cried out as she let her juices ripple over Cori's fingers.

She was lightheaded and felt as though she could slip into a sexual coma. But she managed to stay conscious long enough to feel Cori's arms wrapped around her. They lay there for a while and her body was totally limp in Cori's arms. Eventually, she opened her eyes and smiled contentedly. She sighed heavily. "Wow, that was mind-blowing. Nobody has ever made me feel this way before." She meant it, too. She was no newcomer to the pleasures of sex, but this had been on a different level, and she had experienced deeper feelings. She wasn't sure if it was love, but it sure as hell was magical.

Cori grimaced. "You sure it was okay?"

"Okay?" Steph stroked Cori's hair. "Baby, it was sensational."

Cori gave a half smile.

"Why do you doubt it?"

Cori pulled at a blade of grass where they were laying. "It's just—"

Steph leaned her elbow on the ground and stared down at Cori. "You can tell me. We've shared everything."

Cori took a deep breath. "I've only ever made love to one other woman. Dusty always used to laugh and say at best, she'd give me a six out of ten."

Steph shot up. "Fucking hell. If she wasn't already—you know—I'd kill her." Steph huffed. "I bet she was a selfish bastard too."

"Well, yes, but I suppose it was because I didn't fulfil her needs."

Steph swept Cori into her arms. "Baby. You must get all these negative thoughts out of your head. You are wonderful in every way. Dusty was an abuser."

Cori nodded. "I know, but it's hard to accept that after eight years."

"What worries you the most?"

"Rejection, abandonment. I thought I was doing so much better with my personal

growth, but then—"

"Yes?"

"The thought of a new relationship brings all the fear and insecurities roaring back." Cori sighed. "What if I'm broken? What if I'm not worthy of being loved by someone amazing? What if it all falls apart and I get my heart broken again?" She brushed away a few tears. "I'm scared, Steph."

Steph pulled her close and placed little butterfly kisses all over her face. "Oh, babe. Don't you think I get scared too?"

Cori raised her eyebrows. "What have you got to fear? You're full of confidence."

"Hah! That's just bravado. I guess I get frightened because emotions scare the hell out of me."

"But why?"

"Because of the way I was raised, mostly. I don't want to end up like my cold-blooded family. What if it's in my blood and that's what I become?"

Cori stroked Steph's hair gently. "Sweetie, you will never be cold-blooded. It's not in you. You're the kindest, most considerate person I've ever met."

Steph's chin dropped. "And I worry because I can't help thinking our lives are so different. You're successful and I'm a failure. You have a good education, I don't. You can afford luxury and I have to do stuff on a shoestring."

"Steph, I see none of these things. I care about you for who you are. I've fallen for you because of all your wonderful qualities." Cori smiled.

"In fact, you're a limited edition."

"Thank you." Steph hugged her tightly and they lay in silence for a bit. Steph squeezed her and said, "And we've got each other now, so we'll get through this together."

Cori cheered up after that. Steph knew there was a long way to go before Cori would heal from her wounds, but with the right people by her side, she was confident that one day, Cori would come out at the other end. And so would she.

They took another swim, then ate their snacks. Time had passed by quickly, so they dressed and called Dan the Man. He'd certainly come up trumps on every occasion and Steph made sure she tipped him well when he dropped them off.

***

Over the next few days, they spent as much time as they could with Cori's grandparents. Josh joined them on the odd occasion, and it was like one big happy family. When they weren't doing that, they either lay by the pool or lay in bed making love to each other. It surpassed anything Steph had experienced before and gave her a complete and utter feeling of euphoria. If only they could stay there forever. However, they both knew their wonderful vacation was coming to an end. The day after tomorrow they'd be returning home. Home to face her parents, and back to the cold, damp, miserable weather.

Understandably, Cori and her grandparents wandered around in a state of gloom. There didn't seem to be any way Steph could console Cori. And the closer it got to leaving, the more melancholic she became.

"Now listen, sweet pea," Cori's grandma said. "This is only the beginning. A year isn't that long, and next Christmas is gonna be the best ever. Your mom and dad, me and Errol, Josh…and I sure as heck hope Steph will be coming too." She looked at Steph.

"Hey, that would be brilliant. Thanks so much." It was a long way off, but somehow, Steph knew that they'd be together.

She lifted Cori's chin. "Now let's not have any more of this woefulness. We're going out for dinner tonight, and it's a celebration of your visit, so I want to see happiness…you hear?"

Cori smiled and saluted. "Yes, Grandma."

And that seemed to settle things. The boss had spoken.

Later, Dan turned up to take them to the restaurant. There were five passengers tonight, so he'd borrowed a Jaguar saloon from his cousin. The car was about fifty years old, battered and scruffy, but Dan seemed to be incredibly proud of his cousin's *classic* car.

Josh and Steph sat up front and the others sat in the back. Luckily the journey was only twenty minutes as it was the bumpiest ride she'd ever taken, but nobody complained.

Steph nudged Josh. "What's the restaurant called?"

"The Lobster Wagon. It's my grandparents' favourite place."

"Lobster at last."

They piled out, and around the corner, there was a small cove. Bang in the centre were an assortment of old train carriages, and that was their restaurant. They made their way and commented on the various signs and booths, kept very much in the style of old train journeys.

"Wow," Cori said. "This is so unique."

Cori's grandma nodded. "Been going since the year dot. Errol used to bring me here when we were courting when he could afford it."

"So, as you're familiar with it, what would you order?"

"Josh knows best. He has the appetite."

Josh briefly looked at the menu. "I say we go with a shared seafood platter. That's fish of the day, lobster and shrimp and assorted vegetables in coconut sauce, or any other side orders." He chuckled. "Of course, we'll need ginger beer to go with it."

Steph rubbed her hands together. "All sounds fantastic."

It wasn't long before their food arrived, and they all tucked in. Josh kept them entertained during dinner and talked passionately about his car rental business. "Right now, I'm in the throes of looking for some premises in Montego Bay."

Cori gasped. "No kidding! You're really going for it then. Big businessman and all."

"Well, it's all thanks to our grandparents."

Cori's grandpa waved his hand. "Nonsense. We'd have been plain happy with the little business in Port Antonio, isn't that so, Tianna? Never had the vision you had, my boy."

"Nope. We're small town, Errol, and happy with it."

Josh took a drink and looked at Cori seriously. "When Mum and Dad come over, I want to persuade them to move here and help with the business." Josh tilted his head. "Why don't you two come as well?

Presumably, you can write from anywhere, and Steph would be great running one of the branches. Then I could ease up a bit, go find myself a wife, and have a bunch of kids."

Steph looked at Cori and she shrugged. "Sounds enticing. I don't think it would take much persuading for Mum and Dad to retire here and I certainly wouldn't mind taking a longer vacation. Who knows what the future holds?"

Steph knew Cori and her parents were close. She was sure if Josh lured them out here, Cori would follow, but she didn't see that happening for a while, so there was no panic. But it was way too soon to be planning to not only move in together but to move to a different country altogether. What a dream, though.

They continued chatting about mundane things, and Steph realised it wasn't just to pass the time, but to avoid that lull in conversation, when they'd all start thinking about Cori leaving. Steph had never had those ties to her own family, but every time she looked at *their* world, she realised that family was the core of everything. Love, togetherness, joy and belonging. For once, she felt she belonged, and tears filled her eyes. She so wanted to be wrapped in their family love bubble.

The following day passed by in a flash. Steph and Cori spent the morning packing and then lay by the pool or on their lilos. In the evening they'd had an early dinner together with her grandparents and then the two of them sat on Cori's balcony drinking Red Stripe beer. She'd hardly seen Cori smoke whilst she'd been here, just the odd one after a meal, but after she'd stubbed her cigarette out, she went to light another.

Steph put her hand over the packet. "Baby, you've just put one out. I'm not bothered or anything, but it's not like you."

Cori rubbed her forehead. "I'm so going to miss them."

"Of course you are. They'll be here next time you come, and you'll also have your mum and dad with you. What a reunion, eh?"

Cori nodded. "I hope you'll be there too."

"Just try and stop me." Steph took Cori's hand. "I think you need a distraction, so let's go to bed early. I have some things I want to discuss with your body."

Cori grinned. "Sounds good, I think my body wants to talk to yours too."

Steph pulled Cori up from her seat and led her to the bed. They made love to each other into the early hours until falling to sleep wrapped tightly in each other's arms. There was an urgency to their lovemaking, like they were clinging to a dream that was fast fading.

Steph wondered what the future held for them. Thinking positive was the key to all this. Dogs got excited when they saw you holding a leash and Steph felt a similar excitement, now that the cage had been opened. But what if Cori's world didn't allow for someone like Steph, once they were back?

Chapter Fifteen

Looking back several weeks later, Cori knew she couldn't have got through those goodbyes without Steph. She'd made her safe and given her a strong foundation. She'd supported her through so many difficult times over those weeks, both on the cruise and in Jamaica. She'd leaned on her when she was sick and afraid. She'd given her strength to see into the future. She'd given her faith not to keep harping on the past. Steph was strong and solid, and Cori couldn't imagine her life without Steph in it.

They'd agreed on the long journey back home that they'd temporarily go back to the lives they led before. It wasn't an easy decision, but Cori needed to sort herself out and so did Steph. If they could come through this separation, then they could conquer anything. They'd said they'd talk on the phone every night. Well, that was the plan, but they called each other at least three times a day.

Steph inspired Cori, and it wasn't long before she began her sequel to Scatty the Rat. It was a totally different feeling writing this second book. She no longer had to think about approval because she knew Steph would give her all the encouragement she ever needed. It was strange, but she felt like a different person and her passion for writing increased tenfold.

Life started to feel the way life was supposed to feel. She did what she wanted, when she wanted. She texted or called Steph because she wanted to, not because she was obligated or forced to. She even said yes to a bookseller who wanted her to come read at the shop. Without anyone to put her down or belittle her dreams, she started to feel like she could fly.

***

Steph didn't really miss her parents, or her job. As soon as she'd got back, she'd made an appointment to see them. For anybody else, that would have seemed formal; for Steph it was normal. Of course, word got out and her sister was there too.

They all sat around the table, as if they were waiting for an apology. Steph looked from her mother to her father and then to her sister. "You were all absolutely right. This vacation did me so much good. It gave me time to think about my future."

Her father crossed his arms. "And high time too, young lady."

She could see Hillary was longing to get in there.

"And what exactly have you come up with?" her sister asked.

"I'm making a career change. It's an online course, so I can stay in the business until the end of the year if that suits everyone. Then I'll be moving on to a new job." It suited her because then she'd still be earning.

All three laughed falsely.

Her father looked like he was sucking lemons. "My dear, you have no qualifications. Who would possibly take *you* on? And an online course? May as well get a degree on Facebook."

Steph stared at him. He was such a boost to her morale. She didn't answer. She didn't have to anymore.

"So, you think you can just use us, yet again until it suits you. Ha, there's hundreds of people who'd give their right arm for your job." Her mother's eyes were narrowed, her arms folded across her chest.

Nobody even asked what she was planning to do with her life. That's how much they cared. "I'd hate to deprive anyone of this opportunity, so in that case, I'll leave at the end of the month, and you can hire one of those people lined up to fill my position." She'd find something, anything, rather than take any more of this crap. Steph stood.

Hillary shook her head. "Selfish through and through."

Steph knew she couldn't win. She was damned if she did, and damned if she didn't. "Okay, folks, I'll leave you to get on with your day. See you." There was no point in prolonging this. It hurt that they felt so little for her, but luckily, she'd learned what the love of a normal family was like and somehow it made up for it, and more.

When she walked out of the house, she burst out laughing. She was free, and the feeling was so overwhelming she had to lean against a tree to breathe properly. She'd made her choice, and she was going to become the kind of person she'd always wanted to be. She wanted a life that made it great to get out of bed in the morning. She wanted love that made her tingle and smile, and she wanted a life that meant no regrets when she hit the pearly gates.

And that's just what she was going to have.

***

Steph's mobile phone rang, and she quickly swiped to answer. A wide smile spread across her face, knowing who she was going to see.

Steph grinned and blew her a kiss. "Hello, gorgeous. How you doin'?"

Cori blew a kiss back. "I'm good, thank you. How's my ray of sunshine?"

"Shining brightly. I'm as excited as a kid about to experience her first roller coaster ride."

Cori giggled. "And why would that be?"

"Ha ha. Could have something to do with seeing my girlfriend for the first time in yonks. Christ, you have no idea how much I want to kiss you, hold you, and make love to you."

Cori chuckled. "I thought you did that the other night."

Steph cleared her throat. "Yeah, but that was virtual. Nothing like the real thing."

Cori wiggled her eyebrows. "It was still pretty damn hot. Anyway, what time tomorrow?"

Steph stroked her chin. "Now let me see. Maybe after the twentieth car wax." She'd had a stroke of fortune. One of her friends had opened a new manual car wash business and Steph was her first employee. She loved it…no pressure except for the washer and it gave her a brilliant workout every day, so she even saved on gym fees. And it meant she had a lot of time to devote to her studies, which was what she needed most.

"Is there another clue?"

"About five o'clock."

Cori kissed her finger and placed it on the screen. "Perfect. I'm cooking pasta, so we can eat at any time."

Steph's eyes flashed. "About eight, then."

Cori smiled. "Sounds good to me. And then onto dessert."

Steph winked and pointed her finger at the screen. "You bet, baby." She sat up straight. "So how did it go yesterday?"

"Tell you tomorrow. And how is your project going?"

Steph gave a wicked grin. "Tell you tomorrow."

"Seems like tomorrow is going to be a long day."

Steph snorted. "Getting longer by the minute. What you up to?"

"I've cleaned the house a hundred times and it doesn't even need it. You know me, I'm a tidy and methodical person."

Steph slumped forward. "Unlike me."

"Yes, but yours isn't deliberate. Dusty seemed to go out of her way to mess everything up. However, that's in the past. I'm learning to try and leave it behind, but Rome wasn't built in a day. That's what my new therapist tells me."

"Who originally said that?"

"John Heywood. He was an English playwright. It was about reminding someone that it took time to sow the seeds in order to make something happen. It may take months or even years, but every hour you have to lay the bricks and focus on regularity rather than worry about the end result. Sounds simple, but it's difficult to change the habit of what seems like a lifetime. I've got a long way to go."

"You'll get there, babe."

Cori smiled. "I know, I have you."

"And I have you too." Steph checked her watch. "Best go now. Coming up to chat time with my other girlfriend."

Cori placed her hands together as though praying. "Oh gosh. I don't want to come between you two."

Steph jiggled in her seat. "Ooh, now there's a thought."

"Forget it! Now buzz off, you perv."

Steph bit her bottom lip. "Hmm...I'll be thinking about that all night." She brought her hands up and covered her face. "Don't hit me. I'm going."

"Farewell, sunshine."

Steph blew another kiss and left. Just seeing Cori, even though it was only via video link, always left her with a cheesy grin on her face that lasted the rest of the day. These were happy times, and they weren't just daydreams. For once she was prepared to make changes in her life instead of thinking about missed opportunities. And this was all because of Cori.

The following day seemed like it would last a lifetime. Even the cars seemed like they were passing through in slow motion. But eventually she got away.

At four thirty, she rang the doorbell. Cori opened the door, and there she was, as large as life itself.

Steph lay the bunch of flowers on the step. Her face lit up as she engulfed Cori in her arms and swung her around. "This has been a long time coming. Too bloody long."

Cori seemed short of breath. "But we did agree."

Steph put her down and picked the flowers up. "Yes, but it was a stupid idea. From now on, we see each other every weekend."

Cori took her hand and pulled her inside. "Oh, I do like a strong woman. Anyway, it was only until we got our lives sorted a little."

Once inside, Steph took Cori in her arms and kissed her hard on the lips. "God, I've been waiting for that for so long."

Cori stroked Steph's face. "Well, we'll have plenty of that over the weekend. In the meantime, let's go fetch your stuff in."

Steph picked her up and carried her up the stairs. "No way. First things first." She got to the top and turned left.

Cori wriggled in her arms, but it seemed half-hearted. "Wait. My bedroom's the other way."

Steph made a U-turn and softly struck the door with her foot, and it swung open. She threw Cori on the bed and pounced on top of her. "Now I'm going to show you how much I've missed you."

Several hours later, Cori and Steph returned downstairs. "Well, that was a wonderful appetiser. Now I'm ready for the main course."

Steph wiggled her eyebrows. "Personally, I'd prefer the inter—"

Cori slapped her on the arm. "Yes, one is aware. However, I need sustenance of another kind. We have plenty of time for your shenanigans."

Steph laughed. "Oh, is that what you call it? Please may I have another helping of shenanigans?"

"No."

"Okay, feed me then, woman."

Cori took Steph's hand and led her to the kitchen. She loaded her arms with place mats, cutlery, glasses, and a bottle of wine. "Now go lay the table. You can lay me again later if you behave."

"Whoopee!"

Steph returned to the kitchen. "Chores done. What next?"

"You can take the plates and salad through. Be with you in a minute." Cori followed through with the hot dish. They lifted their glasses and clinked. "Now help yourself."

"Wow, this is fantastic. What's it called?"

"Chicken parmigiana bake. It's good because it can be prepared before then heated. Perfect post-sex-marathon meal."

Steph snorted. "Hope you've got loads of those recipes."

"Yes, I have a spreadsheet. Anyway, tell me how your course is going?"

"You mean I have to go first?"

"Yes."

"Your wish is my command." Steph finished off her mouthful of food and laid her fork down. "It's going really well. My tutor, Amanda, is impressed with my efforts."

"What exactly do you have to do?"

"They give you a residential renovation and you have to upload new flooring, lighting plans, furnishings, fabrics, window treatments, plus upholstery and accessories. Then of course there's the colour schemes. When it's done, you have to make a written quotation, prepare advertisements, and then write a scope of work for your contractors with a preliminary costing for your clients. Lots more other stuff too but that's the gist of it. Of course, it's all hypothetical." Steph was upbeat. "It's fantastic."

"What happens when you've completed it?"

"You upload it onto the site and the tutor marks it. They give you a grade out of ten and give you feedback. It's great because they really deliver what's on the tin. It works because there's also a Student Support Team which operates 24/7. So, when I've finished, they can help me find a good position somewhere, too."

"It sounds terrific and you're obviously loving it. It's wonderful to see you so animated. I'm so happy for you."

"Well, it's you I have to thank. You pointed me in the right direction and gave me that extra push." Steph poked at a last piece of food on her plate. "At the risk of boring you…I could show you some of the work I've done later, or over the weekend. If you wanted to see it."

"Honestly, Steph, I'd love to see it." Cori smiled. "You never know, I may be your first client."

Steph looked around. "You don't need it. Your home is already beautiful."

Cori pushed her chair back, picked up a leaflet, and handed it to Steph.

Steph glanced at it, then at Cori. "Wow, you've actually put the house on the market. I can't believe it."

"I know. Me neither. It only went on the net yesterday and the board isn't up yet, but the estate agent thinks it'll move quickly. It's so handy for everywhere, you know, schools, shops, and transport, etcetera."

Steph reached over and took her hand. "I'm so pleased for you, baby. It must be a terrible wrench, though?"

Cori shook her head. "It's not, actually. It's been much easier than I thought. My counsellor says I'll move on a lot quicker once I can leave it behind."

"So, have you any idea what you're going to look for? Do you want to stay in the same area?"

"I think so. It's quiet here. Maybe an apartment instead, though. There are some new ones not far from mum and dad, and they'll be finished in a couple of months' time. Talking of which, they've invited us over for Sunday lunch because they can't wait to meet you. I hope you don't mind?"

"Mind? I can't wait to meet them."

"Good, then I can show you the property on the way round there. They've got these massive balconies which are more like gardens, and they overlook the duck pond."

"Sounds perfect. Do you want to talk about your counselling, or would you rather not?"

Cori crossed her arms. "For heaven's sake, woman. You're the one who got me involved, did all the spade work for me, and put the wheels in motion. You know practically as much as I've told the counsellor. I'm certainly not going to hold anything back from you."

Steph held her hands up. "Okay, message received."

"Well, I've had four sessions now. On the first occasion, I sat in the waiting room, I fidgeted like crazy and a big part of me wanted to walk out. Luckily a little voice entered my head and resisted the urge to leave. Maria put me at ease, and I thought she was going to ask me loads of questions. She didn't say a word, just waited."

"I guess that's what they're trained to do."

"I said I didn't think she'd want to listen, because really there must be far worse cases and that I was wasting her time." Cori laughed. "All she said was, 'Why?' I can't quite remember my response. I think I started making excuses for Dusty. She made a few remarks…and then I don't know what happened. I just couldn't stop talking and then the flood gates opened. It was the same the next time and then it got easier."

"That sounds encouraging. I'm proud of you, baby. I know it's not going to be fixed overnight, but you'll get there."

Cori smiled and nodded. "I think I will. I'm sure there will be times when doubts creep in—" She took Steph's hand and squeezed it. "But knowing you're there for me has given me strength."

"Works both ways. I know our problems aren't the same, but we're here to help each other."

"Yes, and we're so lucky. How are your parents behaving since you told them? Have you seen them again?"

Steph flinched, and she felt that same flare of frustration whenever she spoke of her parents. "Hah! I went around to collect my stuff and all that came out was a load of crap about how they always saw me taking over the business once I'd finally grown up and how I was letting them down again, and of course how I'd go running back when everything failed."

"But you won't, will you?"

"No way. I find washing cars very therapeutic. Plenty of time to think and when I eventually leave, I'm gonna make this work. I've already made a start on designing my website, but I'm going to work for an established company first. My tutor thinks I should serve an apprenticeship and get some hands-on experience. I suppose the great thing is I can work from home, at least after I've served an apprenticeship or whatever it is I'll have to do." She cocked her head. "I think once I've completed the course and got a job, I'll start thinking about a move myself."

Cori looked down at her hands. "I suppose you'll move to London or a bigger city."

Steph shot up and threw her arms around Cori. "No way, baby. I was thinking about moving somewhere closer to you…in fact, I was thinking more like the same town."

Cori felt her eyes lighting up. "No kidding?"

"Yeah. What do you think? I mean, I'm not rushing stuff too quickly, am I? It won't be until next year, and I'm not saying we'll move in together or anything…"

"I think that would be perfect timing."

Steph stroked Cori's hair. "See, I think we could have a great future. A year will give you time to heal, and it will give me time to get on my feet under me. I want to be able to carry my own weight and be the woman you deserve."

"You're already the woman I need, the one I want. And I can't wait to start our lives together."

Steph cupped Cori's face in her hands. "We've already started, my

love. We've got nothing but adventure ahead of us now."
And all thanks to their Caribbean Dreams.

Epilogue

There was no way Steph was going to cock this one up. She was leaving nothing to chance. She had stuff to prove, and she wanted Cori to be proud of her. So much had changed in the last two years and she was beginning to believe she was an achiever and not a loser. And as she stood in front of her biggest and most important project, it felt true.

Granted, it was all very sneaky. She'd told Cori she had a big job going in London. It was a half-truth as she had been working on the interior design of a boutique hotel there, along with a couple of her colleagues. When she'd finished her course, she'd joined the firm of Kenese Lawrence for a number of reasons. Kenese was from a humble background but had worked her way up the ladder and was now becoming a household name in interior design and ecological architecture, not only in the UK, but internationally. Steph admired her eclectic tastes in design, and she didn't just focus on one area. She diversified, and as she'd told Steph at her interview, she could be working in hospitality, residential, restaurants, private yachts, or aircraft. In fact, she'd just completed a total refurbishment for a celebrity with his own train. Not only that, but Kenese was Jamaican born and bred, and they'd hit it off over their love of the island one day when Kenese had come to guest lecture on Steph's course. Steph had snapped her hand off when Kenese had offered her an apprenticeship six months ago. However, that work had been completed and now Steph was a full employee, with leave to work on the project she'd fallen in love with before she began working for real.

She glanced at her watch. One p.m., their scheduled slot to FaceTime. She grinned when the call came in right on time. "Hi, baby, how's it going?"

Cori kissed her finger and placed it on the screen. "Missing you like crazy."

"Me too, you." Steph smiled. "So come on, tell me what happened?"

Cori shook her head. "You won't believe it. I can't believe it either."

"What. Tell me?"

"It's ridiculous, but my agent says somebody wants to make a movie of Scatty the Rat."

"You're fricking joking?"

Cori rubbed her forehead. "No, and the sequel. Maybe even the final book."

Steph raised her arms. "Awesome, baby. I knew it. You're a genius."

"Am I getting carried away with all this?"

"No way. The books are amazing. You've worked hard and you're *so* talented. Just accept it and embrace it." Steph punched the air with her fist. "I'm over the moon. You're a star."

"I so wish you were here. I have a Zoom meeting with her tomorrow. What should I say?"

"Yes, yes, yes! Trust yourself. You've got this."

Cori laughed. "Okay. If you say so. Won't be until next year so I can discuss it with you. If it's agreed, I want you there with me when we meet up to sign the paperwork."

Steph grinned. "You bet."

Cori grimaced. "Where are you? It looks like there's sunshine in that room?"

"Nah. I'm trying an experiment with some new artificial lighting features. It's amazing how authentic it looks." She'd had that answer prepared, just in case.

"Wouldn't mind some of that here. It's so dark and cold."

Steph cleared her throat. "So, when are you planning to fly?"

"Either the nineteenth or the twentieth. And you?"

"Hopefully, the twenty-second."

"Shame we couldn't have co-ordinated it." Cori smiled. "Still, we'll have plenty of time from now on."

Steph slumped. "Yeah, the sooner I get this finished, the sooner we'll be together." She tilted her head. "I love you so much."

Cori placed her hand on her heart. "I love you too."

Cori sat upright. "Okay, going now. Hurry up and get your job finished. I want you back in my bed."

Thoughts of Cori's smooth body against white sheets made Steph start to sweat, and she grinned in the way that always made Cori blush. They blew kisses to each other and then the screen went blank. Steph looked around. She needed to get moving if the surprise was going to be perfect.

***

A week later, Cori arrived in Jamaica. She crept up the stairs and into the bedroom. Steph was kneeling on the floor with her back to her. *What a sight for sore eyes.* She looked like she was taking measurements by the side of the bed. And what a big bed it was. Super-king at least, and very inviting, along with the vision of Steph. Was she mad at Steph? Not for a second. Once she'd found out, she'd been deeply touched by the romantic nature of her beautiful girlfriend. She tiptoed up behind her, stuck her foot out and kicked her butt. Steph fell forward but instinctively threw her arms out in front of her.

"What the fu—" She sprang to her feet and turned around with her arms stretched in a defensive stance. Her jaw dropped. "Cori! What the hell are you doing here?"

Cori placed her hands on her hips. "I got an earlier flight and had a sleepover in Miami. And I could ask you the same question. You scheming little devil."

"How did you find out?" Steph pouted. "Jeez, all I wanted to do was surprise you." Her eyes widened. "I wanted to be here for the entire build too, but it was out of the question, since I couldn't be away from you that long." Steph took Cori in her arms. "Forgive me, please. I just wanted it to be as ready as it could be before you got here."

"I called the office looking for you, and that new receptionist obviously wasn't in on the secret. She told me where you were, and then I called Josh and threatened him with bodily harm if he didn't tell me what was going on." Cori kissed her. "How can I stay mad at you for doing something so incredible?"

Steph took Cori's hand and pulled her towards the sliding door. "I'll show you the rest of the house in a minute, but for now, just come look at this awesome view from the balcony, babe."

Cori followed her and covered her mouth when she saw the scene spread before her. "Oh wow! It's amazing." She stared down into the garden. "So sad they had to cut the trees down though. Did it upset our grandparents?"

"No. Your grandpa was delighted. A couple were dead, and everyone has a better view of the bay now. Anyway, how come you're here already?

I'd hoped to fit the last bit of furniture tonight. I wanted it to be perfect."

"Once I knew you were here, nothing was going to keep me from getting to you and our new home." Cori put her arms around Steph's neck. "Oh, Steph, aren't we lucky. I can't believe this is happening. I can't believe everything you've done for us."

Steph gave her a lingering kiss. "And now we're going to christen the bed." She swept Cori off her feet, carried her inside, threw her onto the bed and joined her. "Now I'm going to show you how much I've missed you."

An hour or so passed and Cori lay in Steph's arms. She smiled. "Yes, the bed's certainly comfortable. Thank you, darling, for being so thoughtful."

Steph laughed. "I thought I'd been quite selfish, really."

Cori thumped her on the arm playfully. "You're never selfish in any way, shape, or form."

Cori's mum shouted from outside. "Hey there, lovers. The barbeque is almost ready. Hurry up or we'll share your steaks."

"Okay, Mum, down in fifteen." Cori kicked the sheet down. "Come on, you. Best take a shower. I'm starving, and I can't wait to see what kind of house you had built for us."

Steph jumped up. "Yeah, a good workout always makes me hungry too. Might get extras after the loofah."

Cori shook her head and backed towards the shower, swinging her hips. "I can't imagine what you mean." She yelped when Steph ran towards her, grinning.

***

When they finally got outside, Steph rubbed her hands together. "Ooh, is that sorrel and rum I see?"

Cori's grandpa filled all their glasses. "You bet. Reckon all this calls for a big celebration." He wiped his eyes and cleared his throat. "Never thought me and Tianna would see this day, but we have all our family together for Christmas, and hopefully forever. I know we spent it together last year, but then you all went home, and we missed you something fierce."

Cori kissed her grandpa on the forehead. "Well, we're not going anywhere now. We're here for keeps, and I just want to say a big thank you to everybody for making it possible. I honestly never thought we'd be here. When Steph suggested moving, I thought it was a pipe dream. I knew I could work from anywhere, but I didn't think Steph could." She took Steph's hand. "Then you offered us this wonderful piece of land and Steph came up with the brilliant idea of a kit home, although I couldn't have imagined how beautiful she'd make it. And all of you project-managed it for us. It's so perfect, and I'm so excited to spend the rest of my life here." Cori raised her glass. "A massive thank you from both of us. Grandpa, Grandma. It's a truly spectacular gift and we will always be indebted to you."

Cori's grandma waved her hand. "Enough of this crap, pumpkin." She looked up to the sky. "Sorry, Lord, it had to be said." She paused. "We've dreamt of this moment all our lives, haven't we, Errol?"

"You bet. Every day. We're not getting any younger. Our Josh has been a godsend. Looked after us always. But it's time he had a life too. Having our family around us has given us a new lease of life. We goin' to have lotsa fun together." He lifted his glass. "Here's to new beginnings."

They raised their glasses and drank.

Steph blew her nose. "I've never had a family, but you're the bestest anyone could ever ask for. I can't believe it. And all from that cruise. You've all made me feel so welcome."

Cori's mum pulled Steph into an embrace. "We love you like a daughter and couldn't have asked for better. Whenever we look at the happiness on Cori's face, we feel blessed."

"Aww…thank you, Alice."

Josh handed out the plates. "C'mon, you lot, these steaks will get cold."

They tucked in and washed the meal down with plenty of ginger beer. They were embracing their first night together as a family and nothing could wipe the permanent smiles from their faces.

After clearing up the debris, they sat down again to continue their celebrations.

Cori hugged her mum and dad. "Right, it's time for catch-up. You've been living here for three months now, and I've missed you like crazy. And I've missed all the gossip. What's been happening? How is the new business going?"

Cori's mum wrapped her arm around Cori's waist and smiled at her son. "Josh will fill you in. He's far better at telling stories than I am."

Josh winked and clicked his tongue. "Absolutely brilliant, Sis. We've done a bit of a shuffle and Mum's managing the car hire office in Port Antonio. We also offer a short course in driving experiences for the tourists. It works well because a lot of them don't feel confident enough to drive on our roads, so Mum looks after that side too. Steph's had lots of great ideas about the construction, too, you know. She made me promise not to tell you so that you didn't worry she was taking too much on." He grinned when Steph groaned and hung her head.

Cori grimaced. "But what'll happen when Steph starts working? Aside from on our house, I mean."

Josh snorted. "She's working for Kenese Lawrence, the island hero and with the ideas she's come up with for sustainable design and housing, people all over the island already want to adopt Steph into their families. And she's promised to keep helping the family whenever we want to build something new."

Steph nodded in agreement. Requests for her services had already been coming into the office, and Kenese was happy to have Steph in Jamaica to help expand the company.

Cori's grandma turned to Steph. "What did your family say when you told them you were moving to Jamaica? And landing a job with our Kenese, too."

Steph kicked up some gravel on the garden. "Just said I was full of fanciful ideas and living somewhere I didn't belong. They said we were being utterly stupid moving to a country where the laws don't protect us." She looked up and hooted with laughter. "I nearly told them I was opening up a funeral parlour here, just to give them heart attacks. But I didn't, and they didn't ask. I explained that we had family here, and we can be careful living on this beautiful island like we would be anywhere else. And who knows, maybe we can help change things in the future, right?" She shrugged. "They just said I'd come crawling back when it turned out I didn't have anything to offer this family, but my sister said she might be generous and give me my old position back when I had nowhere else to turn, now that she's running the business." Steph squared her shoulders and grinned. "Anyway, I don't need them now. I have you, and blood doesn't make family. Love makes family."

Cori's grandpa scratched his beard stubble. "You know somethin', we're doin' pretty good as a family, and we only just startin'. Let's drink to that."

Steph doubted if they'd ever run out of things to toast. Devon put on some loud reggae, and they danced on the deck to the sound of a bass guitar.

Steph had her arms around Cori and Josh. She hoped one day he too would find the love of his life. This was a billion-dollar experience—but one you certainly couldn't buy. For the first time in many years, she was optimistic about the future. She wanted the night to keep rolling on forever. She looked around at her new family and was certain that would happen as long as they had each other. The stars flickered and a twinkle caught her eye as the Caribbean moonlight danced with them.

What's Your Story?

Global Wordsmiths, CIC, provides an all-encompassing service for all writers, ranging from basic proofreading and cover design to development editing, typesetting, and eBook services. A major part of our work is charity and community focused, delivering writing projects to under-served and under-represented groups across Nottinghamshire, giving voice to the voiceless and visibility to the unseen.

To learn more about what we offer, visit: www.globalwords.co.uk

A selection of books by Global Words Press:
Desire, Love, Identity: with the National Justice Museum
Times Past: with The Workhouse, National Trust
Times Past: Young at Heart with AGE UK
In Different Shoes: Stories of Trans Lives

Self-published authors working with Global Wordsmiths:
E.V. Bancroft
Valden Bush
Dee Griffiths and Ali Holah
Michelle Grubb
Helena Harte
Lee Haven
Iona Kane
Karen Klyne
Ally McGuire
Emma Nichols
Ray Martin
James Merrick
Robyn Nyx
Simon Smalley

Other Great Books by Independent Authors

Music City Dreamers by Robyn Nyx
Music can bring lovers together. In Music City, it can tear them apart.
Available on Amazon (B0994XVDGR)

Scripted Love by Helena Harte
Will Rix and Layla find their way to love? Or is it simply not in their script?
Available on Amazon (ASIN B0993QFLNN)

Nero by Valden Bush
Banished. Abandoned. Lost. Will her destiny reunite her with the love of her life?
Available on Amazon (ASIN B09BXN8VTZ)

Warm Pearls and Paper Cranes by E.V. Bancroft
A family torn apart. The only way forward is love.
Available on Amazon (ASIN B09DTBCQ92)

The Proud Weed by Sam Rawlings
Children's picture book about discovering your place in the world.
Available on Amazon (ASIN B092J6NS38)

The Adventures of Daisy the Boy Sparrow by Dani Lovelady Ryan
Children's illustrated book about chosen family and having the courage to live the life you crave.
Available on Amazon (ASIN B094PDKGNY)

Elodie by Emma Nichols
There's such a thing as a perfect life so why won't she let herself live it?
Available on Amazon (ASIN B08WRFXGRG)

Addie Mae by Addison M. Conley
At the beginning of a bitter divorce, Maddy meets mysterious Jessie Stevens. As their friendship grows, so does the attraction.
Available on Amazon (ISBN 9780998029641)

Printed in Great Britain
by Amazon

57949031R00126